D1601255

YOUTH
HEART OF DARKNESS
TYPHOON

JOSEPH CONRAD

THE MODERN LIBRARY

NEW YORK

Library of Congress Cataloging-in-Publication Data
Conrad, Joseph, 1857–1924.
    Youth; Heart of darkness; Typhoon/Joseph Conrad.
        p.   cm.
    ISBN 0-679-42468-7
I. Title: Youth.   II. Title: Heart of darkness.   III. Title: Typhoon
PR6005.04A6   1993
823'.912 — dc20   92–51069

JOSEPH CONRAD

Joseph Conrad was born Józef Teodor Konrad Korzeniowski in Russian-occupied Poland on December 3, 1857. His parents were aristocrats and intensely nationalistic political activists who were exiled to Vologda, northeast of Moscow, for their opposition to tsarist rule. Józef's mother, Ewa, died in 1865 of tuberculosis, and his father, Apollo, succumbed to the same disease four years later. Józef was cared for by his uncle, Tadeusz Bobrowski, until the young man acted on a long-expressed desire to go to sea. In 1874 he left for Marseilles, where he began sailing for the French merchant service.

In 1878, in money difficulties and no longer able to sail on French vessels because he had not secured an exemption from military service in Russia, Conrad attempted suicide. After his recovery, he left Marseilles on a British ship and went to England, where he worked the route between Lowestoft and Newcastle. He arrived in England virtually without qualifications and with very little English, but he was able in a few years to earn his master's certificate in the British merchant marine and became a British national. Conrad traveled to Mauritius and Constantinople, worked on wool clippers from London to Australia, and sailed the waters of the Far East. These voyages were punctuated by long periods when he could not find suitable positions because of the decline in sail-powered transport in the age of the steamship.

Conrad began writing in English, which became his language of choice after his native Polish and French, although he complained of difficulties with English grammar and syntax. His voyages provided the background for much of his fiction. "Youth" and "Typhoon" draw on Conrad's personal experience with disasters at sea. In 1881, he became second mate on the *Palestine*, a ship that was rammed, caught in tempestuous gales in the English Channel, had its cargo of coal catch fire, and sank off Sumatra. His captaincy of the *Otago* from Bangkok in 1888 informs *The Shadow-Line* (1917) and the stories "Falk" and "The Secret Sharer." "Heart of Darkness" (1899) is drawn from an expedition to the Belgian Congo in 1890. He was already working on a novel when he traveled to the Congo, where he expected to take command of a river steamer. The assignment failed to materialize and Conrad fell dangerously ill. On his return to England, he was forced to find work as a ship's mate. He was able during this period of intermittent employment to devote more time to his writing, and in 1894 he submitted the novel *Almayer's Folly* to the publisher Fisher Unwin. Unwin published it in 1895 under the anglicized version of Conrad's Polish name.

Conrad was encouraged to continue to write by Unwin's reader Edward Garnett, although he went on applying for posts as a ship's captain. He finished *The Outcast of the*

Islands in 1895 and in 1896 married Jessie George. They had two sons, Borys and John, born in 1898 and 1906. Constantly in need of more money, Conrad produced short stories and serialized his novels. Although plagued by physical illness and psychological problems, he established one of the most formidable bodies of work in the English language. His longer works include *The Nigger of the "Narcissus"* (1897), *Lord Jim* (1900), *Nostromo* (1904), *The Secret Agent* (1907), *Under Western Eyes* (1911), and *Victory* (1915). From early in his career Conrad had the admiration of fellow writers—Stephen Crane, John Galsworthy, Henry James, and Ford Madox Ford, with whom Conrad collaborated on *The Inheritors* (1901) and *Romance* (1903). It was only after the success of *Chance* (1913), however, that his writing afforded him widespread recognition and relative financial security. He spent his declining years in Kent, often in ill health, and died on August 3, 1924, at his home near Canterbury.

Contents

Youth

A Narrative

This could have occurred nowhere but in England, where men and sea interpenetrate, so to speak—the sea entering into the life of most men, and the men knowing something or everything about the sea, in the way of amusement, of travel, or of bread-winning.

We were sitting round a mahogany table that reflected the bottle, the claret-glasses, and our faces as we leaned on our elbows. There was a director of companies, an accountant, a lawyer, Marlow, and myself. The director had been a *Conway* boy, the accountant had served four years at sea, the lawyer—a fine crusted Tory, High Churchman, the best of old fellows, the soul of honour—had been chief officer in the P. & O. service in the good old days when mail-boats were square-rigged at least on two masts, and used to come down the China Sea before a fair monsoon with stun'-sails set alow and aloft. We all began life in the merchant service. Between the five of us there was the strong bond of the sea, and also the fellowship of the craft, which no amount of enthusiasm for yachting, cruising, and so on can give, since one is only the amusement of life and the other is life itself.

Marlow (at least I think that is how he spelt his name) told the story, or rather the chronicle, of a voyage:—

'Yes, I have seen a little of the Eastern seas; but what I remember best is my first voyage there. You fellows know there are those voyages that seem ordered for the

3

illustration of life, that might stand for a symbol of existence. You fight, work, sweat, nearly kill yourself, sometimes do kill yourself, trying to accomplish something—and you can't. Not from any fault of yours. You simply can do nothing, neither great nor little—not a thing in the world—not even marry an old maid, or get a wretched 600-ton cargo of coal to its port of destination.

'It was altogether a memorable affair. It was my first voyage to the East, and my first voyage as second mate; it was also my skipper's first command. You'll admit it was time. He was sixty if a day; a little man, with a broad, not very straight back, with bowed shoulders and one leg more bandy than the other, he had that queer twisted-about appearance you see so often in men who work in the fields. He had a nut-cracker face—chin and nose trying to come together over a sunken mouth—and it was framed in iron-gray fluffy hair, that looked like a chin-strap of cotton-wool sprinkled with coal-dust. And he had blue eyes in that old face of his, which were amazingly like a boy's, with that candid expression some quite common men preserve to the end of their days by a rare internal gift of simplicity of heart and rectitude of soul. What induced him to accept me was a wonder. I had come out of a crack Australian clipper, where I had been third officer, and he seemed to have a prejudice against crack clippers as aristocratic and high-toned. He said to me, "You know, in this ship you will have to work." I said I had to work in every ship I had

ever been in. "Ah, but this is different, and you gentle-
men out of them big ships; . . . but there! I dare say
you will do. Join tomorrow."

'I joined tomorrow. It was twenty-two years ago; and
I was just twenty. How time passes! It was one of the
happiest days of my life. Fancy! Second mate for the
first time—a really responsible officer! I wouldn't have
thrown up my new billet for a fortune. The mate looked
me over carefully. He was also an old chap, but of
another stamp. He had a Roman nose, a snow-white,
long beard, and his name was Mahon, but he insisted
that it should be pronounced Mann. He was well con-
nected; yet there was something wrong with his luck,
and he had never got on.

'As to the captain, he had been for years in coasters,
then in the Mediterranean, and last in the West Indian
trade. He had never been round the Capes. He could
just write a kind of sketchy hand, and didn't care for
writing at all. Both were thorough good seamen of
course, and between those two old chaps I felt like a
small boy between two grandfathers.

'The ship also was old. Her name was the *Judea*.
Queer name, isn't it? She belonged to a man Wilmer,
Wilcox—some name like that; but he has been bankrupt
and dead these twenty years or more, and his name
don't matter. She had been laid up in Shadwell basin for
ever so long. You may imagine her state. She was all
rust, dust, grime—soot aloft, dirt on deck. To me it was
like coming out of a palace into a ruined cottage. She

was about 400 tons, had a primitive windlass, wooden
latches to the doors, not a bit of brass about her, and a
big square stern. There was on it, below her name in big
letters, a lot of scrollwork, with the gilt off, and some
sort of a coat of arms, with the motto "Do or Die'
underneath. I remember it took my fancy immensely.
There was a touch of romance in it, something that
made me love the old thing—something that appealed to
my youth!

'We left London in ballast—sand ballast—to load a
cargo of coal in a northern port for Bankok. Bankok! I
thrilled. I had been six years at sea, but had only seen
Melbourne and Sydney, very good places, charming
places in their way—but Bankok!

'We worked out of the Thames under canvas, with a
North Sea pilot on board. His name was Jermyn, and he
dodged all day long about the galley drying his handkerchief before the stove. Apparently he never slept. He
was a dismal man, with a perpetual tear sparkling at the
end of his nose, who either had been in trouble, or was
in trouble, or expected to be in trouble—couldn't be
happy unless something went wrong. He mistrusted my
youth, my common-sense, and my seamanship, and
made a point of showing it in a hundred little ways. I
dare say he was right. It seems to me I knew very little
then, and I know not much more now; but I cherish a
hate for that Jermyn to this day.

'We were a week working up as far as Yarmouth
Roads, and then we got into a gale—the famous Octo-

ber gale of twenty-two years ago. It was wind, lightning, sleet, snow, and a terrific sea. We were flying light, and you may imagine how bad it was when I tell you we had smashed bulwarks and a flooded deck. On the second night she shifted her ballast into the lee bow, and by that time we had been blown off somewhere on the Dogger Bank. There was nothing for it but to go below with shovels and try to right her, and there we were in that vast hold, gloomy like a cavern, the tallow dips stuck and flickering on the beams, the gale howling above, the ship tossing about like mad on her side; there we all were, Jermyn, the captain, every one, hardly able to keep our feet, engaged on that gravedigger's work, and trying to toss shovelfuls of wet sand up to windward. At every tumble of the ship you could see vaguely in the dim light men falling down with a great flourish of shovels. One of the ship's boys (we had two), impressed by the weirdness of the scene, wept as if his heart would break. We could hear him blubbering somewhere in the shadows.

'On the third day the gale died out, and by-and-by a north-country tug picked us up. We took sixteen days in all to get from London to the Tyne! When we got into dock we had lost our turn for loading, and they hauled us off to a tier where we remained for a month. Mrs Beard (the captain's name was Beard) came from Colchester to see the old man. She lived on board. The crew of runners had left, and there remained only the officers, one boy and the steward, a mulatto who answered to the name of Abraham. Mrs Beard was an old woman, with a face all wrinkled and ruddy like a winter apple, and the figure of a young girl. She caught sight of me once, sewing on a button, and insisted on having my shirts to repair. This was something different from the captains' wives I had known on board crack clippers. When I brought her the shirts, she said: "And the socks? They want mending, I am sure, and John's— Captain Beard's—things are all in order now. I would be glad of something to do." Bless the old woman. She overhauled my outfit for me, and meantime I read for the first time *Sartor Resartus* and Burnaby's *Ride to Khiva*. I didn't understand much of the first then; but I remember I preferred the soldier to the philosopher at the time; a preference which life has only confirmed. One was a man, and the other was either more—or less. However, they are both dead and Mrs Beard is dead, and youth, strength, genius, thoughts, achievements, simple hearts—all dies . . . No matter.

'They loaded us at last. We shipped a crew. Eight able seamen and two boys. We hauled off one evening to the buoys at the dock-gates, ready to go out, and with a fair prospect of beginning the voyage next day. Mrs Beard was to start for home by a late train. When the ship was fast we went to tea. We sat rather silent through the meal—Mahon, the old couple, and I. I finished first, and slipped away for a smoke, my cabin being in a deck-house just against the poop. It was high

water, blowing fresh with a drizzle; the double dock-
gates were opened, and the steam-colliers were going in
and out in the darkness with their lights burning bright,
a great plashing of propellers, rattling of winches, and a
lot of hailing on the pier-heads. I watched the procession of head-lights gliding high and of green lights gliding low in the night, when suddenly a red gleam flashed
at me, vanished, came into view again, and remained.
The fore-end of a steamer loomed up close. I shouted
down the cabin, "Come up, quick!" and then heard a
startled voice saying afar in the dark, "Stop her, sir." A
bell jingled. Another voice cried warningly, "We are
going right into that barque, sir." The answer to this was
a gruff "All right," and the next thing was a heavy crash
as the steamer struck a glancing blow with the bluff of
her bow about our fore-rigging. There was a moment of
confusion, yelling, and running about. Steam roared.
Then somebody was heard saying, "All clear, sir" . . .
"Are you all right?" asked the gruff voice. I had jumped
forward to see the damage, and hailed back, "I think so."
"Easy astern," said the gruff voice. A bell jingled. "What
steamer is that?" screamed Mahon. By that time she was
no more to us than a bulky shadow manoeuvring a little
way off. They shouted at us some name—a woman's
name, Miranda or Melissa—or some such thing. "This
means another month in this beastly hole," said Mahon
to me, as we peered with lamps about the splintered bulwarks and broken braces. "But where's the captain?"

'We had not heard or seen anything of him all that time. We went aft to look. A doleful voice arose hailing somewhere in the middle of the dock, *"Judea* ahoy!" . . . How the devil did he get there? . . . "Hallo!" we shouted. "I am adrift in our boat without oars," he cried. A belated water-man offered his services, and Mahon struck a bargain with him for half-a-crown to tow our skipper alongside; but it was Mrs Beard that came up the ladder first. They had been floating about the dock in that mizzly cold rain for nearly an hour. I was never so surprised in my life.

'It appears that when he heard my shout "Come up" he understood at once what was the matter, caught up his wife, ran on deck, and across, and down into our boat, which was fast to the ladder. Not bad for a sixty-year-old. Just imagine that old fellow saving heroically in his arms that old woman—the woman of his life. He set her down on a thwart, and was ready to climb back on board when the painter came adrift somehow, and away they went together. Of course in the confusion we did not hear him shouting. He looked abashed. She said cheerfully, "I suppose it does not matter my losing the train now?" "No, Jenny—you go below and get warm," he growled. Then to us: "A sailor has no business with a wife—I say. There I was, out of the ship. Well, no harm done this time. Let's go and look at what that fool of a steamer smashed."

'It wasn't much, but it delayed us three weeks. At the end of that time, the captain being engaged with his agents, I carried Mrs Beard's bag to the railway-station and put her all comfy into a third-class carriage. She lowered the window to say, "You are a good young man. If you see John—Captain Beard—without his muffler at night, just remind him from me to keep his throat well wrapped up." "Certainly, Mrs Beard," I said. "You are a good young man; I noticed how attentive you are to John—to Captain—" The train pulled out suddenly; I took my cap off to the old woman: I never saw her again . . . Pass the bottle.

'We went to sea next day. When we made that start for Bankok we had been already three months out of London. We had expected to be a fortnight or so—at the outside.

'It was January, and the weather was beautiful—the beautiful sunny winter weather that has more charm than in the summer-time, because it is unexpected, and crisp, and you know it won't, it can't, last long. It's like a windfall, like a godsend, like an unexpected piece of luck.

'It lasted all down the North Sea, all down Channel; and it lasted till we were three hundred miles or so to the westward of the Lizards: then the wind went round to the sou'west and began to pipe up. In two days it blew a gale. The *Judea*, hove to, wallowed on the Atlantic like an old candle-box. It blew day after day: it blew with spite, without interval, without mercy, without rest. The world was nothing but an immensity of great foaming waves rushing at us, under a sky low enough to touch with the hand and dirty like a smoked ceiling. In the stormy space surrounding us there was as much flying spray as air. Day after day and night after night there was nothing round the ship but the howl of the wind, the tumult of the sea, the noise of water pouring over her deck. There was no rest for her and no rest for us. She tossed, she pitched, she stood on her head, she sat on her tail, she rolled, she groaned, and we had to hold on while on deck and cling to our bunks when below, in a constant effort of body and worry of mind.

'One night Mahon spoke through the small window of my berth. It opened right into my very bed, and I was lying there sleepless, in my boots, feeling as though I had not slept for years, and could not if I tried. He said excitedly—

' "You got the sounding-rod in here, Marlow? I can't get the pumps to suck. By God! it's no child's play."

'I gave him the sounding-rod and lay down again, trying to think of various things—but I thought only of the pumps. When I came on deck they were still at it, and my watch relieved at the pumps. By the light of the lantern brought on deck to examine the sounding-rod I caught a glimpse of their weary, serious faces. We pumped all the four hours. We pumped all night, all day, all the week—watch and watch. She was working herself loose, and leaked badly—not enough to drown us at once, but enough to kill us with the work at the pumps. And while we pumped the ship was going from us piecemeal: the bulwarks went, the stanchions were

torn out, the ventilators smashed, the cabin-door burst
in. There was not a dry spot in the ship. She was being
gutted bit by bit. The long-boat changed, as if by
magic, into matchwood where she stood in her gripes. I
had lashed her myself, and was rather proud of my
handiwork, which had withstood so long the malice of
the sea. And we pumped. And there was no break in the
weather. The sea was white like a sheet of foam, like a
caldron of boiling milk; there was not a break in the
clouds, no—not the size of a man's hand—no, not for so
much as ten seconds. There was for us no sky, there
were for us no stars, no sun, no universe—nothing but
angry clouds and an infuriated sea. We pumped watch
and watch, for dear life; and it seemed to last for
months, for years, for all eternity, as though we had
been dead and gone to a hell for sailors. We forgot the
day of the week, the name of the month, what year it
was, and whether we had ever been ashore. The sails
blew away, she lay broadside on under a weather-cloth,
the ocean poured over her, and we did not care. We
turned those handles, and had the eyes of idiots. As
soon as we had crawled on deck I used to take a round
turn with a rope about the men, the pumps, and the
mainmast, and we turned, we turned incessantly, with
the water to our waists, to our necks, over our heads. It
was all one. We had forgotten how it felt to be dry.

'And there was somewhere in me the thought: By
Jove! this is the deuce of an adventure—something you
read about; and it is my first voyage as second mate—

and I am only twenty—and here I am lasting it out as well as any of these men, and keeping my chaps up to the mark. I was pleased. I would not have given up the experience for worlds. I had moments of exultation. Whenever the old dismantled craft pitched heavily with her counter high in the air, she seemed to me to throw up, like an appeal, like a defiance, like a cry to the clouds without mercy, the words written on her stern: "*Judea*, London. Do or Die."

'O youth! The strength of it, the faith of it, the imagination of it! To me she was not an old rattle-trap carting about the world a lot of coal for a freight—to me she was the endeavour, the test, the trial of life. I think of her with pleasure, with affection, with regret—as you would think of someone dead you have loved. I shall never forget her . . . Pass the bottle.

'One night when tied to the mast, as I explained, we were pumping on, deafened with the wind, and without spirit enough in us to wish ourselves dead, a heavy sea crashed aboard and swept clean over us. As soon as I got my breath I shouted, as in duty bound, "Keep on, boys!" when suddenly I felt something hard floating on deck strike the calf of my leg. I made a grab at it and missed. It was so dark we could not see each other's faces within a foot—you understand.

'After that thump the ship kept quiet for a while, and the thing, whatever it was, struck my leg again. This time I caught it—and it was a saucepan. At first, being stupid with fatigue and thinking of nothing but the pumps, I did not understand what I had in my hand. Suddenly it dawned upon me, and I shouted, "Boys, the house on deck is gone. Leave this, and let's look for the cook."

'There was a deck-house forward, which contained the galley, the cook's berth, and the quarters of the crew. As we had expected for days to see it swept away, the hands had been ordered to sleep in the cabin—the only safe place in the ship. The steward, Abraham, however, persisted in clinging to his berth, stupidly, like a mule—from sheer fright I believe, like an animal that won't leave a stable falling in an earthquake. So we went to look for him. It was chancing death, since once out of our lashings we were as exposed as if on a raft. But we went. The house was shattered as if a shell had exploded inside. Most of it had gone overboard—stove, men's quarters, and their property, all was gone; but two posts, holding a portion of the bulkhead to which Abraham's bunk was attached, remained as if by a miracle. We groped in the ruins and came upon this, and there he was, sitting in his bunk, surrounded by foam and wreckage, jabbering cheerfully to himself. He was out of his mind; completely and for ever mad, with this sudden shock coming upon the fag-end of his endurance. We snatched him up, lugged him aft, and pitched him head-first down the cabin companion. You understand there was no time to carry him down with infinite precautions and wait to see how he got on. Those below would pick him up at the bottom of the

stairs all right. We were in a hurry to go back to the
pumps. That business could not wait. A bad leak is an
inhuman thing.

'One would think that the sole purpose of that
fiendish gale had been to make a lunatic of that poor
devil of a mulatto. It eased before morning, and next
day the sky cleared, and as the sea went down the leak
took up. When it came to bending a fresh set of sails the
crew demanded to put back—and really there was nothing else to do. Boats gone, decks swept clean, cabin gutted, men without a stitch but what they stood in, stores
spoiled, ship strained. We put her head for home, and—
would you believe it? The wind came east right in our
teeth. It blew fresh, it blew continuously. We had to
beat up every inch of the way, but she did not leak so
badly, the water keeping comparatively smooth. Two
hours' pumping in every four is no joke—but it kept her
afloat as far as Falmouth.

'The good people there live on casualties of the sea,
and no doubt were glad to see us. A hungry crowd of
shipwrights sharpened their chisels at the sight of that
carcass of a ship. And, by Jove! they had pretty pickings
off us before they were done. I fancy the owner was
already in a tight place. There were delays. Then it was
decided to take part of the cargo out and caulk her top-
sides. This was done, the repairs finished, cargo
reshipped; a new crew came on board, and we went
out—for Bankok. At the end of a week we were back
again. The crew said they weren't going to Bankok—a

hundred and fifty days' passage—in a something hooker that wanted pumping eight hours out of the twenty-four; and the nautical papers inserted again the little paragraph: *"Judea.* Barque. Tyne to Bankok; coals; put back to Falmouth leaky and with crew refusing duty."

'There were more delays—more tinkering. The owner came down for a day, and said she was as right as a little fiddle. Poor old Captain Beard looked like the ghost of a Geordie skipper through the worry and humiliation of it. Remember he was sixty, and it was his first command. Mahon said it was a foolish business, and would end badly. I loved the ship more than ever, and wanted awfully to get to Bankok. To Bankok! Magic name, blessed name. Mesopotamia wasn't a patch on it. Remember I was twenty, and it was my first second-mate's billet, and the East was waiting for me.

'We went out and anchored in the outer roads with a fresh crew—the third. She leaked worse than ever. It was as if those confounded shipwrights had actually made a hole in her. This time we did not even go outside. The crew simply refused to man the windlass.

'They towed us back to the inner harbour, and we became a fixture, a feature, an institution of the place. People pointed us out to visitors as "That 'ere barque that's going to Bankok has been here six months—put back three times." On holidays the small boys pulling about in boats would hail, *"Judea,* ahoy!" and if a head showed above the rail shouted, "Where you bound to?— Bankok?" and jeered. We were only three on board. The poor old skipper mooned in the cabin. Mahon undertook the cooking, and unexpectedly developed all a Frenchman's genius for preparing nice little messes. I looked languidly after the rigging. We became citizens of Falmouth. Every shopkeeper knew us. At the barber's or tobacconist's they asked familiarly, "Do you think you will ever get to Bankok?" Meantime the owner, the underwriters, and the charterers squabbled amongst themselves in London, and our pay went on . . . Pass the bottle.

'It was horrid. Morally it was worse than pumping for life. It seemed as though we had been forgotten by the world, belonged to nobody, would get nowhere; it seemed that, as if bewitched, we would have to live for ever and ever in that inner harbour, a derision and a byword to generations of long-shore loafers and dishonest boatmen. I obtained three months' pay and a five days' leave, and made a rush for London. It took me a day to get there and pretty well another to come back—but three months' pay went all the same. I don't know what I did with it. I went to a music-hall, I believe, lunched, dined, and supped in a swell place in Regent Street, and was back to time, with nothing but a complete set of Byron's works and a new railway rug to show for three months' work. The boat-man who pulled me off to the ship said: "Hallo! I thought you had left the old thing. *She* will never get to Bankok." "That's all *you* know about it," I said, scornfully—but I didn't like that prophecy at all.

'Suddenly a man, some kind of agent to somebody, appeared with full powers. He had grog-blossoms all over his face, an indomitable energy, and was a jolly soul. We leaped into life again. A hulk came alongside, took our cargo, and then we went into dry dock to get our copper stripped. No wonder she leaked. The poor thing, strained beyond endurance by the gale, had, as if in disgust, spat out all the oakum of her lower seams. She was recaulked, new coppered, and made as tight as a bottle. We went back to the hulk and reshipped our cargo.

'Then, on a fine moonlight night, all the rats left the ship.

'We had been infested with them. They had destroyed our sails, consumed more stores than the crew, affably shared our beds and our dangers, and now, when the ship was made seaworthy, concluded to clear out. I called Mahon to enjoy the spectacle. Rat after rat appeared on our rail, took a last look over his shoulder, and leaped with a hollow thud into the empty hulk. We tried to count them, but soon lost the tale. Mahon said: "Well, well! don't talk to me about the intelligence of rats. They ought to have left before, when we had that narrow squeak from foundering. There you have the proof how silly is the superstition about them. They leave a good ship for an old rotten hulk, where there is nothing to eat, too, the fools! . . . I don't believe they know what is safe or what is good for them, any more than you or I."

'And after some more talk we agreed that the wisdom

of rats had been grossly overrated, being in fact no greater than that of men.

'The story of the ship was known, by this, all up the Channel from Land's End to the Forelands, and we could get no crew on the south coast. They sent us one all complete from Liverpool, and we left once more—for Bankok.

'We had fair breezes, smooth water right into the tropics, and the old *Judea* lumbered along in the sunshine. When she went eight knots everything cracked aloft, and we tied our caps to our heads; but mostly she strolled on at the rate of three miles an hour. What could you expect? She was tired—that old ship. Her youth was where mine is—where yours is—you fellows who listen to this yarn; and what friend would throw your years and your weariness in your face? We didn't grumble at her. To us aft, at least, it seemed as though we had been born in her, reared in her, had lived in her for ages, had never known any other ship. I would just as soon have abused the old village church at home for not being a cathedral.

'And for me there was also my youth to make me patient. There was all the East before me, and all life, and the thought that I had been tried in that ship and had come out pretty well. And I thought of men of old who, centuries ago, went that road in ships that sailed no better, to the land of palms, and spices, and yellow sands, and of brown nations ruled by kings more cruel than Nero the Roman, and more splendid than Solomon the Jew. The old bark lumbered on, heavy with her age and the burden of her cargo, while I lived the life of youth in ignorance and hope. She lumbered on through an interminable procession of days; and the fresh gilding flashed back at the setting sun, seemed to cry out over the darkening sea the words painted on her stern, "*Judea*, London. Do or Die."

'Then we entered the Indian Ocean and steered northerly for Java Head. The winds were light. Weeks slipped by. She crawled on, do or die, and people at home began to think of posting us as overdue.

'One Saturday evening, I being off duty, the men asked me to give them an extra bucket of water or so—for washing clothes. As I did not wish to screw on the fresh-water pump so late, I went forward whistling, and with a key in my hand to unlock the forepeak scuttle, intending to serve the water out of a spare tank we kept there.

'The smell down below was as unexpected as it was frightful. One would have thought hundreds of paraffin-lamps had been flaring and smoking in that hole for days. I was glad to get out. The man with me coughed and said, "Funny smell, sir." I answered negligently, "It's good for the health they say," and walked aft.

'The first thing I did was to put my head down the square of the midship ventilator. As I lifted the lid a visible breath, something like a thin fog, a puff of faint haze, rose from the opening. The ascending air was hot, and had a heavy, sooty, paraffiny smell. I gave one sniff, and put down the lid gently. It was no use choking myself. The cargo was on fire.

'Next day she began to smoke in earnest. You see it was to be expected, for though the coal was of a safe kind, that cargo had been so handled, so broken up with handling, that it looked more like smithy coal than anything else. Then it had been wetted—more than once. It rained all the time we were taking it back from the hulk, and now with this long passage it got heated, and there was another case of spontaneous combustion.

'The captain called us into the cabin. He had a chart spread on the table, and looked unhappy. He said, "The coast of West Australia is near, but I mean to proceed to our destination. It is the hurricane month, too; but we will just keep her head for Bankok, and fight the fire. No more putting back anywhere, if we all get roasted. We will try first to stifle this 'ere damned combustion by want of air."

'We tried. We battened down everything, and still she smoked. The smoke kept coming out through imperceptible crevices; it forced itself through bulkheads and covers; it oozed here and there and everywhere in slender threads, in an invisible film, in an incomprehensible manner. It made its way into the cabin, into the forecastle; it poisoned the sheltered places on the deck, it could be sniffed as high as the mainyard. It was clear that if the smoke came out the air came in. This was disheartening. This combustion refused to be stifled.

'We resolved to try water, and took the hatches off.

Enormous volumes of smoke, whitish, yellowish, thick, greasy, misty, choking, ascended as high as the trucks. All hands cleared out aft. Then the poisonous cloud blew away, and we went back to work in a smoke that was no thicker now than that of an ordinary factory chimney.

'We rigged the force-pump, got the hose along, and by-and-by it burst. Well, it was as old as the ship—a prehistoric hose, and past repair. Then we pumped with the feeble head-pump, drew water with buckets, and in this way managed in time to pour lots of Indian Ocean into the main hatch. The bright stream flashed in sunshine, fell into a layer of white crawling smoke, and vanished on the black surface of coal. Steam ascended mingling with the smoke. We poured salt water as into a barrel without a bottom. It was our fate to pump in that ship, to pump out of her, to pump into her; and after keeping water out of her to save ourselves from being drowned, we frantically poured water into her to save ourselves from being burnt.

'And she crawled on, do or die, in the serene weather. The sky was a miracle of purity, a miracle of azure. The sea was polished, was blue, was pellucid, was sparkling like a precious stone, extending on all sides, all round to the horizon—as if the whole terrestrial globe had been one jewel, one colossal sapphire, a single gem fashioned into a planet. And on the lustre of the great calm waters the *Judea* glided imperceptibly, enveloped in languid and unclean vapours, in a lazy cloud that drifted to leeward, light and slow; a pestiferous cloud defiling the splendour of sea and sky.

'All this time of course we saw no fire. The cargo smouldered at the bottom somewhere. Once Mahon, as we were working side by side, said to me with a queer smile: "Now, if she only would spring a tidy leak—like that time when we first left the Channel—it would put a stopper on this fire. Wouldn't it?" I remarked irrelevantly, "Do you remember the rats?"

'We fought the fire and sailed the ship too as carefully as though nothing had been the matter The steward cooked and attended on us. Of the other twelve men, eight worked while four rested. Everyone took his turn, captain included. There was equality, and if not exactly fraternity, then a deal of good feeling. Sometimes a man, as he dashed a bucketful of water down the hatchway, would yell out, "Hurrah for Bankok!" and the rest laughed. But generally we were taciturn and serious—and thirsty. Oh! how thirsty! And we had to be careful with the water. Strict allowance. The ship smoked, the sun blazed . . . Pass the bottle.

'We tried everything. We even made an attempt to dig down to the fire. No good, of course. No man could remain more than a minute below. Mahon, who went first, fainted there, and the man who went to fetch him out did likewise. We lugged them out on deck. Then I leaped down to show how easily it could be done. They had learned wisdom by that time, and contented themselves by fishing for me with a chain-hook tied to a broom-handle, I believe. I did not offer to go and fetch up my shovel, which was left down below.

'Things began to look bad. We put the long boat into the water. The second boat was ready to swing out. We had also another, a 14-foot thing on davits aft, where it was quite safe.

'Then, behold, the smoke suddenly decreased. We redoubled our efforts to flood the bottom of the ship. In two days there was no smoke at all. Everybody was on the broad grin. This was on a Friday. On Saturday no work, but sailing the ship of course, was done. The men washed their clothes and their faces for the first time in a fortnight, and had a special dinner given them. They spoke of spontaneous combustion with contempt, and implied *they* were the boys to put out combustions. Somehow we all felt as though we each had inherited a large fortune. But a beastly smell of burning hung about the ship. Captain Beard had hollow eyes and sunken cheeks. I had never noticed so much before how twisted and bowed he was. He and Mahon prowled soberly about hatches and ventilators, sniffing. It struck me suddenly poor Mahon was a very, very old chap. As to me, I was as pleased and proud as though I had helped to win a great naval battle. O! Youth!

'The night was fine. In the morning a homeward-bound ship passed us hull down—the first we had seen for months; but we were nearing the land at last, Java Head being about 190 miles off, and nearly due north.

'Next day it was my watch on deck from eight to

twelve. At breakfast the captain observed, "It's wonderful how that smell hangs about the cabin." About ten, the mate being on the poop, I stepped down on the main-deck for a moment. The carpenter's bench stood abaft the mainmast: I leaned against it sucking at my pipe, and the carpenter, a young chap, came to talk to me. He remarked, "I think we have done very well, haven't we?" and then I perceived with annoyance the fool was trying to tilt the bench. I said curtly, "Don't, Chips," and immediately became aware of a queer sensation, of an absurd delusion,—I seemed somehow to be in the air. I heard all round me like a pent-up breath released—as if a thousand giants simultaneously had said Phoo!—and felt a dull concussion which made my ribs ache suddenly. No doubt about it—I was in the air, and my body was describing a short parabola. But short as it was, I had the time to think several thoughts in, as far as I can remember, the following order: "This can't be the carpenter—What is it?—Some accident—Submarine volcano?—Coals, gas!—By Jove! we are being blown up—Everybody's dead—I am falling into the after-hatch—I see fire in it."

'The coal-dust suspended in the air of the hold had glowed dull-red at the moment of the explosion. In the twinkling of an eye, in an infinitesimal fraction of a second since the first tilt of the bench, I was sprawling full length on the cargo. I picked myself up and scrambled out. It was quick like a rebound. The deck was a wilderness of smashed timber, lying crosswise like trees in a

wood after a hurricane; an immense curtain of soiled
rags waved gently before me—it was the main-sail
blown to strips. I thought, The masts will be toppling
over directly; and to get out of the way bolted on all-
fours towards the poop-ladder. The first person I saw
was Mahon, with eyes like saucers, his mouth open, and
the long white hair standing straight on end round his
head like a silver halo. He was just about to go down
when the sight of the main-deck stirring, heaving up,
and changing into splinters before his eyes, petrified him
on the top step. I stared at him in unbelief, and he
stared at me with a queer kind of shocked curiosity. I
did not know that I had no hair, no eyebrows, no eye-
lashes, that my young moustache was burnt off, that my
face was black, one cheek laid open, my nose cut, and
my chin bleeding. I had lost my cap, one of my slippers,
and my shirt was torn to rags. Of all this I was not
aware. I was amazed to see the ship still afloat, the
poop-deck whole—and, most of all, to see anybody
alive. Also the peace of the sky and the serenity of the
sea were distinctly surprising. I suppose I expected to
see them convulsed with horror . . . Pass the bottle.

'There was a voice hailing the ship from somewhere—in the air, in the sky—I couldn't tell. Presently
I saw the captain and he was mad. He asked me eagerly,
"Where's the cabin-table?" and to hear such a question
was a frightful shock. I had just been blown up, you
understand, and vibrated with that experience,—I
wasn't quite sure whether I was alive. Mahon began to

stamp with both feet and yelled at him, "Good God!
don't you see the deck's blown out of her?" I found my
voice, and stammered out as if conscious of some gross
neglect of duty, "I don't know where the cabin-table is."
It was like an absurd dream.

'Do you know what he wanted next? Well, he wanted
to trim the yards. Very placidly, and as if lost in
thought, he insisted on having the foreyard squared. "I
don't know if there's anybody alive," said Mahon,
almost tearfully. "Surely," he said, gently, "there will
be enough left to square the foreyard."

'The old chap, it seems, was in his own berth winding
up the chronometers, when the shock sent him spinning.
Immediately it occurred to him—as he said afterwards—
that the ship had struck something, and ran out into the
cabin. There, he saw, the cabin-table had vanished
somewhere. The deck being blown up, it had fallen
down into the lazarette of course. Where we had our
breakfast that morning he saw only a great hole in the
floor. This appeared to him so awfully mysterious, and
impressed him so immensely, that what he saw and
heard after he got on deck were mere trifles in compar-
ison. And, mark, he noticed directly the wheel deserted
and his barque off her course—and his only thought was
to get that miserable, stripped, undecked, smouldering
shell of a ship back again with her head pointing at her
port of destination. Bankok! That's what he was after.
I tell you this quiet, bowed, bandy-legged, almost
deformed little man was immense in the singleness of

his idea and in his placid ignorance of our agitation. He motioned us forward with a commanding gesture, and went to take the wheel himself.

'Yes; that was the first thing we did—trim the yards of that wreck! No one was killed, or even disabled, but everyone was more or less hurt. You should have seen them! Some were in rags, with black faces, like coal-heavers, like sweeps, and had bullet heads that seemed closely cropped, but were in fact singed to the skin. Others of the watch below, awakened by being shot out from their collapsing bunks, shivered incessantly, and kept on groaning even as we went about our work. But they all worked. That crew of Liverpool hard cases had in them the right stuff. It's my experience they always have. It is the sea that gives it—the vastness, the lone-liness surrounding their dark stolid souls. Ah! Well! we stumbled, we crept, we fell, we barked our shins on the wreckage, we hauled. The masts stood, but we did not know how much they might be charred down below. It was nearly calm, but a long swell ran from the west and made her roll. They might go at any moment. We looked at them with apprehension. One could not fore-see which way they would fall.

'Then we retreated aft and looked about us. The deck was a tangle of planks on edge, of planks on end, of splinters, of ruined woodwork. The masts rose from that chaos like big trees above a matted undergrowth. The interstices of that mass of wreckage were full of some-thing whitish, sluggish, stirring—of something that was

like a greasy fog. The smoke of the invisible fire was
coming up again, was trailing, like a poisonous thick
mist in some valley choked with dead wood. Already
lazy wisps were beginning to curl upwards amongst the
mass of splinters. Here and there a piece of timber,
stuck upright, resembled a post. Half of a fife-rail had
been shot through the foresail, and the sky made a patch
of glorious blue in the ignobly soiled canvas. A portion
of several boards holding together had fallen across the
rail, and one end protruded overboard, like a gangway
leading upon nothing, like a gangway leading over the
deep sea, leading to death—as if inviting us to walk the
plank at once and be done with our ridiculous troubles.
And still the air, the sky—a ghost, something invisible
was hailing the ship.

'Someone had the sense to look over, and there was
the helmsman, who had impulsively jumped overboard,
anxious to come back. He yelled and swam lustily like
a merman, keeping up with the ship. We threw him a
rope, and presently he stood amongst us streaming with
water and very crestfallen. The captain had surrendered
the wheel, and apart, elbow on rail and chin in hand,
gazed at the sea wistfully. We asked ourselves, What
next? I thought, Now, this is something like. This is
great. I wonder what will happen. O youth!

'Suddenly Mahon sighted a steamer far astern. Captain Beard said, We may do something with her yet.'
We hoisted two flags, which said in the international
language of the sea, "On fire. Want immediate assis-

tance." The steamer grew bigger rapidly, and by-and-by spoke with two flags on her foremast, "I am coming to your assistance."

'In half an hour she was abreast, to windward, within hail, and rolling slightly, with her engines stopped. We lost our composure, and yelled all together with excitement, "We've been blown up." A man in a white helmet, on the bridge, cried "Yes! All right! all right!" and he nodded his head, and smiled, and made soothing motions with his hand as though at a lot of frightened children. One of the boats dropped in the water, and walked towards us upon the sea with her long oars. Four Calashes pulled a swinging stroke. This was my first sight of Malay seamen. I've known them since, but what struck me then was their unconcern: they came alongside, and even the bowman standing up and holding to our main-chains with the boat-hook did not deign to lift his head for a glance. I thought people who had been blown up deserved more attention.

'A little man, dry like a chip and agile like a monkey, cIambered up. It was the mate of the steamer. He gave one look, and cried, "O boys—you had better quit."

'We were silent. He talked apart with the captain for a time, seemed to argue with him. Then they went away together to the steamer.

'When our skipper came back we learned that the steamer was the *Somerville*, Captain Nash, from West Australia to Singapore *via* Batavia with mails, and that the agreement was she should tow us to Anjer or

Batavia, if possible, where we could extinguish the fire
by scuttling, and then proceed on our voyage—to
Bankok! The old man seemed excited. "We will do it
yet," he said to Mahon, fiercely. He shook his fist at the
sky. Nobody else said a word.

'At noon the steamer began to tow. She went ahead
slim and high, and what was left of the *Judea* followed at
the end of seventy fathom of tow-rope,—followed her
swiftly like a cloud of smoke with mast-heads protrud-
ing above. We went aloft to furl the sails. We coughed
on the yards, and were careful about the bunts. Do you
see the lot of us there, putting a neat furl on the sails
of that ship doomed to arrive nowhere? There was not
a man who didn't think that at any moment the masts
would topple over. From aloft we could not see the ship
for smoke, and they worked carefully, passing the gaskets with even turns. "Harbour furl—aloft there!" cried
Mahon from below.

'You understand this? I don't think one of those
chaps expected to get down in the usual way. When we
did I heard them saying to each other, "Well, I thought
we would come down overboard, in a lump—sticks and
all—blame me if I didn't." "That's what I was thinking
to myself," would answer wearily another battered and
bandaged scarecrow. And, mind, these were men without the drilled-in habit of obedience. To an onlooker
they would be a lot of profane scallywags without a
redeeming point. What made them do it—what made
them obey me when I, thinking consciously how fine

it was, made them drop the bunt of the foresail twice to try and do it better? What? They had no professional reputation—no examples, no praise. It wasn't a sense of duty; they all knew well enough how to shirk, and laze, and dodge—when they had a mind to it—and mostly they had. Was it the two pounds ten a-month that sent them there? They didn't think their pay half good enough. No; it was something in them, something inborn and subtle and everlasting. I don't say positively that the crew of a French or German merchantman wouldn't have done it, but I doubt whether it would have been done in the same way. There was a completeness in it, something solid like a principle, and masterful like an instinct—a disclosure of something secret—of that hidden something, that gift of good or evil that makes racial difference, that shapes the fate of nations.

'It was that night at ten that, for the first time since we had been fighting it, we saw the fire. The speed of the towing had fanned the smouldering destruction. A blue gleam appeared forward, shining below the wreck of the deck. It wavered in patches, it seemed to stir and creep like the light of a glowworm. I saw it first, and told Mahon. "Then the game's up," he said. "We had better stop this towing, or she will burst out suddenly fore and aft before we can clear out." We set up a yell; rang bells to attract their attention; they towed on. At last Mahon and I had to crawl forward and cut the rope with an axe. There was no time to cast off the lashings. Red tongues could be seen licking the wilderness of splinters under our feet as we made our way back to the poop.

'Of course they very soon found out in the steamer that the rope was gone. She gave a loud blast of her whistle, her lights were seen sweeping in a wide circle, she came up ranging close alongside, and stopped. We were all in a tight group on the poop looking at her. Every man had saved a little bundle or a bag. Suddenly a conical flame with a twisted top shot up forward and threw upon the black sea a circle of light, with the two vessels side by side and heaving gently in its centre. Captain Beard had been sitting on the gratings still and mute for hours, but now he rose slowly and advanced in front of us, to the mizzen-shrouds. Captain Nash hailed: "Come along! Look sharp. I have mail-bags on board. I will take you and your boats to Singapore."

' "Thank you! No!" said our skipper. "We must see the last of the ship."

' "I can't stand by any longer," shouted the other. "Mails—you know."

' "Ay! ay! We are all right."

' "Very well! I'll report you in Singapore . . . Good-bye!"

'He waved his hand. Our men dropped their bundles quietly. The steamer moved ahead, and passing out of the circle of light, vanished at once from our sight, dazzled by the fire which burned fiercely. And then I knew that I would see the East first as commander of a small boat. I thought it fine; and the fidelity to the old ship was fine. We should see the last of her. Oh, the glamour of youth! Oh, the fire of it, more dazzling than the flames of the burning ship, throwing a magic light on the wide earth, leaping audaciously to the sky, presently to be quenched by time, more cruel, more pitiless, more bitter than the sea—and like the flames of the burning ship surrounded by an impenetrable night.

'The old man warned us in his gentle and inflexible way that it was part of our duty to save for the underwriters as much as we could of the ship's gear. Accordingly we went to work aft, while she blazed forward to give us plenty of light. We lugged out a lot of rubbish. What didn't we save? An old barometer fixed with an absurd quantity of screws nearly cost me my life: a sudden rush of smoke came upon me, and I just got away in time. There were various stores, bolts of canvas, coils of rope; the poop looked like a marine bazaar, and the boats were lumbered to the gunwales. One would have thought the old man wanted to take as much as he could of his first command with him. He was very, very quiet, but off his balance evidently. Would you believe it? He wanted to take a length of old stream-cable and a kedge-anchor with him in the long-boat. We said, "Ay, ay, sir," deferentially, and on the quiet let the things slip overboard. The heavy medicine-chest went that way, two bags of green coffee, tins of paint—fancy, paint!— a whole lot of things. Then I was ordered with two hands into the boats to make a stowage and get them

ready against the time it would be proper for us to leave
the ship.

'We put everything straight, stepped the long-boat's
mast for our skipper, who was to take charge of her,
and I was not sorry to sit down for a moment. My face
felt raw, every limb ached as if broken, I was aware of
all my ribs, and would have sworn to a twist in the
backbone. The boats, fast astern, lay in a deep shadow,
and all around I could see the circle of the sea lighted
by the fire. A gigantic flame arose forward straight and
clear. It flared fierce, with noises like the whirr of
wings, with rumbles as of thunder. There were cracks,
detonations, and from the cone of flame the sparks flew
upwards, as man is born to trouble, to leaky ships, and
to ships that burn.

'What bothered me was that the ship, lying broadside
to the swell and to such wind as there was—a mere
breath—the boats would not keep astern where they
were safe, but persisted, in a pig-headed way boats have,
in getting under the counter and then swinging alongside. They were knocking about dangerously and coming near the flame, while the ship rolled on them, and,
of course, there was always the danger of the masts
going over the side at any moment. I and my two boat-
keepers kept them off as best we could, with oars and
boat-hooks; but to be constantly at it became exasperating, since there was no reason why we should not
leave at once. We could not see those on board nor
could we imagine what caused the delay. The boat-

keepers were swearing feebly, and I had not only my share of the work but also had to keep at it two men who showed a constant inclination to lay themselves down and let things slide.

'At last I hailed, "On deck there," and someone looked over "We're ready here," I said. The head disappeared, and very soon popped up again. "The captain says, All right, sir, and to keep the boats well clear of the ship."

'Half an hour passed. Suddenly there was a frightful racket, rattle, clanking of chain, hiss of water, and millions of sparks flew up into the shivering column of smoke that stood leaning slightly above the ship. The cat-heads had burned away, and the two red-hot anchors had gone to the bottom, tearing out after them two hundred fathom of red-hot chain. The ship trembled, the mass of flame swayed as if ready to collapse, and the fore top-gallant-mast fell. It darted down like an arrow of fire, shot under, and instantly leaping up within an oar's-length of the boats, floated quietly, very black on the luminous sea. I hailed the deck again. After some time a man in an unexpectedly cheerful but also muffled tone, as though he had been trying to speak with his mouth shut, informed me, "Coming directly, sir," and vanished. For a long time I heard nothing but the whirr and roar of the fire. There were also whistling sounds. The boats jumped, tugged at the painters, ran at each other playfully, knocked their sides together, or, do what we would, swung in a bunch against the ship's side. I couldn't stand it any longer, and swarming up a rope, clambered aboard over the stern.

'It was as bright as day. Coming up like this, the sheet of fire facing me was a terrifying sight, and the heat seemed hardly bearable at first. On a settee cushion dragged out of the cabin Captain Beard, his legs drawn up and one arm under his head, slept with the light playing on him. Do you know what the rest were busy about? They were sitting on deck right aft, round an open case, eating bread and cheese and drinking bottled stout.

'On the background of flames twisting in fierce tongues above their heads they seemed at home like salamanders, and looked like a band of desperate pirates. The fire sparkled in the whites of their eyes, gleamed on patches of white skin seen through the torn shirts. Each had the marks as of a battle about him—bandaged heads, tied-up arms, a strip of dirty rag round a knee—and each man had a bottle between his legs and a chunk of cheese in his hand. Mahon got up. With his handsome and disreputable head, his hooked profile, his long white beard, and with an uncorked bottle in his hand, he resembled one of those reckless sea-robbers of old making merry amidst violence and disaster. "The last meal on board," he explained solemnly. "We had nothing to eat all day, and it was no use leaving all this." He flourished the bottle and indicated the sleeping skipper. "He said he couldn't swallow anything, so I got him to lie down," he went on; and as I stared, "I don't know whether you are aware, young fellow, the man had no sleep to speak of for days—and there will be dam' little sleep in the boats." "There will be no boats by-and-by if you fool about much longer," I said, indignantly. I walked up to the skipper and shook him by the shoulder. At last he opened his eyes, but did not move. "Time to leave her, sir," I said quietly.

'He got up painfully, looked at the flames, at the sea sparkling round the ship, and black, black as ink farther away; he looked at the stars shining dim through a thin veil of smoke in a sky black, black as Erebus.

' "Youngest first," he said.

'And the ordinary seaman, wiping his mouth with the back of his hand, got up, clambered over the taffrail, and vanished. Others followed. One, on the point of going over, stopped short to drain his bottle, and with a great swing of his arm flung it at the fire. "Take this!" he cried.

'The skipper lingered disconsolately, and we left him to commune for a while with his first command. Then I went up again and brought him away at last. It was time. The ironwork on the poop was hot to the touch.

'Then the painter of the long-boat was cut, and the three boats, tied together, drifted clear of the ship. It was just sixteen hours after the explosion when we abandoned her. Mahon had charge of the second boat, and I had the smallest—the 14-foot thing. The long-boat would have taken the lot of us; but the skipper said we must save as much property as we could—for the under-

writers—and so I got my first command. I had two men
with me, a bag of biscuits, a few tins of meat, and a
breaker of water. I was ordered to keep close to the long-
boat, that in case of bad weather we might be taken into
her.

'And do you know what I thought? I thought I
would part company as soon as I could. I wanted to
have my first command all to myself. I wasn't going to
sail in a squadron if there were a chance of independent
cruising. I would make land by myself. I would beat
the other boats. Youth! All youth! The silly charming,
beautiful youth.

'But we did not make a start at once. We must see
the last of the ship. And so the boats drifted about that
night, heaving and setting on the swell. The men dozed,
waked, sighed, groaned. I looked at the burning ship.

'Between the darkness of earth and heaven she was
burning fiercely upon a disc of purple sea shot by the
blood-red play of gleams; upon a disc of water glittering and sinister. A high, clear flame, an immense and
lonely flame, ascended from the ocean, and from its
summit the black smoke poured continuously at the sky.
She burned furiously; mournful and imposing like a
funeral pile kindled in the night, surrounded by the sea,
watched over by the stars. A magnificent death had
come like a grace, like a gift, like a reward to that old
ship at the end of her laborious days. The surrender of
her weary ghost to the keeping of stars and sea was stirring like the sight of a glorious triumph. The masts fell

just before daybreak, and for a moment there was a burst and turmoil of sparks that seemed to fill with flying fire the night patient and watchful, the vast night lying silent upon the sea. At daylight she was only a charred shell, floating still under a cloud of smoke and bearing a glowing mass of coal within.

'Then the oars were got out, and the boats forming in a line moved round her remains as if in procession— the long-boat leading. As we pulled across her stern a slim dart of fire shot out viciously at us, and suddenly she went down, head first, in a great hiss of steam. The unconsumed stern was the last to sink; but the paint had gone, had cracked, had peeled off, and there were no letters, there was no word, no stubborn device that was like her soul, to flash at the rising sun her creed and her name.

'We made our way north. A breeze sprang up, and about noon all the boats came together for the last time. I had no mast or sail in mine, but I made a mast out of a spare oar and hoisted a boat-awning for a sail, with a boat-hook for a yard. She was certainly over-masted, but I had the satisfaction of knowing that with the wind aft I could beat the other two. I had to wait for them. Then we all had a look at the captain's chart, and, after a sociable meal of hard bread and water, got our last instructions. These were simple: steer north, and keep together as much as possible. "Be careful with that jury-rig, Marlow," said the captain; and Mahon, as I sailed proudly past his boat, wrinkled his curved nose and hailed, "You will sail that ship of yours under water, if you don't look out, young fellow." He was a malicious old man—and may the deep sea where he sleeps now rock him gently, rock him tenderly to the end of time!

'Before sunset a thick rain-squall passed over the two boats, which were far astern, and that was the last I saw of them for a time. Next day I sat steering my cockle-shell—my first command—with nothing but water and sky around me. I did sight in the afternoon the upper sails of a ship far away, but said nothing, and my men did not notice her. You see I was afraid she might be homeward bound, and I had no mind to turn back from the portals of the East. I was steering for Java—another blessed name—like Bankok, you know. I steered many days.

'I need not tell you what it is to be knocking about in an open boat. I remember nights and days of calm, when we pulled, we pulled, and the boat seemed to stand still, as if bewitched within the circle of the sea horizon. I remember the heat, the deluge of rain-squalls that kept us baling for dear life (but filled our water-cask), and I remember sixteen hours on end with a mouth dry as a cinder and a steering-oar over the stern to keep my first command head on to a breaking sea. I did not know how good a man I was till then. I remember the drawn faces, the dejected figures of my two men, and I remember my youth and the feeling that will never come back any more—the feeling that I could last for ever, outlast the sea, the earth, and all men; the deceitful feeling that lures us on to joys, to perils, to love, to vain effort—to death; the triumphant conviction of strength, the heat of life in the handful of dust, the glow in the heart that with every year grows dim, grows cold, grows small, and expires—and expires, too soon, too soon—before life itself.

'And this is how I see the East. I have seen its secret places and have looked into its very soul; but now I see it always from a small boat, a high outline of mountains, blue and afar in the morning; like faint mist at noon; a jagged wall of purple at sunset. I have the feel of the oar in my hand, the vision of a scorching blue sea in my eyes. And I see a bay, a wide bay, smooth as glass and polished like ice, shimmering in the dark. A red light burns far off upon the gloom of the land, and the night is soft and warm. We drag at the oars with aching arms, and suddenly a puff of wind, a puff faint and tepid and laden with strange odours of blossoms, of aromatic wood, comes out of the still night—the first sigh of the East on my face. That I can never forget. It was impalpable and enslaving, like a charm, like a whispered promise of mysterious delight.

'We had been pulling this finishing spell for eleven hours. Two pulled, and he whose turn it was to rest sat at the tiller. We had made out the red light in that bay and steered for it, guessing it must mark some small coasting port. We passed two vessels, outlandish and high-sterned, sleeping at anchor, and, approaching the light, now very dim, ran the boat's nose against the end of a jutting wharf. We were blind with fatigue. My men dropped the oars and fell off the thwarts as if dead. I made fast to a pile. A current rippled softly. The scented obscurity of the shore was grouped into vast masses, a density of colossal clumps of vegetation, probably—mute and fantastic shapes. And at their foot the semicircle of a bench gleamed faintly, like an illusion. There was not a light, not a stir, not a sound. The mysterious East faced me, perfumed like a flower, silent like death, dark like a grave.

'And I sat weary beyond expression, exulting like a conqueror, sleepless and entranced as if before a profound, a fateful enigma.

'A splashing of oars, a measured dip reverberating on the level of water, intensified by the silence of the shore into loud claps, made me jump up. A boat, a European boat, was coming in. I invoked the name of the dead; I hailed: *Judea* ahoy! A thin shout answered.

'It was the captain. I had beaten the flagship by three hours, and I was glad to hear the old man's voice again, tremulous and tired. "Is it you, Marlow?" "Mind the end of that jetty, sir," I cried.

'He approached cautiously, and brought up with the deep-sea lead-line which he had saved—for the underwriters. I eased my painter and fell alongside. He sat, a broken figure at the stern, wet with dew, his hands clasped in his lap. His men were asleep already. "I had a terrible time of it," he murmured. "Mahon is behind—not very far." We conversed in whispers, in low whispers, as if afraid to wake up the land. Guns, thunder, earthquakes would not have awakened the men just then.

'Looking round as we talked, I saw away at sea a bright light travelling in the night. "There's a steamer passing the bay," I said. She was not passing, she was entering, and she even came close and anchored. "I wish," said the old man, "you would find out whether she is English. Perhaps they could give us a passage somewhere." He seemed nervously anxious. So by dint of punching and kicking I started one of my men into a state of somnambulism, and giving him an oar, took another and pulled towards the lights of the steamer.

'There was a murmur of voices in her, metallic hollow clangs of the engine-room, footsteps on the deck. Her ports shone, round like dilated eyes. Shapes moved about, and there was a shadowy man high up on the bridge. He heard my oars.

'And then, before I could open my lips, the East spoke to me, but it was in a Western voice. A torrent of words was poured into the enigmatical, the fateful silence; outlandish, angry words, mixed with words and even whole sentences of good English, less strange but even more surprising. The voice swore and cursed violently; it riddled the solemn peace of the bay by a volley of abuse. It began by calling me Pig, and from that went crescendo into unmentionable adjectives—in English. The man up there raged aloud in two languages, and with a sincerity in his fury that almost convinced

me I had, in some way, sinned against the harmony of
the universe. I could hardly see him, but began to think
he would work himself into a fit.

'Suddenly he ceased, and I could hear him snorting
and blowing like a porpoise. I said—

' "What steamer is this, pray?"

' "Eh? What's this? And who are you?"

' "Castaway crew of an English barque burnt at sea.
We came here tonight. I am the second mate. The captain is in the long-boat, and wishes to know if you
would give us a passage somewhere."

' "Oh, my goodness! I say ... This is the *Celestial*
from Singapore on her return trip. I'll arrange with your
captain in the morning, . . . and, . . . I say, . . . did you
hear me just now?"

' "I should think the whole bay heard you."

' "I thought you were a shore-boat. Now, look here—
this infernal lazy scoundrel of a caretaker has gone to
sleep again—curse him. The light is out, and I nearly
ran foul of the end of this damned jetty. This is the
third time he plays me this trick. Now, I ask you, can
anybody stand this kind of thing? It's enough to drive
a man out of his mind. I'll report him . . . I'll get the
Assistant Resident to give him the sack, by . . . ! See—
there's no light. It's out, isn't it? I take you to witness
the light's out. There should be a light, you know. A
red light on the—"

' "There was a light," I said, mildly.

' "But it's out, man! What's the use of talking like

this? You can see for yourself it's out—don't you? If you had to take a valuable steamer along this Godforsaken coast you would want a light, too. I'll kick him from end to end of his miserable wharf. You'll see if I don't. I will—"

' "So I may tell my captain you'll take us ?" I broke in.

' "Yes, I'll take you. Good night," he said, brusquely.

'I pulled back, made fast again to the jetty, and then went to sleep at last. I had faced the silence of the East. I had heard some of its language. But when I opened my eyes again the silence was as complete as though it had never been broken. I was lying in a flood of light, and the sky had never looked so far, so high, before. I opened my eyes and lay without moving.

'And then I saw the men of the East—they were looking at me. The whole length of the jetty was full of people. I saw brown, bronze, yellow faces, the black eyes, the glitter, the colour of an Eastern crowd. And all these beings stared without a murmur, without a sigh, without a movement. They stared down at the boats, at the sleeping men who at night had come to them from the sea. Nothing moved. The fronds of palms stood still against the sky. Not a branch stirred along the shore, and the brown roofs of hidden houses peeped through the green foliage, through the big leaves that hung shining and still like leaves forged of heavy metal. This was the East of the ancient navigators, so old, so mysterious, resplendent and sombre, living and unchanged, full of danger and promise. And these were the men. I sat up suddenly. A wave of movement passed through the crowd from end to end, passed along the heads, swayed the bodies, ran along the jetty like a ripple on the water, like a breath of wind on a field—and all was still again. I see it now—the wide sweep of the bay, the glittering sands, the wealth of green infinite and varied, the sea blue like the sea of a dream, the crowd of attentive faces, the blaze of vivid colour—the water reflecting it all, the curve of the shore, the jetty, the high-sterned outlandish craft floating still, and the three boats with the tired men from the West sleeping, unconscious of the land and the people and of the violence of sunshine. They slept thrown across the thwarts, curled on bottom-boards, in the careless attitudes of death. The head of the old skipper, leaning back in the stern of the long-boat, had fallen on his breast, and he looked as though he would never wake. Farther out old Mahon's face was upturned to the sky, with the long white beard spread out on his breast, as though he had been shot where he sat at the tiller; and a man, all in a heap in the bows of the boat, slept with both arms embracing the stem-head and with his cheek laid on the gunwale. The East looked at them without a sound.

'I have known its fascination since; I have seen the mysterious shores, the still water, the lands of brown nations, where a stealthy Nemesis lies in wait, pursues, overtakes so many of the conquering race, who are proud of their wisdom, of their knowledge, of their strength. But for me all the East is contained in that vision of my youth. It is all in that moment when I opened my young eyes on it. I came upon it from a tussle with the sea—and I was young—and I saw it looking at me. And this is all that is left of it! Only a moment; a moment of strength, of romance, of glamour—of youth! . . . A flick of sunshine upon a strange shore, the time to remember, the time for a sigh, and—good-bye!—Night—Good-bye . . . !'

He drank.

'Ah! The good old time—the good old time. Youth and the sea. Glamour and the sea! The good, strong sea, the salt, bitter sea, that could whisper to you and roar at you and knock your breath out of you.'

He drank again.

'By all that's wonderful it is the sea, I believe, the sea itself—or is it youth alone? Who can tell? But you here—you all had something out of life: money, love— whatever one gets on shore—and, tell me, wasn't that the best time, that time when we were young at sea; young and had nothing, on the sea that gives nothing, except hard knocks—and sometimes a chance to feel your strength—that only—what you all regret?'

And we all nodded at him: the man of finance, the man of accounts, the man of law, we all nodded at him over the polished table that like a still sheet of brown water reflected our faces, lined, wrinkled; our faces marked by toil, by deceptions, by success, by love; our weary eyes looking still, looking always, looking anxiously for something out of life, that while it is expected is already gone—has passed unseen, in a sigh, in a flash—together with the youth, with the strength, with the romance of illusions.

Heart of Darkness

I

The *Nellie*, a cruising yawl, swung to her anchor without a flutter of the sails, and was at rest. The flood had made, the wind was nearly calm, and being bound down the river, the only thing for it was to come to and wait for the turn of the tide.

The sea-reach of the Thames stretched before us like the beginning of an interminable waterway. In the offing the sea and the sky were welded together without a joint, and in the luminous space the tanned sails of the barges drifting up with the tide seemed to stand still in red clusters of canvas sharply peaked, with gleams of varnished sprits. A haze rested on the low shores that ran out to sea in vanishing flatness. The air was dark above Gravesend, and farther back still seemed condensed into a mournful gloom, brooding motionless over the biggest, and the greatest, town on earth.

The Director of Companies was our captain and our host. We four affectionately watched his back as he stood in the bows looking to seaward. On the whole river there was nothing that looked half so nautical. He resembled a pilot, which to a seaman is trustworthiness personified. It was difficult to realize his work was not out there in the luminous estuary, but behind him, within the brooding gloom.

Between us there was, as I have already said somewhere, the bond of the sea. Besides holding our hearts together through long periods of separation, it had the effect of making us tolerant of each other's yarns—and even convictions. The Lawyer—the best of old fellows—had, because of his many years and many virtues, the only cushion on deck, and was lying on the only rug. The Accountant had brought out already a box of dominoes, and was toying architecturally with the bones. Marlow sat cross-legged right aft, leaning against the mizzen-mast. He had sunken cheeks, a yellow complexion, a straight back. an ascetic aspect, and, with his arms dropped, the palms of hands outwards, resembled an idol. The Director, satisfied the anchor had good hold, made his way aft and sat down amongst us. We exchanged a few words lazily. Afterwards there was silence on board the yacht. For some reason or other we did not begin that game of dominoes. We felt meditative, and fit for nothing but placid staring. The day was ending in a serenity of still and exquisite brilliance. The water shone pacifically; the sky, without a speck, was a benign immensity of unstained light; the very mist on the Essex marshes was like a gauzy and radiant fabric, hung from the wooded rises inland, and draping the low shores in diaphanous folds. Only the gloom to the west, brooding over the upper reaches, became more sombre every minute, as if angered by the approach of the sun.

And at last, in its curved and imperceptible fall, the sun sank low, and from glowing white changed to a dull red without rays and without heat, as if about to go out suddenly, stricken to death by the touch of that gloom brooding over a crowd of men.

Forthwith a change came over the waters, and the serenity became less brilliant but more profound. The old river in its broad reach rested unruffled at the decline of day, after ages of good service done to the race that peopled its banks, spread out in the tranquil dignity of a waterway leading to the uttermost ends of the earth. We looked at the venerable stream not in the vivid flush of a short day that comes and departs for ever, but in the august light of abiding memories. And indeed nothing is easier for a man who has, as the phrase goes, 'followed the sea' with reverence and affection, than to evoke the great spirit of the past upon the lower reaches of the Thames. The tidal current runs tö and fro in its unceasing service, crowded with memories of men and ships it had borne to the rest of home or to the battles of the sea. It had known and served all the men of whom the nation is proud, from Sir Francis Drake to Sir John Franklin, knights all, titled and untitled—the great knights-errant of the sea. It had borne all the ships whose names are like jewels flashing in the night of time, from the *Golden Hind* returning with her round flanks full of treasure, to be visited by the Queen's Highness and thus pass out of the gigantic tale, to the *Erebus* and *Terror*, bound on other conquests—and that never returned. It had known the ships and the men. They had sailed from Deptford, from Greenwich, from Erith—the adventurers and the settlers; kings' ships and

the ships of men on 'Change; captains, admirals, the
dark 'interlopers' of the Eastern trade, and the commis-
sioned 'generals' of East India fleets. Hunters for gold or
pursuers of fame, they all had gone out on that stream,
bearing the sword, and often the torch, messengers of
the might within the land, bearers of a spark from the
sacred fire. What greatness had not floated on the ebb
of that river into the mystery of an unknown earth! . . .
The dreams of men, the seed of commonwealths, the
germs of empires.

The sun set; the dusk fell on the stream, and lights
began to appear along the shore. The Chapman light-
house, a three-legged thing erect on a mud-flat, shone
strongly. Lights of ships moved in the fairway—a great
stir of lights going up and going down. And farther west
on the upper reaches the place of the monstrous town
was still marked ominously on the sky, a brooding
gloom in sunshine, a lurid glare under the stars.

'And this also,' said Marlow suddenly, 'has been one
of the dark places of the earth.'

He was the only man of us who still 'followed the
sea'. The worst that could be said of him was that he
did not represent his class. He was a seaman, but he was
a wanderer, too, while most seamen lead, if one may so
express it, a sedentary life. Their minds are of the stay-
at-home order, and their home is always with them—the
ship; and so is their country—the sea. One ship is very
much like another, and the sea is always the same. In
the immutability of their surroundings the foreign

shores, the foreign faces, the changing immensity of life, glide past, veiled not by a sense of mystery but by a slightly disdainful ignorance; for there is nothing mysterious to a seaman unless it be the sea itself, which is the mistress of his existence and as inscrutable as Destiny. For the rest, after his hours of work, a casual stroll or a casual spree on shore suffices to unfold for him the secret of a whole continent, and generally he finds the secret not worth knowing. The yarns of seamen have a direct simplicity, the whole meaning of which lies within the shell of a cracked nut. But Marlow was not typical (if his propensity to spin yarns be excepted), and to him the meaning of an episode was not inside like a kernel but outside, enveloping the tale which brought it out only as a glow brings out a haze, in the likeness of one of these misty halos that sometimes are made visible by the spectral illumination of moonshine.

His remark did not seem at all surprising. It was just like Marlow. It was accepted in silence. No one took the trouble to grunt even; and presently he said, very slow—

'I was thinking of very old times, when the Romans first came here, nineteen hundred years ago—the other day . . . Light came out of this river since—you say Knights? Yes; but it is like a running blaze on a plain, like a flash of lightning in the clouds. We live in the flicker—may it last as long as the old earth keeps rolling! But darkness was here yesterday. Imagine the feelings of a commander of a fine—what d'ye call 'em?—trireme in the Mediterranean, ordered suddenly to the north; run overland across the Gauls in a hurry; put in charge of one of these craft the legionaries—a wonderful lot of handy men they must have been, too—used to build, apparently by the hundred, in a month or two, if we may believe what we read. Imagine him here—the very end of the world, a sea the colour of lead, a sky the colour of smoke, a kind of ship about as rigid as a concertina—and going up this river with stores, or orders, or what you like. Sand-banks, marshes, forests, savages,—precious little to eat fit for a civilized man, nothing but Thames water to drink. No Falernian wine here, no going ashore. Here and there a military camp lost in a wilderness, like a needle in a bundle of hay—cold, fog, tempests, disease, exile, and death—death skulking in the air, in the water, in the bush. They must have been dying like flies here. Oh, yes—he did it. Did it very well, too, no doubt, and without thinking much about it either, except afterwards to brag of what he had done through his time, perhaps. They were men enough to face the darkness. And perhaps he was cheered by keeping his eye on a chance of promotion to the fleet at Ravenna by-and-by, if he had good friends in Rome and survived the awful climate. Or think of a decent young citizen in a toga—perhaps too much dice, you know—coming out here in the train of some prefect, or tax-gatherer, or trader even, to mend his fortunes. Land in a swamp, march through the woods, and in some inland post feel the savagery, the utter savagery, had closed round him,—all that mysterious life of the wilderness that stirs in the forest, in the jungles, in the hearts of wild men. There's no initiation either into such mysteries. He has to live in the midst of the incomprehensible, which is also detestable. And it has a fascination, too, that goes to work upon him. The fascination of the abomination—you know, imagine the growing regrets, the longing to escape, the powerless disgust, the surrender, the hate.'

He paused.

'Mind,' he began again, lifting one arm from the elbow, the palm of the hand outwards, so that, with his legs folded before him, he had the pose of a Buddha preaching in European clothes and without a lotusflower- 'Mind, none of us would feel exactly like this. What saves us is efficiency—the devotion to efficiency. But these chaps were not much account, really. They were no colonists; their administration was merely a squeeze, and nothing more, I suspect. They were conquerors, and for that you want only brute force—nothing to boast of, when you have it, since your strength is just an accident arising from the weakness of others. They grabbed what they could get for the sake of what was to be got. It was just robbery with violence, aggravated murder on a great scale, and men going at it blind—as is very proper for those who tackle a darkness. The conquest of the earth, which mostly means the taking it away from those who have a different complexion or slightly flatter noses than ourselves, is not a pretty

thing when you look into it too much. What redeems
it is the idea only. An idea at the back of it; not a sen-
timental pretence but an idea; and an unselfish belief in
the idea—something you can set up, and bow down
before, and offer a sacrifice to . . .'

He broke off. Flames glided in the river, small green
flames, red flames, white flames, pursuing, overtaking,
joining, crossing each other—then separating slowly or
hastily. The traffic of the great city went on in the deepening night upon the sleepless river. We looked on, waiting patiently—there was nothing else to do till the end of
the flood; but it was only after a long silence, when he
said, in a hesitating voice, 'I suppose you fellows
remember I did once turn fresh-water sailor for a bit,'
that we knew we were fated, before the ebb began to run,
to hear about one of Marlow's inconclusive experiences.

'I don't want to bother you much with what happened
to me personally,' he began, showing in this remark the
weakness of many tellers of tales who seem so often
unaware of what their audience would best like to hear;
'yet to understand the effect of it on me you ought to
know how I got out there, what I saw, how I went up
that river to the place where I first met the poor chap.
It was the farthest point of navigation and the culminating point of my experience. It seemed somehow to throw
a kind of light on everything about me—and into my
thoughts. It was sombre enough, too—and pitiful—not
extraordinary in any way—not very clear either. No, not
very clear. And yet it seemed to throw a kind of light.

'I had then, as you remember, just returned to London after a lot of Indian Ocean, Pacific, China Seas—a regular dose of the East—six years or so, and I was loafing about, hindering you fellows in your work and invading your homes, just as though I had got a heavenly mission to civilize you. It was very fine for a time, but after a bit I did get tired of resting. Then I began to look for a ship—I should think the hardest work on earth. But the ships wouldn't even look at me. And I got tired of that game, too.

'Now when I was a little chap I had a passion for maps. I would look for hours at South America, or Africa, or Australia, and lose myself in all the glories of exploration. At that time there were many blank spaces on the earth, and when I saw one that looked particularly inviting on a map (but they all look that) I would put my finger on it and say, When I grow up I will go there. The North Pole was one of these places, I remember. Well, I haven't been there yet, and shall not try now. The glamour's off. Other places were scattered about the Equator, and in every sort of latitude all over the two hemispheres. I have been in some of them, and . . . well, we won't talk about that. But there was one yet—the biggest, the most blank, so to speak—that I had a hankering after.

'True, by this time it was not a blank space any more. It had got filled since my boyhood with rivers and lakes and names. It had ceased to be a blank space of delightful mystery—a white patch for a boy to dream gloriously over. It had become a place of darkness. But there was in it one river especially, a mighty big river, that you could see on the map, resembling an immense snake uncoiled, with its head in the sea, its body at rest curving afar over a vast country, and its tail lost in the depths of the land. And as I looked at the map of it in a shop-window, it fascinated me as a snake would a bird—a silly little bird. Then I remembered there was a big concern, a Company for trade on that river. Dash it all! I thought to myself, they can't trade without using some kind of craft on that lot of fresh water—steamboats! Why shouldn't I try to get charge of one? I went on along Fleet Street, but could not shake off the idea. The snake had charmed me.

'You understand it was a Continental concern, that Trading society; but I have a lot of relations living on the Continent, because it's cheap and not so nasty as it looks, they say.

'I am sorry to own I began to worry them. This was already a fresh departure for me. I was not used to get things that way, you know. I always went my own road and on my own legs where I had a mind to go. I wouldn't have believed it of myself; but, then—you see—I felt somehow I must get there by hook or by crook. So I worried them. The men said "My dear fellow," and did nothing. Then—would you believe it?—I tried the women. I, Charlie Marlow, set the women to work—to get a job. Heavens! Well, you see, the notion drove me. I had an aunt, a dear enthusiastic soul. She wrote: "It will be delightful. I am ready to do anything, anything for you. It is a glorious idea. I know the wife of a very high personage in the Administration, and also a man who has lots of influence with," etc., etc. She was determined to make no end of fuss to get me appointed skipper of a river steamboat, if such was my fancy.

'I got my appointment—of course; and I got it very quick. It appears the Company had received news that one of their captains had been killed in a scuffle with the natives. This was my chance, and it made me the more anxious to go. It was only months and months afterwards, when I made the attempt to recover what was left of the body, that I heard the original quarrel arose from a misunderstanding about some hens. Yes, two black hens. Fresleven—that was the fellow's name, a Dane—thought himself wronged somehow in the bargain, so he went ashore and started to hammer the chief of the village with a stick. Oh, it didn't surprise me in the least to hear this, and at the same time to be told that Fresleven was the gentlest, quietest creature that ever walked on two legs. No doubt he was; but he had been a couple of years already out there engaged in the noble cause, you know, and he probably felt the need at last of asserting his self-respect in some way. Therefore he whacked the old nigger mercilessly, while a big crowd of his people watched him, thunderstruck, till some man—I was told the chief's son—in desperation at hearing the old chap yell, made a tentative jab with a spear at the white man—and of course it went quite easy between the shoulder-blades. Then the whole population cleared into the forest, expecting all kinds of calamities to happen, while, on the other hand, the steamer Fresleven commanded left also in a bad panic, in charge of the engineer, I believe. Afterwards nobody seemed to trouble much about Fresleven's remains, till I got out and stepped into his shoes. I couldn't let it rest, though; but when an opportunity offered at last to meet my predecessor, the grass growing through his ribs was tall enough to hide his bones. They were all there. The supernatural being had not been touched after he fell. And the village was deserted, the huts gaped black, rotting, all askew within the fallen enclosures. A calamity had come to it, sure enough. The people had vanished. Mad terror had scattered them, men, women, and children, through the bush, and they had never returned. What became of the hens I don't know either. I should think the cause of progress got them, anyhow. However, through this glorious affair I got my appointment, before I had fairly begun to hope for it.

'I flew around like mad to get ready, and before forty-eight hours I was crossing the Channel to show myself to my employers, and sign the contract. In a very few hours I arrived in a city that always makes me think of a whited sepulchre. Prejudice no doubt. I had no difficulty in finding the Company's offices. It was the biggest thing in the town, and everybody I met was full of it. They were going to run an over-sea empire, and make no end of coin by trade.

'A narrow and deserted street in deep shadow, high houses, innumerable windows with venetian blinds, a dead silence, grass sprouting between the stones, imposing carriage archways right and left, immense double doors standing ponderously ajar. I slipped through one of these cracks, went up a swept and ungarnished staircase, as arid as a desert, and opened the first door I came to. Two women, one fat and the other slim, sat on straw-bottomed chairs, knitting black wool. The slim one got up and walked straight at me—still knitting with downcast eyes—and only just as I began to think of getting out of her way, as you would for a somnambulist, stood still, and looked up. Her dress was as plain as an umbrella-cover, and she turned round without a word and preceded me into a waiting-room. I gave my name, and looked about. Deal table in the middle, plain chairs all round the walls, on one end a large shining map, marked with all the colours of a rainbow. There was a vast amount of red—good to see at any time, because one knows that some real work is done in there, a deuce of a lot of blue, a little green, smears of orange, and, on the East Coast, a purple patch, to show where the jolly pioneers of progress drink the jolly lager-beer. However, I wasn't going into any of these. I was going into the yellow. Dead in the centre. And the river was there—fascinating—deadly—like a snake. Ough! A door opened, a white-haired secretarial head, but wearing a compassionate expression, appeared, and a skinny forefinger beckoned me into the sanctuary. Its light was

dim, and a heavy writing-desk squatted in the middle.
From behind that structure came out an impression of
pale plumpness in a frock-coat. The great man himself.
He was five feet six, I should judge, and had his grip
on the handle-end of ever so many millions. He shook
hands, I fancy, murmured vaguely, was satisfied with
my French. *Bon voyage.*

'In about forty-five seconds I found myself again in
the waiting-room with the compassionate secretary, who,
full of desolation and sympathy, made me sign some
document. I believe I undertook amongst other things
not to disclose any trade secrets. Well, I am not going to.

'I began to feel slightly uneasy. You know I am not
used to such ceremonies, and there was something ominous in the atmosphere. It was just as though I had
been let into some conspiracy—I don't know—something not quite right; and I was glad to get out. In the
outer room the two women knitted black wool feverishly. People were arriving, and the younger one was
walking back and forth introducing them. The old one
sat on her chair. Her flat cloth slippers were propped
up on a foot-warmer, and a cat reposed on her lap. She
wore a starched white affair on her head, had a wart on
one cheek, and silver-rimmed spectacles hung on the
tip of her nose. She glanced at me above the glasses.
The swift and indifferent placidity of that look troubled
me. Two youths with foolish and cheery countenances
were being piloted over, and she threw at them the
same quick glance of unconcerned wisdom. She seemed

to know all about them and about me, too. An eerie feeling came over me. She seemed uncanny and fateful. Often far away there I thought of these two, guarding the door of Darkness, knitting black wool as for a warm pall, one introducing, introducing continuously to the unknown, the other scrutinizing the cheery and foolish faces with unconcerned old eyes. *Ave!* Old knitter of black wool. *Morituri te salutant.* Not many of those she looked at ever saw her again—not half, by a long way.

'There was yet a visit to the doctor. "A simple formality," assured me the secretary, with an air of taking an immense part in all my sorrows. Accordingly a young chap wearing his hat over the left eyebrow, some clerk I suppose—there must have been clerks in the business, though the house was as still as a house in a city of the dead—came from somewhere upstairs, and led me forth. He was shabby and careless, with ink-stains on the sleeves of his jacket, and his cravat was large and billowy, under a chin shaped like the toe of an old boot. It was a little too early for the doctor, so I proposed a drink, and thereupon he developed a vein of joviality As we sat over our vermouths he glorified the Company's business, and by-and-by I expressed casually my surprise at him not going out there. He became very cool and collected all at once. "I am not such a fool as I look, quoth Plato to his disciples," he said sententiously, emptied his glass with great resolution, and we rose.

'The old doctor felt my pulse, evidently thinking of

something else the while. "Good, good for there," he mumbled, and then with a certain eagerness asked me whether I would let him measure my head. Rather surprised, I said Yes, when he produced a thing like calipers and got the dimensions back and front and every way taking notes carefully. He was an unshaven little man in a threadbare coat like a gaberdine, with his feet in slippers, and I thought him a harmless fool. "I always ask leave, in the interests of science, to measure the crania of those going out there," he said. "And when they come back, too?" I asked. "Oh, I never see them," he remarked; "and, moreover, the changes take place inside, you know." He smiled. as if at some quiet joke. "So you are going out there. Famous. Interesting, too." He gave me a searching glance, and made another note. "Ever any madness in your family?" he asked, in a matter-of-fact tone. I felt very annoyed. "Is that question in the interests of science, too?" "It would be," he said, without taking notice of my irritation, "interesting for science to watch the mental changes of individuals, on the spot, but . . ." "Are you an alienist?" I interrupted. "Every doctor should be—a little," answered that original, imperturbably. "I have a little theory which you Messieurs who go out there must help me to prove. This is my share in the advantages my country shall reap from the possession of such a magnificent dependency. The mere wealth I leave to others. Pardon my questions, but you are the first Englishman coming under my observation . . ." I hastened to assure him I

was not in the least typical. "If I were," said I, "I
wouldn't be talking like this with you." "What you say
is rather profound, and probably erroneous," he said,
with a laugh. "Avoid irritation more than exposure to
the sun. Adieu. How do you English say, eh? Good-bye.
Ah! Good-bye. Adieu. In the tropics one must before
everything keep calm." . . . He lifted a warning forefinger . . . *"Du calme, du calme. Adieu."*

'One thing more remained to do—say good-bye to
my excellent aunt. I found her triumphant. I had a cup
of tea—the last decent cup of tea for many days—and in
a room that most soothingly looked just as you would
expect a lady's drawing-room to look, we had a long
quiet chat by the fireside. In the course of these confi-
dences it became quite plain to me I had been repre-
sented to the wife of the high dignitary, and goodness
knows to how many more people besides, as an exceptional and gifted creature—a piece of good fortune for
the Company—a man you don't get hold of every day.
Good heavens! and I was going to take charge of a two-
penny-half-penny river steamboat with a penny whistle
attached! It appeared, however, I was also one of the
Workers, with a capital—you know. Something like an
emissary of light, something like a lower sort of apos-
tle. There had been a lot of such rot let loose in print
and talk just about that time, and the excellent woman,
living right in the rush of all that humbug, got carried
off her feet. She talked about "weaning those ignorant
millions from their horrid ways", till, upon my word,

she made me quite uncomfortable. I ventured to hint that the Company was run for profit.

' "You forget, dear Charlie, that the labourer is worthy of his hire," she said, brightly. It's queer how out of touch with truth women are. They live in a world of their own, and there has never been anything like it, and never can be. It is too beautiful altogether, and if they were to set it up it would go to pieces before the first sunset. Some confounded fact we men have been living contentedly with ever since the day of creation would start up and knock the whole thing over.

'After this I got embraced, told to wear flannel, be sure to write often, and so on—and I left. In the street— I don't know why—a queer feeling came to me that I was an impostor. Odd thing that I, who used to clear out for any part of the world at twenty-four hours' notice, with less thought than most men give to the crossing of a street, had a moment—I won't say of hesitation, but of startled pause, before this commonplace affair. The best way I can explain it to you is by saying that, for a second or two, I felt as though, instead of going to the centre of a continent, I were about to set off for the centre of the earth.

'I left in a French steamer, and she called in every blamed port they have out there, for, as far as I could see, the sole purpose of landing soldiers and custom-house officers. I watched the coast. Watching a coast as it slips by the ship is like thinking about an enigma. There it is before you—smiling, frowning, inviting,

grand, mean, insipid, or savage, and always mute with
an air of whispering, Come and find out. This one was
almost featureless, as if still in the making, with an
aspect of monotonous grimness. The edge of a colossal
jungle, so dark-green as to be almost black, fringed with
white surf, ran straight, like a ruled line, far, far away
along a blue sea whose glitter was blurred by a creep-
ing mist. The sun was fierce, the land seemed to glis-
ten and drip with steam. Here and there greyish-whitish
specks showed up clustered inside the white surf, with
a flag flying above them perhaps. Settlements some centuries old, and still no bigger than pinheads on the
untouched expanse of their background. We pounded
along, stopped, landed soldiers; went on, landed custom-house clerks to levy toll in what looked like a God-
forsaken wilderness, with a tin shed and a flag-pole lost
in it; landed more soldiers—to take care of the custom-
house clerks, presumably. Some, I heard, got drowned
in the surf; but whether they did or not, nobody seemed
particularly to care. They were just flung out there, and
on we went. Every day the coast looked the same, as
though we had not moved; but we passed various
places—trading places—with names like Gran' Bassam,
Little Popo; names that seemed to belong to some sordid farce acted in front of a sinister back-cloth. The
idleness of a passenger, my isolation amongst all these
men with whom I had no point of contact, the oily and
languid sea, the uniform sombreness of the coast,
seemed to keep me away from the truth of things,

within the toil of a mournful and senseless delusion. The voice of the surf now and then was a positive pleasure, like the speech of a brother. It was something natural, that had its reason, that had a meaning. Now and then a boat from the shore gave one a momentary contact with reality. It was paddled by black fellows. You could see from afar the white of their eyeballs glistening. They shouted, sang; their bodies streamed with perspiration; they had faces like grotesque masks—these chaps; but they had bone, muscle, a wild vitality, an intense energy of movement, that was as natural and true as the surf along their coast. They wanted no excuse for being there. They were a great comfort to look at. For a time I would feel I belonged still to a world of straightforward facts; but the feeling would not last long. Something would turn up to scare it away. Once, I remember, we came upon a man-of-war anchored off the coast. There wasn't even a shed there, and she was shelling the bush. It appears the French had one of their wars going on thereabouts. Her ensign drooped limp like a rag; the muzzles of the long six-inch guns stuck out all over the low hull; the greasy, slimy swell swung her up lazily and let her down, swaying her thin masts. In the empty immensity of earth, sky, and water, there she was, incomprehensible, firing into a continent. Pop, would go one of the six-inch guns; a small flame would dart and vanish, a little white smoke would disappear, a tiny projectile would give a feeble screech—and nothing happened. Nothing could happen. There was a touch of

insanity in the proceeding, a sense of lugubrious drollery
in the sight; and it was not dissipated by somebody on
board assuring me earnestly there was a camp of
natives—he called them enemies!—hidden out of sight
somewhere.

'We gave her her letters (I heard the men in that
lonely ship were dying of fever at the rate of three a-
day) and went on. We called at some more places with
farcical names, where the merry dance of death and
trade goes on in a still and earthy atmosphere as of an
overheated catacomb; all along the formless coast bor-
dered by dangerous surf, as if Nature herself had tried
to ward off intruders; in and out of rivers, streams of
death in life, whose banks were rotting into mud, whose
waters, thickened into slime, invaded the contorted
mangroves, that seemed to writhe at us in the extremity of an impotent despair. Nowhere did we stop long
enough to get a particularized impression, but the general sense of vague and oppressive wonder grew upon
me. It was like a weary pilgrimage amongst hints for
nightmares.

'It was upward of thirty days before I saw the mouth
of the big river. We anchored off the seat of the government. But my work would not begin till some two
hundred miles farther on. So as soon as I could I made
a start for a place thirty miles higher up.

'I had my passage on a little sea-going steamer. Her
captain was a Swede, and knowing me for a seaman,
invited me on the bridge. He was a young man, lean,

fair, and morose, with lanky hair and a shuffling gait. As
we left the miserable little wharf, he tossed his head
contemptuously at the shore. "Been living there?" he
asked. I said, "Yes." "Fine lot these government chaps—
are they not?" he went on, speaking English with great
precision and considerable bitterness. "It is funny what
some people will do for a few francs a-month. I wonder what becomes of that kind when it goes up country?" I said to him I expected to see that soon. "So-o-o!"
he exclaimed. He shuffled athwart, keeping one eye
ahead vigilantly. "Don't be too sure," he continued.
"The other day I took up a man who hanged himself
on the road. He was a Swede, too." "Hanged himself!
Why, in God's name?" I cried. He kept on looking out
watchfully. "Who knows? The sun too much for him,
or the country perhaps."

'At last we opened a reach. A rocky cliff appeared,
mounds of turned-up earth by the shore, houses on a
hill, others with iron roofs, amongst a waste of excava-
tions, or hanging to the declivity. A continuous noise
of the rapids above hovered over this scene of inhabited
devastation. A lot of people, mostly black and naked,
moved about like ants. A jetty projected into the river.
A blinding sunlight drowned all this at times in a sudden recrudescence of glare. "There's your Company's
station," said the Swede, pointing to three wooden bar-
rack-like structures on the rocky slope. "I will send your
things up. Four boxes did you say? So. Farewell."

'I came upon a boiler wallowing in the grass, then

found a path leading up the hill. It turned aside for the boulders, and also for an undersized railway-truck lying there on its back with its wheels in the air. One was off. The thing looked as dead as the carcass of some animal. I came upon more pieces of decaying machinery, a stack of rusty rails. To the left a clump of trees made a shady spot, where dark things seemed to stir feebly. I blinked, the path was steep. A horn tooted to the right, and I saw the black people run. A heavy and dull detonation shook the ground, a puff of smoke came out of the cliff, and that was all. No change appeared on the face of the rock. They were building a railway. The cliff was not in the way of anything; but this objectless blasting was all the work going on.

'A slight clinking behind me made me turn my head. Six black men advanced in a file, toiling up the path. They walked erect and slow, balancing small baskets full of earth on their heads, and the clink kept time with their footsteps. Black rags were wound round their loins, and the short ends behind waggled to and fro like tails. I could see every rib, the joints of their limbs were like knots in a rope; each had an iron collar on his neck, and all were connected together with a chain whose bights swung between them, rhythmically clinking. Another report from the cliff made me think suddenly of that ship of war I had seen firing into a continent. It was the same kind of ominous voice; but these men could by no stretch of imagination be called enemies. They were called criminals, and the outraged law, like the bursting shells, had come to them, an insoluble mystery from the sea. All their meagre breasts panted together, the violently dilated nostrils quivered, the eyes stared stonily uphill. They passed me within six inches, without a glance, with that complete, deathlike indifference of unhappy savages. Behind this raw matter one of the reclaimed, the product of the new forces at work, strolled despondently, carrying a rifle by its middle. He had a uniform jacket with one button off, and seeing a white man on the path, hoisted his weapon to his shoulder with alacrity. This was simple prudence, white men being so much alike at a distance that he could not tell who I might be. He was speedily reassured, and with a large, white, rascally grin, and a glance at his charge, seemed to take me into partnership in his exalted trust. After all, I also was a part of the great cause of these high and just proceedings.

'Instead of going up, I turned and descended to the left. My idea was to let that chain-gang get out of sight before I climbed the hill. You know I am not particularly tender; I've had to strike and to fend off. I've had to resist and to attack sometimes—that's only one way of resisting—without counting the exact cost, according to the demands of such sort of life as I had blundered into. I've seen the devil of violence, and the devil of greed, and the devil of hot desire; but, by all the stars! these were strong, lusty, red-eyed devils, that swayed and drove men—men, I tell you. But as I stood on this hillside, I foresaw that in the blinding sunshine of that land I would become acquainted with a flabby, pre-tending, weak-eyed devil of a rapacious and pitiless folly. How insidious he could be, too, I was only to find out several months later and a thousand miles farther. For a moment I stood appalled, as though by a warning. Finally I descended the hill, obliquely, towards the trees I had seen.

'I avoided a vast artificial hole somebody had been digging on the slope, the purpose of which I found it impossible to divine. It wasn't a quarry or a sandpit, anyhow. It was just a hole. It might have been con-nected with the philanthropic desire of giving the crim-inals something to do. I don't know. Then I nearly fell into a very narrow ravine, almost no more than a scar in the hillside. I discovered that a lot of imported drainage-pipes for the settlement had been tumbled in there. There wasn't one that was not broken. It was a wanton smash-up. At last I got under the trees. My purpose was to stroll into the shade for a moment; but no sooner within than it seemed to me I had stepped into the gloomy circle of some Inferno. The rapids were near, and an uninterrupted, uniform, headlong, rushing noise filled the mournful stillness of the grove, where not a breath stirred, not a leaf moved, with a mysteri-ous sound—as though the tearing pace of the launched earth had suddenly become audible.

'Black shapes crouched, lay, sat between the trees leaning against the trunks, clinging to the earth, half coming out, half effaced within the dim light, in all the

78   JOSEPH CONRAD

attitudes of pain, abandonment, and despair. Another
mine on the cliff went off, followed by a slight shudder
of the soil under my feet. The work was going on. The
work! And this was the place where some of the helpers
had withdrawn to die.

'They were dying slowly—it was very clear. They
were not enemies, they were not criminals, they were
nothing earthly now,—nothing but black shadows of
disease and starvation, lying confusedly in the greenish
gloom. Brought from all the recesses of the coast in all
the legality of time contracts, lost in uncongenial surroundings, fed on unfamiliar food, they sickened,
became inefficient, and were then allowed to crawl away
and rest. These moribund shapes were free as air—and
nearly as thin. I began to distinguish the gleam of the
eyes under the trees. Then, glancing down, I saw a face
near my hand. The black bones reclined at full length
with one shoulder against the tree, and slowly the eyelids rose and the sunken eyes looked up at me, enormous and vacant, a kind of blind, white flicker in the
depths of the orbs, which died out slowly. The man
seemed young—almost a boy—but you know with them
it's hard to tell. I found nothing else to do but to offer
him one of my good Swede's ship's biscuits I had in my
pocket. The fingers closed slowly on it and held—there
was no other movement and no other glance. He had
tied a bit of white worsted round his neck—Why?
Where did he get it? Was it a badge—an ornament—a
charm—a propitiatory act? Was there any idea at all

connected with it? It looked startling round his black neck, this bit of white thread from beyond the seas.

'Near the same tree two more bundles of acute angles sat with their legs drawn up. One, with his chin propped on his knees, stared at nothing, in an intolerable and appalling manner: his brother phantom rested its forehead, as if overcome with a great weariness; and all about others were scattered in every pose of contorted collapse, as in some picture of a massacre or a pestilence. While I stood horror-struck, one of these creatures rose to his hands and knees, and went off on all-fours towards the river to drink. He lapped out of his hand, then sat up in the sunlight, crossing his shins in front of him, and after a time let his woolly head fall on his breastbone.

'I didn't want any more loitering in the shade, and I made haste towards the station. When near the buildings I met a white man, in such an unexpected elegance of get-up that in the first moment I took him for a sort of vision. I saw a high starched collar, white cuffs, a light alpaca jacket, snowy trousers, a clean necktie, and varnished boots. No hat. Hair parted, brushed, oiled, under a green-lined parasol held in a big white hand. He was amazing, and had a penholder behind his ear.

'I shook hands with this miracle, and I learned he was the Company's chief accountant, and that all the book-keeping was done at this station. He had come out for a moment, he said, "to get a breath of fresh air." The expression sounded wonderfully odd, with its suggestion

of sedentary desk-life. I wouldn't have mentioned the
fellow to you at all, only it was from his lips that I first
heard the name of the man who is so indissolubly con-
nected with the memories of that time. Moreover, I
respected the fellow. Yes; I respected his collars, his vast
cuffs, his brushed hair. His appearance was certainly
that of a hairdresser's dummy; but in the great demor-
alization of the land he kept up his appearance. That's
backbone. His starched collars and got-up shirt-fronts
were achievements of character. He had been out nearly
three years; and later, I could not help asking him how
he managed to sport such linen. He had just the faintest
blush, and said modestly, "I've been teaching one of the
native women about the station. It was difficult. She had
a distaste for the work." Thus this man had verily
accomplished something. And he was devoted to his
books, which were in apple-pie order.

'Everything else in the station was in a muddle—
heads, things, buildings. Strings of dusty niggers with
splay feet arrived and departed; a stream of manufac-
tured goods, rubbishy cottons, beads, and brass wire
sent into the depths of darkness, and in return came a
precious trickle of ivory.

'I had to wait in the station for ten days—an eternity. I lived in a hut in the yard, but to be out of the
chaos I would sometimes get into the accountant's
office. It was built of horizontal planks, and so badly put
together that, as he bent over his high desk, he was
barred from neck to heels with narrow strips of sunlight.

There was no need to open the big shutters to see. It was hot there, too; big flies buzzed fiendishly, and did not sting, but stabbed. I sat generally on the floor, while, of faultless appearance (and even slightly scented), perching on a high stool, he wrote. Sometimes he stood up for exercise. When a truckle-bed with a sick man (some invalid agent from up-country) was put in there, he exhibited a gentle annoyance. "The groans of this sick person," he said, "distract my attention. And without that it is extremely difficult to guard against clerical errors in this climate."

'One day he remarked, without lifting his head, "In the interior you will no doubt meet Mr Kurtz." On my asking who Mr Kurtz was, he said he was a first-class agent; and seeing my disappointment at this information, he added slowly, laying down his pen, "He is a very remarkable person." Further questions elicited from him that Mr Kurtz was at present in charge of a trading post, a very important one, in the true ivory-country, at "the very bottom of there. Sends in as much ivory as all the others put together . . ." He began to write again. The sick man was too ill to groan. The flies buzzed in a great peace.

'Suddenly there was a growing murmur of voices and a great tramping of feet. A caravan had come in. A violent babble of uncouth sounds burst out on the other side of the planks. All the carriers were speaking together, and in the midst of the uproar the lamentable voice of the chief agent was heard "giving it up" tearfully

for the twentieth time that day . . . He rose slowly.
"What a frightful row," he said. He crossed the room
gently to look at the sick man, and returning, said to me,
"He does not hear." "What! Dead?" I asked, startled.
"No, not yet," he answered, with great composure.
Then, alluding with a toss of the head to the tumult in
the station yard, "When one has got to make correct
entries, one comes to hate those savages—hate them to
the death." He remained thoughtful for a moment.
"When you see Mr Kurtz," he went on, "tell him from
me that everything here"—he glanced at the desk—"is
very satisfactory. I don't like to write to him—with those
messengers of ours you never know who may get hold
of your letter—at that Central Station." He stared at me
for a moment with his mild, bulging eyes. "Oh, he will
go far, very far," he began again. "He will be a somebody in the Administration before long. They, above—
the Council in Europe, you know—mean him to be."

'He turned to his work. The noise outside had ceased,
and presently in going out I stopped at the door. In the
steady buzz of flies the homeward-bound agent was
lying flushed and insensible; the other, bent over his
books, was making correct entries of perfectly correct
transactions; and fifty feet below the doorstep I could
see the still tree-tops of the grove of death.

'Next day I left that station at last, with a caravan of
sixty men, for a two-hundred-mile tramp.

'No use telling you much about that. Paths, paths,
everywhere; a stamped-in network of paths spreading

over the empty land, through long grass, through burnt grass, through thickets, down and up chilly ravines, up and down stony hills ablaze with heat; and a solitude, a solitude, nobody, not a hut. The population had cleared out a long time ago. Well, if a lot of mysterious niggers armed with all kinds of fearful weapons suddenly took to travelling on the road between Deal and Gravesend, catching the yokels right and left to carry heavy loads for them, I fancy every farm and cottage thereabouts would get empty very soon. Only here the dwellings were gone, too. Still I passed through several abandoned villages. There's something pathetically childish in the ruins of grass walls. Day after day, with the stamp and shuffle of sixty pair of bare feet behind me, each pair under a 60-lb. load. Camp, cook, sleep, strike camp, march. Now and then a carrier dead in harness, at rest in the long grass near the path, with an empty water-gourd and his long staff lying by his side. A great silence around and above. Perhaps on some quiet night the tremor of far-off drums, sinking, swelling, a tremor vast, faint; a sound weird, appealing, suggestive, and wild—and perhaps with as profound a meaning as the sound of bells in a Christian country. Once a white man in an unbuttoned uniform, camping on the path with an armed escort of lank Zanzibaris, very hospitable and festive—not to say drunk. Was looking after the upkeep of the road, he declared. Can't say I saw any road or any upkeep, unless the body of a middle-aged negro, with a bullet-hole in the forehead, upon which I absolutely stumbled three miles farther on, may be considered as a permanent improvement. I had a white companion, too, not a bad chap, but rather too fleshy and with the exasperating habit of fainting on the hot hillsides, miles away from the least bit of shade and water. Annoying, you know, to hold your own coat like a parasol over a man's head while he is coming-to. I couldn't help asking him once what he meant by coming there at all. "To make money, of course. What do you think?" he said, scornfully. Then he got fever, and had to be carried in a hammock slung under a pole. As he weighed sixteen stone I had no end of rows with the carriers. They jibbed, ran away, sneaked off with their loads in the night—quite a mutiny. So, one evening, I made a speech in English with gestures, not one of which was lost to the sixty pairs of eyes before me, and the next morning I started the hammock off in front all right. An hour afterwards I came upon the whole concern wrecked in a bush—man, hammock, groans, blankets, horrors. The heavy pole had skinned his poor nose. He was very anxious for me to kill somebody, but there wasn't the shadow of a carrier near. I remembered the old doctor,—"It would be interesting for science to watch the mental changes of individuals, on the spot." I felt I was becoming scientifically interesting. However, all that is to no purpose. On the fifteenth day I came in sight of the big river again, and hobbled into the Central Station. It was on a backwater surrounded by scrub and forest, with a pretty border of smelly mud on one side, and on the three others enclosed by a crazy fence of rushes. A neglected gap was all the gate it had, and the first glance at the place was enough to let you see the flabby devil was running that show. White men with long staves in their hands appeared languidly from amongst the buildings, strolling up to take a look at me, and then retired out of sight somewhere. One of them, a stout, excitable chap with black moustaches, informed me with great volubility and many digressions, as soon as I told him who I was, that my steamer was at the bottom of the river. I was thunderstruck. What, how, why? Oh, it was "all right". The "manager himself" was there. All quite correct. "Everybody had behaved splendidly! splendidly!"—"You must," he said in agitation, "go and see the general manager at once. He is waiting!"

'I did not see the real significance of that wreck at once. I fancy I see it now, but I am not sure—not at all. Certainly the affair was too stupid—when I think of it— to be altogether natural. Still . . . But at the moment it presented itself simply as a confounded nuisance. The steamer was sunk. They had started two days before in a sudden hurry up the river with the manager on board, in charge of some volunteer skipper, and before they had been out three hours they tore the bottom out of her on stones, and she sank near the south bank. I asked myself what I was to do there, now my boat was lost. As a matter of fact, I had plenty to do in fishing my command out of the river. I had to set about it the very next day. That, and the repairs when I brought the pieces to the station, took some months.

'My first interview with the manager was curious. He did not ask me to sit down after my twenty-mile walk that morning. He was commonplace in complexion, in feature, in manners, and in voice. He was of middle size and of ordinary build. His eyes, of the usual blue, were perhaps remarkably cold, and he certainly could make his glance fall on one as trenchant and heavy as an axe. But even at these times the rest of his person seemed to disclaim the intention. Otherwise there was only an indefinable, faint expression of his lips, something stealthy—a smile—not a smile—I remember it, but I can't explain. It was unconscious, this smile was, though just after he had said something it got intensified for an instant. It came at the end of his speeches like a seal applied on the words to make the meaning of the commonest phrase appear absolutely inscrutable. He was a common trader, from his youth up employed in these parts—nothing more. He was obeyed, yet he inspired neither love nor fear. nor even respect. He inspired uneasiness. That was it! Uneasiness. Not a definite mistrust—just uneasiness—nothing more. You have no idea how effective such a . . . a . . . faculty can be. He had no genius for organizing, for initiative, or for order even. That was evident in such things as the deplorable state of the station. He had no learning, and no intelligence. His position had come to him—why? Perhaps because he

was never ill . . . He had served three terms of three years
out there . . . Because triumphant health in the general
rout of constitutions is a kind of power in itself. When
he went home on leave he rioted on a large scale—
pompously. Jack ashore—with a difference—in externals
only. This one could gather from his casual talk. He
originated nothing, he could keep the routine going—
that's all. But he was great. He was great by this little
thing that it was impossible to tell what could control
such a man. He never gave that secret away. Perhaps
there was nothing within him. Such a suspicion made
one pause—for out there there were no external checks.
Once when various tropical diseases had laid low almost
every "agent" in the station, he was heard to say, "Men
who come out here should have no entrails." He sealed
the utterance with that smile of his, as though it had
been a door opening into a darkness he had in his keeping. You fancied you had seen things—but the seal was
on. When annoyed at meal-times by the constant quar-
rels of the white men about precedence, he ordered an
immense round table to be made, for which a special
house had to be built. This was the station's mess-room.
Where he sat was the first place—the rest were
nowhere. One felt this to be his unalterable conviction.
He was neither civil nor uncivil. He was quiet. He
allowed his "boy"—an overfed young Negro from the
coast—to treat the white men, under his very eyes, with
provoking insolence.

'He began to speak as soon as he saw me. I had been

very long on the road. He could not wait. Had to start without me. The up-river stations had to be relieved. There had been so many delays already that he did not know who was dead and who was alive, and how they got on—and so on, and so on. He paid no attention to my explanations, and, playing with a stick of sealing-wax, repeated several times that the situation was "very grave, very grave". There were rumours that a very important station was in jeopardy, and its chief, Mr Kurtz, was ill. Hoped it was not true. Mr Kurtz was . . . I felt weary and irritable. Hang Kurtz, I thought. I interrupted him by saying I had heard of Mr Kurtz on the coast. "Ah! So they talk of him down there," he murmured to himself. Then he began again, assuring me Mr Kurtz was the best agent he had, an exceptional man, of the greatest importance to the Company; therefore I could understand his anxiety. He was, he said, "very, very uneasy". Certainly he fidgeted on his chair a good deal, exclaimed, "Ah, Mr Kurtz!", broke the stick of sealingwax and seemed dumbfounded by the accident. Next thing he wanted to know "how long it would take to" . . . I interrupted him again. Being hungry, you know, and kept on my feet, too, I was getting savage. "How could I tell?" I said. "I hadn't even seen the wreck yet—some months, no doubt." All this talk seemed to me so futile. "Some months," he said. "Well, let us say three months before we can make a start. Yes. That ought to do the affair." I flung out of his hut (he lived all alone in a clay hut with a sort of verandah) muttering to myself my opinion of him. He was a chattering idiot. Afterwards I took it back when it was borne in upon me startlingly with what extreme nicety he had estimated the time requisite for the "affair".

'I went to work the next day, turning, so to speak, my back on that station. In that way only it seemed to me I could keep my hold on the redeeming facts of life. Still, one must look about sometimes; and then I saw this station, these men strolling aimlessly about in the sunshine of the yard. I asked myself sometimes what it all meant. They wandered here and there with their absurd long staves in their hands, like a lot of faithless pilgrims bewitched inside a rotten fence. The word "ivory" rang in the air, was whispered, was sighed. You would think they were praying to it. A taint of imbecile rapacity blew through it all, like a whiff from some corpse. By Jove! I've never seen anything so unreal in my life. And outside, the silent wilderness surrounding this cleared speck on the earth struck me as something great and invincible, like evil or truth, waiting patiently for the passing away of this fantastic invasion.

'Oh, these months! Well, never mind. Various things happened. One evening a grass shed full of calico, cotton print, beads, and I don't know what else, burst into a blaze so suddenly that you would have thought the earth had opened to let an avenging fire consume all that trash. I was smoking my pipe quietly by my dismantled steamer, and saw them all cutting capers in the light, with their arms lifted high, when the stout man

with moustaches came tearing down to the river, a tin
pail in his hand, assured me that everybody was "behav-
ing splendidly, splendidly", dipped about a quart of
water and tore back again. I noticed there was a hole in
the bottom of his pail.

'I strolled up. There was no hurry. You see the thing
had gone off like a box of matches. It had been hopeless from the very first. The flame had leaped high,
driven everybody back, lighted up everything—and collapsed. The shed was already a heap of embers glowing
fiercely. A nigger was being beaten near by. They said
he had caused the fire in some way; be that as it may, he
was screeching most horribly. I saw him, later, for several days, sitting in a bit of shade looking very sick and
trying to recover himself: afterwards he arose and went
out—and the wilderness without a sound took him into
its bosom again. As I approached the glow from the
dark I found myself at the back of two men, talking. I
heard the name of Kurtz pronounced, then the words,
"take advantage of this unfortunate accident". One of
the men was the manager. I wished him a good evening.
"Did you ever see anything like it—eh? it is incredible,"
he said, and walked off. The other man remained. He
was a first-class agent, young, gentlemanly, a bit
reserved, with a forked little beard and a hooked nose.
He was stand-offish with the other agents, and they on
their side said he was the manager's spy upon them. As
to me, I had hardly ever spoken to him before. We got
into talk, and by-and-by we strolled away from the hiss-

ing ruins. Then he asked me to his room, which was in the main building of the station. He struck a match, and I perceived that this young aristocrat had not only a silver-mounted dressing-case but also a whole candle all to himself. Just at that time the manager was the only man supposed to have any right to candles. Native mats covered the clay walls; a collection of spears, assegais, shields, knives was hung up in trophies. The business entrusted to this fellow was the making of bricks—so I had been informed; but there wasn't a fragment of a brick anywhere in the station, and he had been there more than a year—waiting. It seems he could not make bricks without something, I don't know what—straw maybe. Anyway, it could not be found there, and as it was not likely to be sent from Europe, it did not appear clear to me what he was waiting for. An act of special creation perhaps. However, they were all waiting—all the sixteen or twenty pilgrims of them—for something; and upon my word it did not seem an uncongenial occupation, from the way they took it, though the only thing that ever came to them was disease—as far as I could see. They beguiled the time by backbiting and intriguing against each other in a foolish kind of way. There was an air of plotting about that station, but nothing came of it, of course. It was as unreal as everything else—as the philanthropic pretence of the whole concern, as their talk, as their government, as their show of work. The only real feeling was a desire to get appointed to a trading post where ivory was to be had, so that they could earn percentages. They intrigued and slandered and hated each other only on that account—but as to effectually lifting a little finger—oh, no. By heavens! there is something after all in the world allowing one man to steal a horse while another must not look at a halter. Steal a horse straight out. Very well. He has done it. Perhaps he can ride. But there is a way of looking at a halter that would provoke the most charitable of saints into a kick.

'I had no idea why he wanted to be sociable, but as we chatted in there it suddenly occurred to me the fellow was trying to get at something—in fact, pumping me. He alluded constantly to Europe, to the people I was supposed to know there—putting leading questions as to my acquaintances in the sepulchral city, and so on. His little eyes glittered like mica discs—with curiosity—though he tried to keep up a bit of superciliousness. At first I was astonished, but very soon I became awfully curious to see what he would find out from me. I couldn't possibly imagine what I had in me to make it worth his while. It was very pretty to see how he baffled himself, for in truth my body was full only of chills, and my head had nothing in it but that wretched steamboat business. It was evident he took me for a perfectly shameless prevaricator. At last he got angry, and to conceal a movement of furious annoyance, he yawned. I rose. Then I noticed a small sketch in oils, on a panel, representing a woman, draped and blindfolded, carrying a lighted torch. The background was sombre—

almost black. The movement of the woman was stately, and the effect of the torch-light on the face was sinister.

'It arrested me, and he stood by civilly, holding an empty half-pint champagne bottle (medical comforts) with the candle stuck in it. To my question he said Mr Kurtz had painted this—in this very station more than a year ago—while waiting for means to go to his trading post. "Tell me, pray," said I, "who is this Mr Kurtz?"

' "The chief of the Inner Station," he answered in a short tone, looking away. "Much obliged," I said, laughing. "And you are the brickmaker of the Central Station. Everyone knows that." He was silent for a while. "He is a prodigy," he said at last. "He is an emissary of pity, and science, and progress, and devil knows what else. We want," he began to declaim suddenly, "for the guidance of the cause entrusted to us by Europe, so to speak, higher intelligence, wide sympathies, a singleness of purpose." "Who says that?" I asked. "Lots of them," he replied. "Some even write that; and so *he* comes here, a special being, as you ought to know." "Why ought I to know?" I interrupted, really surprised. He paid no attention. "Yes. Today he is chief of the best station, next year he will be assistant-manager, two years more and . . . but I daresay you know what he will be in two years' time. You are of the new gang—the gang of virtue. The same people who sent him specially also recommended you. Oh, don't say no. I've my own eyes to trust." Light dawned upon me. My dear aunt's influential acquaintances were producing an unexpected effect upon that young man. I nearly burst into a laugh. "Do you read the Company's confidential correspondence?" I asked. He hadn't a word to say. It was great fun. "When Mr Kurtz," I continued, severely, "is General Manager, you won't have the opportunity."

'He blew the candle out suddenly, and we went outside. The moon had risen. Black figures strolled about listlessly, pouring water on the glow, whence proceeded a sound of hissing; steam ascended in the moonlight, the beaten nigger groaned somewhere. "What a row the brute makes!" said the indefatigable man with the moustaches, appearing near us. "Serve him right. Transgression—punishment—bang! Pitiless, pitiless. That's the only way. This will prevent all conflagrations for the future. I was just telling the manager . . ." He noticed my companion, and became crestfallen all at once. "Not in bed yet," he said, with a kind of servile heartiness; "it's so natural. Ha! Danger—agitation." He vanished. I went on to the river-side, and the other followed me. I heard a scathing murmur at my ear, "Heap of muffs—go to." The pilgrims could be seen in knots gesticulating, discussing. Several had still their staves in their hands. I verily believe they took these sticks to bed with them. Beyond the fence the forest stood up spectrally in the moonlight, and through the dim stir, through the faint sounds of that lamentable courtyard, the silence of the land went home to one's very heart—its mystery, its greatness, the amazing reality of its concealed life. The hurt nigger moaned feebly somewhere near by, and then fetched a deep sigh that made me mend my pace away from there. I felt a hand introducing itself under my arm. "My dear sir," said the fellow, "I don't want to be misunderstood, and especially by you, who will see Mr Kurtz long before I can have that pleasure. I wouldn't like him to get a false idea of my disposition . . ."

'I let him run on, this papier-mâché Mephistopheles, and it seemed to me that if I tried I could poke my fore-finger through him, and would find nothing inside but a little loose dirt, maybe. He, don't you see, had been planning to be assistant-manager by-and-by under the present man, and I could see that the coming of that Kurtz had upset them both not a little. He talked pre-cipitately, and I did not try to stop him. I had my shoul-ders against the wreck of my steamer, hauled up on the slope like a carcass of some big river animal. The smell of mud, of primeval mud, by Jove! was in my nostrils, the high stillness of primeval forest was before my eyes; there were shiny patches on the black creek. The moon had spread over everything a thin layer of silver—over the rank grass, over the mud, upon the wall of matted vegetation standing higher than the wall of a temple, over the great river I could see through a sombre gap glittering, glittering, as it flowed broadly by without a murmur. All this was great, expectant, mute, while the man jabbered about himself. I wondered whether the stillness on the face of the immensity looking at us two were meant as an appeal or as a menace. What were we who had strayed in here? Could we handle that dumb

thing, or would it handle us? I felt how big, how confoundedly big, was that thing that couldn't talk, and
perhaps was deaf as well. What was in there? I could see
a little ivory coming out from there, and I had heard Mr
Kurtz was in there. I had heard enough about it, too—
God knows! Yet somehow it didn't bring any image
with it—no more than if I had been told an angel or a
fiend was in there. I believed it in the same way one of
you might believe there are inhabitants in the planet
Mars. I knew once a Scotch sailmaker who was certain,
dead sure, there were people in Mars. If you asked him
for some idea how they looked and behaved, he would
get shy and mutter something about "walking on all
fours". If you as much as smiled, he would—though a
man of sixty—offer to fight you. I would not have gone
so far as to fight for Kurtz, but I went for him near
enough to a lie. You know I hate, detest, and can't bear
a lie, not because I am straighter than the rest of us, but
simply because it appalls me. There is a taint of death,
a flavour of mortality in lies—which is exactly what I
hate and detest in the world—what I want to forget. It
makes me miserable and sick, like biting something rotten would do. Temperament, I suppose. Well, I went
near enough to it by letting the young fool there believe
anything he liked to imagine as to my influence in
Europe. I became in an instant as much of a pretence
as the rest of the bewitched pilgrims. This simply
because I had a notion it somehow would be of help to
that Kurtz whom at the time I did not see—you under-

stand. He was just a word for me. I did not see the man in the name any more than you do. Do you see him? Do you see the story? Do you see anything? It seems to me I am trying to tell you a dream—making a vain attempt, because no relation of a dream can convey the dream-sensation, that commingling of absurdity, surprise, and bewilderment in a tremor of struggling revolt, that notion of being captured by the incredible which is of the very essence of dreams . . .'

He was silent for a while.

'. . . No, it is impossible; it is impossible to convey the life-sensation of any given epoch of one's existence—that which makes its truth, its meaning—its subtle and penetrating essence. It is impossible. We live, as we dream—alone . . .'

He paused again as if reflecting, then added—

'Of course in this you fellows see more than I could then. You see me, whom you know . . .'

It had become so pitch dark that we listeners could hardly see one another. For a long time already he, sitting apart, had been no more to us than a voice. There was not a word from anybody. The others might have been asleep, but I was awake. I listened, I listened on the watch for the sentence, for the word, that would give me the clue to the faint uneasiness inspired by this narrative that seemed to shape itself without human lips in the heavy night-air of the river.

'. . . Yes—I let him run on,' Marlow began again, 'and think what he pleased about the powers that were behind me. I did! And there was nothing behind me! There was nothing but that wretched, old, mangled steamboat I was leaning against, while he talked fluently about "the necessity for every man to get on". "And when one comes out here, you conceive, it is not to gaze at the moon." Mr Kurtz was a "universal genius", but even a genius would find it easier to work with "adequate tools—intelligent men". He did not make bricks—why, there was a physical impossibility in the way—as I was well aware; and if he did secretarial work for the manager, it was because "no sensible man rejects wantonly the confidence of his superiors". Did I see it? I saw it. What more did I want? What I really wanted was rivets, by heaven! Rivets. To get on with the work—to stop the hole. Rivets I wanted. There were cases of them down at the coast—cases—piled up—burst—split! You kicked a loose rivet at every second step in that station yard on the hillside. Rivets had rolled into the grove of death. You could fill your pockets with rivets for the trouble of stooping down—and there wasn't one rivet to be found where it was wanted. We had plates that would do, but nothing to fasten them with. And every week the messenger, a lone negro, letter-bag on shoulder and staff in hand, left our station for the coast. And several times a week a coast caravan came in with trade goods—ghastly glazed calico that made you shudder only to look at it, glass beads value about a penny a quart, confounded spotted cotton handkerchiefs. And no rivets. Three carriers could have brought all that was wanted to set that steamboat afloat.

'He was becoming confidential now, but I fancy my unresponsive attitude must have exasperated him at last, for he judged it necessary to inform me he feared neither God nor devil, let alone any mere man. I said I could see that very well, but what I wanted was a certain quantity of rivets—and rivets were what really Mr Kurtz wanted, if he had only known it. Now letters went to the coast every week . . . "My dear sir," he cried, "I write from dictation." I demanded rivets. There was a way—for an intelligent man. He changed his manner; became very cold, and suddenly began to talk about a hippopotamus; wondered whether sleeping on board the steamer (I stuck to my salvage night and day) I wasn't disturbed. There was an old hippo that had the bad habit of getting out on the bank and roaming at night over the station grounds. The pilgrims used to turn out in a body and empty every rifle they could lay hands on at him. Some even had sat up o' nights for him. All this energy was wasted, though. "That animal has a charmed life," he said; "but you can say this only of brutes in this country. No man—you apprehend me?—no man here bears a charmed life." He stood there for a moment in the moonlight with his delicate hooked nose set a little askew, and his mica eyes glittering without a wink, then, with a curt Good-night, he strode off. I could see he was disturbed and considerably puzzled, which made me feel more hopeful than I had been for days. It was a great comfort to turn from that chap to my influential friend, the battered, twisted ruined, tin-pot steamboat. I clambered on board. She rang under my feet like an empty Huntley & Palmers biscuit-tin kicked along a gutter; she was nothing so solid in make, and rather less pretty in shape, but I had expended enough hard work on her to make me love her. No influential friend would have served me better. She had given me a chance to come out a bit—to find out what I could do. No, I don't like work. I had rather laze about and think of all the fine things that can be done. I don't like work,—no man does—but I like what is in the work,—the chance to find yourself. Your own reality—for yourself, not for others—what no other man can ever know. They can only see the mere show, and never can tell what it really means.

'I was not surprised to see somebody sitting aft, on the deck, with his legs dangling over the mud. You see I rather chummed with the few mechanics there were in that station, whom the other pilgrims naturally despised—on account of their imperfect manners, I suppose. This was the foreman—a boiler-maker by trade— a good worker. He was a lank, bony, yellow-faced man, with big intense eyes. His aspect was worried, and his head was as bald as the palm of my hand; but his hair in falling seemed to have stuck to his chin, and had prospered in the new locality, for his beard hung down to his waist. He was a widower with six young children (he had left them in charge of a sister of his to come out there), and the passion of his life was pigeon-flying. He was an enthusiast and a connoisseur. He would rave about pigeons. After work hours he used sometimes to come over from his hut for a talk about his children and his pigeons; at work, when he had to crawl in the mud under the bottom of the steamboat, he would tie up that beard of his in a kind of white serviette he brought for the purpose. It had loops to go over his ears. In the evening he could be seen squatted on the bank rinsing that wrapper in the creek with great care, then spreading it solemnly on a bush to dry.

'I slapped him on the back and shouted "We shall have rivets!" He scrambled to his feet exclaiming "No! Rivets!" as though he couldn't believe his ears. Then in a low voice, "You . . . eh?" I don't know why we behaved like lunatics. I put my finger to the side of my nose and nodded mysteriously. "Good for you!" he cried, snapped his fingers above his head, lifting one foot. I tried a jig. We capered on the iron deck. A frightful clatter came out of that hulk, and the virgin forest on the other bank of the creek sent it back in a thundering roll upon the sleeping station. It must have made some of the pilgrims sit up in their hovels. A dark figure obscured the lighted doorway of the manager's hut, vanished, then, a second or so after, the doorway itself vanished, too. We stopped, and the silence driven away by the stamping of our feet flowed back again from the recesses of the land. The great wall of vegetation, an exuberant and entangled mass of trunks, branches, leaves, boughs, festoons, motionless in the moonlight, was like a rioting invasion of soundless life, a rolling wave of plants, piled up, crested, ready to topple over the creek, to sweep every little man of us out of his little existence. And it moved not. A deadened burst of mighty splashes and snorts reached us from afar, as though an ichthyosaurus had been taking a bath of glitter in the great river. "After all," said the boiler-maker in a reasonable tone, "why shouldn't we get the rivets?" Why not, indeed! I did not know of any reason why we shouldn't. "They'll come in three weeks," I said, confidently.

'But they didn't. Instead of rivets there came an invasion, an infliction, a visitation. It came in sections during the next three weeks, each section headed by a donkey carrying a white man in new clothes and tan shoes. bowing from that elevation right and left to the impressed pilgrims. A quarrelsome band of footsore sulky niggers trod on the heels of the donkey; a lot of tents, camp-stools, tin boxes, white cases, brown bales would be shot down in the courtyard, and the air of mystery would deepen a little over the muddle of the station. Five such instalments came, with their absurd air of disorderly flight with the loot of innumerable outfit shops and provision stores, that, one would think, they were lugging, after a raid, into the wilderness for equitable division. It was an inextricable mess of things decent in themselves but that human folly made look like spoils of thieving.

'This devoted band called itself the Eldorado Exploring Expedition, and I believe they were sworn to secrecy. Their talk, however, was the talk of sordid buccaneers: it was reckless without hardihood, greedy without audacity, and cruel without courage; there was not an atom of foresight or of serious intention in the whole batch of them, and they did not seem aware these things are wanted for the work of the world. To tear treasure out of the bowels of the land was their desire, with no more moral purpose at the back of it than there is in burglars breaking into a safe. Who paid the expenses of the noble enterprise I don't know; but the uncle of our manager was leader of that lot.

'In exterior he resembled a butcher in a poor neighbourhood, and his eyes had a look of sleepy cunning. He carried his fat paunch with ostentation on his short legs, and during the time his gang infested the station spoke to no one but his nephew. You could see these two roaming about all day long with their heads close together in an everlasting confab.

'I had given up worrying myself about the rivets. One's capacity for that kind of folly is more limited than you would suppose. I said Hang!—and let things slide. I had plenty of time for meditation, and now and then I would give some thought to Kurtz. I wasn't very interested in him. No. Still, I was curious to see whether this man, who had come out equipped with moral ideas of some sort, would climb to the top after all and how he would set about his work when there.'

II

'One evening as I was lying flat on the deck of my steamboat, I heard voices approaching—and there were the nephew and the uncle strolling along the bank. I laid my head on my arm again, and had nearly lost myself in a doze, when somebody said in my ear, as it were; "I am as harmless as a little child, but I don't like to be dictated to. Am I the manager—or am I not? I was ordered to send him there. It's incredible." . . . I became aware that the two were standing on the shore alongside the forepart of the steamboat, just below my head. I did not move; it did not occur to me to move: I was sleepy. "It *is* unpleasant," grunted the uncle. "He has asked the Administration to be sent there," said the other, "with the idea of showing what he could do; and I was instructed accordingly. Look at the influence that man must have. Is it not frightful?" They both agreed it was frightful, then made several bizarre remarks: "Make rain and fine weather—one man—the Council—by the nose"—bits of absurd sentences that got the better of my drowsiness, so that I had pretty near the whole of my wits about me when the uncle said, "The climate may do away with this difficulty for you. Is he alone there?" "Yes," answered the manager; "he sent his assistant down the river with a note to me in these terms: 'Clear this poor devil out of the country, and don't bother sending more of that sort. I had rather be alone

104

than have the kind of men you can dispose of with me.' It was more than a year ago. Can you imagine such impudence!" "Anything since then?" asked the other, hoarsely. "Ivory," jerked the nephew; "lots of it—prime sort—lots—most annoying, from him." "And with that?" questioned the heavy rumble. "Invoice," was the reply fired out, so to speak. Then silence. They had been talking about Kurtz.

'I was broad awake by this time, but, lying perfectly at ease, remained still, having no inducement to change my position. "How did that ivory come all this way?" growled the elder man, who seemed very vexed. The other explained that it had come with a fleet of canoes in charge of an English half-caste clerk Kurtz had with him; that Kurtz had apparently intended to return himself, the station being by that time bare of goods and stores, but after coming three hundred miles, had suddenly decided to go back, which he started to do alone in a small dugout with four paddlers, leaving the half-caste to continue down the river with the ivory. The two fellows there seemed astounded at anybody attempting such a thing. They were at a loss for an adequate motive. As to me, I seemed to see Kurtz for the first time. It was a distinct glimpse: the dugout, four paddling savages, and the lone white man turning his back suddenly on the headquarters, on relief, on thoughts of home—perhaps; setting his face towards the depths of the wilderness, towards his empty and desolate station. I did not know the motive. Perhaps he was just simply a fine fellow who

stuck to his work for its own sake. His name, you understand, had not been pronounced once. He was "that
man". The half-caste, who, as far as I could see, had
conducted a difficult trip with great prudence and pluck,
was invariably alluded to as "that scoundrel". The
"scoundrel" had reported that the "man" had been very
ill—had recovered imperfectly . . . The two below me
moved away then a few paces, and strolled back and
forth at some little distance. I heard: "Military post—
doctor—two hundred miles—quite alone now—unavoidable delays—nine months—no news—strange rumours."
They approached again, just as the manager was saying, "No one, as far as I know, unless a species of wandering trader—a pestilential fellow, snapping ivory from
the natives." Who was it they were talking about now?
I gathered in snatches that this was some man supposed
to be in Kurtz's district, and of whom the manager did
not approve. "We will not be free from unfair compe-
tition till one of these fellows is hanged for an example,"
he said. "Certainly," grunted the other; "get him
hanged! Why not? Anything—anything can be done in
this country. That's what I say; nobody here, you
understand, *here*, can endanger your position. And why?
You stand the climate—you outlast them all The danger
is in Europe; but there before I left I took care to—'
They moved off and whispered, then their voices rose
again. "The extraordinary series of delays is not my
fault. I did my best." The fat man sighed. "Very sad."

"And the pestiferous absurdity of his talk," continued
the other; "he bothered me enough when he was here.
'Each station should be like a beacon on the road
towards better things, a centre for trade of course, but
also for humanizing, improving, instructing.' Conceive
you—that ass! And he wants to be manager! No, it's—"
Here he got choked by excessive indignation, and I
lifted my head the least bit. I was surprised to see how
near they were—right under me. I could have spat upon
their hats. They were looking on the ground, absorbed
in thought. The manager was switching his leg with a
slender twig: his sagacious relative lifted his head. "You
have been well since you came out this time?" he asked.
The other gave a start. "Who? I? Oh! Like a charm—
like a charm. But the rest—oh, my goodness! All sick.
They die so quick, too, that I haven't the time to send
them out of the country—it's incredible!" "H'm. Just
so," grunted the uncle. "Ah! my boy, trust to this—I
say, trust to this." I saw him extend his short flipper of
an arm for a gesture that took in the forest, the creek,
the mud, the river—seemed to beckon with a dishonouring flourish before the sunlit face of the land a
treacherous appeal to the lurking death, to the hidden
evil, to the profound darkness of its heart. It was so startling that I leaped to my feet and looked back at the
edge of the forest, as though I had expected an answer
of some sort to that black display of confidence. You
know the foolish notions that come to one sometimes.

The high stillness confronted these two figures with its ominous patience, waiting for the passing away of a fantastic invasion.

'They swore aloud together—out of sheer fright, I believe—then pretending not to know anything of my existence, turned back to the station. The sun was low; and leaning forward side by side, they seemed to be tugging painfully uphill their two ridiculous shadows of unequal length, that trailed behind them slowly over the tall grass without bending a single blade.

'In a few days the Eldorado Expedition went into the patient wilderness, that closed upon it as the sea closes over a diver. Long afterwards the news came that all the donkeys were dead. I know nothing as to the fate of the less valuable animals. They, no doubt, like the rest of us, found what they deserved. I did not inquire. I was then rather excited at the prospect of meeting Kurtz very soon. When I say very soon I mean it comparatively. It was just two months from the day we left the creek when we came to the bank below Kurtz's station.

'Going up that river was like travelling back to the earliest beginnings of the world, when vegetation rioted on the earth and the big trees were kings. An empty stream, a great silence, an impenetrable forest. The air was warm, thick, heavy, sluggish. There was no joy in the brilliance of sunshine. The long stretches of the waterway ran on, deserted, into the gloom of overshadowed distances. On silvery sandbanks hippos and alligators sunned themselves side by side. The broadening waters flowed through a mob of wooded islands; you lost your way on that river as you would in a desert, and butted all day long against shoals, trying to find the channel, till you thought yourself bewitched and cut off for ever from everything you had known once—somewhere—far away—in another existence perhaps. There were moments when one's past came back to one, as it will sometimes when you have not a moment to spare to yourself; but it came in the shape of an unrestful and noisy dream, remembered with wonder amongst the overwhelming realities of this strange world of plants, and water, and silence. And this stillness of life did not in the least resemble a peace. It was the stillness of an implacable force brooding over an inscrutable intention. It looked at you with a vengeful aspect. I got used to it afterwards; I did not see it any more; I had no time. I had to keep guessing at the channel; I had to discern, mostly by inspiration, the signs of hidden banks; I watched for sunken stones; I was learning to clap my teeth smartly before my heart flew out, when I shaved by a fluke some infernal sly old snag that would have ripped the life out of the tin-pot steamboat and drowned all the pilgrims; I had to keep a look-out for the signs of dead wood we could cut up in the night for next day's steaming. When you have to attend to things of that sort, to the mere incidents of the surface, the reality—the reality, I tell you—fades. The inner truth is hidden—luckily, luckily. But I felt it all the same; I felt often its mysterious stillness watching me at my monkey tricks, just as it watches you fellows performing on your respective tight-ropes for—what is it? half-a-crown a tumble —'

'Try to be civil, Marlow,' growled a voice, and I knew there was at least one listener awake besides myself.

'I beg your pardon. I forgot the heartache which makes up the rest of the price. And indeed what does the price matter, if the trick be well done? You do your tricks very well. And I didn't do badly either, since I managed not to sink that steamboat on my first trip. It's a wonder to me yet. Imagine a blindfolded man set to drive a van over a bad road. I sweated and shivered over that business considerably, I can tell you. After all, for a seaman, to scrape the bottom of the thing that's supposed to float all the time under his care is the unpardonable sin. No one may know of it, but you never forget the thump—eh? A blow on the very heart. You remember it, you dream of it, you wake up at night and think of it—years after—and go hot and cold all over. I don't pretend to say that steamboat floated all the time. More than once she had to wade for a bit, with twenty cannibals splashing around and pushing. We had enlisted some of these chaps on the way for a crew. Fine fellows—cannibals—in their place. They were men one could work with, and I am grateful to them. And, after all, they did not eat each other before my face: they had brought along a provision of hippo-meat which went rotten, and made the mystery of the wilderness stink in my nostrils. Phoo! I can sniff it now.

I had the manager on board and three or four pilgrims with their staves—all complete. Sometimes we came upon a station close by the bank, clinging to the skirts of the unknown, and the white men rushing out of a tumbledown hovel, with great gestures of joy and surprise and welcome, seemed very strange—had the appearance of being held there captive by a spell. The word ivory would ring in the air for a while—and on we went again into the silence, along empty reaches, round the still bends, between the high walls of our winding way, reverberating in hollow claps the ponderous beat of the stern-wheel. Trees, trees, millions of trees, massive, immense, running up high; and at their foot, hugging the bank against the stream, crept the little begrimed steamboat, like a sluggish beetle crawling on the floor of a lofty portico. It made you feel very small, very lost, and yet it was not altogether depressing, that feeling. After all, if you were small, the grimy beetle crawled on—which was just what you wanted it to do. Where the pilgrims imagined it crawled to I don't know. To some place where they expected to get something, I bet! For me it crawled towards Kurtz—exclusively; but when the steam-pipes started leaking we crawled very slow. The reaches opened before us and closed behind, as if the forest had stepped leisurely across the water to bar the way for our return. We penetrated deeper and deeper into the heart of darkness. It was very quiet there. At night sometimes the roll of drums behind the curtain of trees would run up the

river and remain sustained faintly, as if hovering in the
air high over our heads, till the first break of day.
Whether it meant war, peace, or prayer we could not
tell. The dawns were heralded by the descent of a chill
stillness; the wood-cutters slept, their fires burned low;
the snapping of a twig would make you start. We were
wanderers on prehistoric earth, on an earth that wore
the aspect of an unknown planet. We could have fancied ourselves the first of men taking possession of an
accursed inheritance, to be subdued at the cost of profound anguish and of excessive toil. But suddenly, as
we struggled round a bend, there would be a glimpse of
rush walls, of peaked grass-roofs, a burst of yells, a
whirl of black limbs, a mass of hands clapping, of feet
stamping, of bodies swaying, of eyes rolling, under the
droop of heavy and motionless foliage. The steamer
toiled along slowly on the edge of a black and incomprehensible frenzy. The prehistoric man was cursing us,
praying to us, welcoming us—who could tell? We were
cut off from the comprehension of our surroundings;
we glided past like phantoms, wondering and secretly
appalled, as sane men would be before an enthusiastic
outbreak in a madhouse. We could not understand
because we were too far and could not remember,
because we were travelling in the night of first ages, of
those ages that are gone, leaving hardly a sign—and no
memories.

'The earth seemed unearthly. We are accustomed to
look upon the shackled form of a conquered monster,

but there—there you could look at a thing monstrous
and free. It was unearthly, and the men were—No, they
were not inhuman. Well, you know, that was the worst
of it—this suspicion of their not being inhuman. It
would come slowly to one. They howled and leaped,
and spun, and made horrid faces; but what thrilled you
was just the thought of their humanity—like yours—the
thought of your remote kinship with this wild and passionate uproar. Ugly. Yes, it was ugly enough; but if
you were man enough you would admit to yourself that
there was in you just the faintest trace of a response to
the terrible frankness of that noise, a dim suspicion of
there being a meaning in it which you—you so remote
from the night of first ages—could comprehend. And
why not? The mind of man is capable of anything—
because everything is in it, all the past as well as all the
future. What was there after all? Joy, fear, sorrow, devotion, valour, rage—who can tell?—but truth—truth
stripped of its cloak of time. Let the fool gape and shudder—the man knows, and can look on without a wink.
But he must at least be as much of a man as these on the
shore. He must meet that truth with his own true
stuff—with his own inborn strength. Principles won't
do. Acquisitions, clothes, pretty rags—rags that would
fly off at the first good shake. No; you want a deliberate belief. An appeal to me in this fiendish row—is
there? Very well; I hear; I admit, but I have a voice, too,
and for good or evil mine is the speech that cannot be
silenced. Of course, a fool, what with sheer fright and

fine sentiments, is always safe. Who's that grunting?
You wonder I didn't go ashore for a howl and a dance?
Well, no—I didn't. Fine sentiments, you say? Fine sentiments, be hanged! I had no time. I had to mess about
with white-lead and strips of woollen blanket helping to
put bandages on those leaky steam-pipes—I tell you. I
had to watch the steering, and circumvent those snags,
and get the tin-pot along by hook or by crook. There
was surface-truth enough in these things to save a wiser
man. And between whiles I had to look after the savage who was fireman. He was an improved specimen; he
could fire up a vertical boiler. He was there below me,
and, upon my word, to look at him was as edifying as
seeing a dog in a parody of breeches and a feather hat,
walking on his hind-legs. A few months of training had
done for that really fine chap. He squinted at the steam-
gauge and at the water-gauge with an evident effort of
intrepidity—and he had filed teeth, too, the poor devil,
and the wool of his pate shaved into queer patterns, and
three ornamental scars on each of his cheeks. He ought
to have been clapping his hands and stamping his feet
on the bank, instead of which he was hard at work, a
thrall to strange witchcraft, full of improving knowledge.
He was useful because he had been instructed; and what
he knew was this—that should the water in that trans-
parent thing disappear, the evil spirit inside the boiler
would get angry through the greatness of his thirst, and
take a terrible vengeance. So he sweated and fired up
and watched the glass fearfully (with an impromptu

charm, made of rags, tied to his arm, and a piece of polished bone, as big as a watch, stuck flatways through his
lower lip), while the wooded banks slipped past us
slowly, the short noise was left behind, the interminable
miles of silence—and we crept on, towards Kurtz. But
the snags were thick, the water was treacherous and
shallow, the boiler seemed indeed to have a sulky devil
in it, and thus neither that fireman nor I had any time
to peer into our creepy thoughts.

'Some fifty miles below the Inner Station we came
upon a hut of reeds, an inclined and melancholy pole,
with the unrecognizable tatters of what had been a flag
of some sort flying from it, and a neatly stacked wood-
pile. This was unexpected. We came to the bank, and
on the stack of firewood found a flat piece of board with
some faded pencil-writing on it. When deciphered it
said: "Wood for you. Hurry up. Approach cautiously."
There was a signature, but it was illegible—not Kurtz—
a much longer word. Hurry up. Where? Up the river?
"Approach cautiously." We had not done so. But the
warning could not have been meant for the place where
it could be only found after approach. Something was
wrong above. But what—and how much? That was the
question. We commented adversely upon the imbecility of that telegraphic style. The bush around said nothing, and would not let us look very far, either. A torn
curtain of red twill hung in the doorway of the hut, and
flapped sadly in our faces. The dwelling was dismantled; but we could see a white man had lived there not

very long ago. There remained a rude table—a plank on two posts; a heap of rubbish reposed in a dark corner, and by the door I picked up a book. It had lost its covers, and the pages had been thumbed into a state of extremely dirty softness; but the back had been lovingly stitched afresh with white cotton thread, which looked clean yet. It was an extraordinary find. Its title was, *An Inquiry into some Points of Seamanship*, by a man, Tower, Towson—some such name—Master in His Majesty's Navy. The matter looked dreary reading enough, with illustrative diagrams and repulsive tables of figures, and the copy was sixty years old. I handled this amazing antiquity with the greatest possible tenderness, lest it should dissolve in my hands. Within, Towson or Towser was inquiring earnestly into the breaking strain of ships' chains and tackle, and other such matters. Not a very enthralling book; but at the first glance you could see there a singleness of intention, an honest concern for the right way of going to work, which made these humble pages, thought out so many years ago, luminous with another than a professional light. The simple old sailor, with his talk of chains and purchases, made me forget the jungle and the pilgrims in a delicious sensation of having come upon something unmistakably real. Such a book being there was wonderful enough; but still more astounding were the notes pencilled in the margin, and plainly referring to the text. I couldn't believe my eyes! They were in cipher! Yes, it looked like cipher. Fancy a man lugging with him a book of that description into this nowhere and studying it—and making notes—in cipher at that! It was an extravagant mystery.

'I had been dimly aware for some time of a worrying noise, and when I lifted my eyes I saw the wood-pile was gone, and the manager, aided by all the pilgrims, was shouting at me from the river-side. I slipped the book into my pocket. I assure you to leave off reading was like tearing myself away from the shelter of an old and solid friendship.

'I started the lame engine ahead. "It must be this miserable trader—this intruder," exclaimed the manager, looking back malevolently at the place we had left. "He must be English," I said. "It will not save him from getting into trouble if he is not careful," muttered the manager darkly. I observed with assumed innocence that no man was safe from trouble in this world.

'The current was more rapid now, the steamer seemed at her last gasp, the stern-wheel flopped languidly, and I caught myself listening on tiptoe for the next beat of the float, for in sober truth I expected the wretched thing to give up every moment. It was like watching the last flickers of a life. But still we crawled. Sometimes I would pick out a tree a little way ahead to measure our progress towards Kurtz by, but I lost it invariably before we got abreast. To keep the eyes so long on one thing was too much for human patience. The manager displayed a beautiful resignation. I fretted and fumed and took to arguing with myself whether or no I would talk openly with Kurtz; but before I could come to any conclusion it occurred to me that my speech or my silence, indeed any action of mine, would be a mere futility. What did it matter what anyone knew or ignored? What did it matter who was manager? One gets sometimes such a flash of insight. The essentials of this affair lay deep under the surface, beyond my reach, and beyond my power of meddling.

'Towards the evening of the second day we judged ourselves about eight miles from Kurtz's station. I wanted to push on; but the manager looked grave, and told me the navigation up there was so dangerous that it would be advisable, the sun being very low already, to wait where we were till next morning. Moreover, he pointed out that if the warning to approach cautiously were to be followed, we must approach in daylight—not at dusk, or in the dark. This was sensible enough. Eight miles meant nearly three hours' steaming for us, and I could also see suspicious ripples at the upper end of the reach. Nevertheless, I was annoyed beyond expression at the delay, and most unreasonably, too, since one night more could not matter much after so many months. As we had plenty of wood, and caution was the word, I brought up in the middle of the stream. The reach was narrow, straight, with high sides like a railway cutting. The dusk came gliding into it long before the sun had set. The current ran smooth and swift, but a dumb immobility sat on the banks. The living trees, lashed together by the creepers and every living bush of the undergrowth, might have been changed into stone, even to the slenderest twig, to the lightest leaf. It was not sleep—it seemed unnatural. Like a state of trance. Not the faintest sound of any kind could be heard. You looked on amazed, and began to suspect yourself of being deaf—then the night came suddenly, and struck you blind as well. About three in the morning some large fish leaped, and the loud splash made me jump as though a gun had been fired. When the sun rose there was a white fog, very warm and clammy, and more blinding than the night. It did not shift or drive; it was just there, standing all round you like something solid. At eight or nine, perhaps, it lifted as a shutter lifts. We had a glimpse of the towering multitude of trees, of the immense matted jungle, with the blazing little ball of the sun hanging over it—all perfectly still—and then the white shutter came down again, smoothly, as if sliding in greased grooves. I ordered the chain, which we had begun to heave in, to be paid out again. Before it stopped running with a muffled rattle, a cry, a very loud cry, as of infinite desolation, soared slowly in the opaque air. It ceased. A complaining clamour, modulated in savage discords, filled our ears. The sheer unexpectedness of it made my hair stir under my cap. I don't know how it struck the others: to me it seemed as though the mist itself had screamed, so suddenly, and apparently from all sides at once, did this tumultuous and mournful uproar arise. It culminated in a hurried outbreak of almost intolerably excessive shrieking, which stopped short, leaving us stiffened in a variety of silly attitudes, and obstinately listening to the nearly as appalling and excessive silence. "Good God! What is the meaning—" stammered at my elbow one of the pilgrims,—a little fat man, with sandy hair and red whiskers, who wore side-spring boots, and pink pyjamas tucked into his socks. Two others remained open-mouthed a whole minute, then dashed into the little cabin, to rush out incontinently and stand darting scared glances, with Winchesters at "ready" in their hands. What we could see was just the steamer we were on, her outlines blurred as though she had been on the point of dissolving, and a misty strip of water, perhaps two feet broad, around her—and that was all. The rest of the world was nowhere, as far as our eyes and ears were concerned. Just nowhere. Gone, disappeared; swept off without leaving a whisper or a shadow behind.

'I went forward, and ordered the chain to be hauled in short, so as to be ready to trip the anchor and move the steamboat at once if necessary. "Will they attack?" whispered an awed voice. "We will be all butchered in this fog," murmured another. The faces twitched with the strain, the hands trembled slightly, the eyes forgot to wink. It was very curious to see the contrast of expressions of the white men and of the black fellows of our crew, who were as much strangers to that part of the river as we, though their homes were only eight hundred miles away. The whites, of course greatly discomposed, had besides a curious look of being painfully shocked by such an outrageous row. The others had an alert, naturally interested expression; but their faces were essentially quiet, even those of the one or two who grinned as they hauled at the chain. Several exchanged short, grunting phrases, which seemed to settle the matter to their satisfaction. Their headman, a young, broad-chested black, severely draped in dark-blue fringed cloths, with fierce nostrils and his hair all done up artfully in oily ringlets, stood near me. "Aha!" I said, just for good fellowship's sake. "Catch 'im," he snapped, with a bloodshot widening of his eyes and a flash of sharp teeth—"catch 'im. Give 'im to us." "To you, eh?" I asked; "what would you do with them?" "Eat 'im!" he said, curtly, and, leaning his elbow on the rail, looked out into the fog in a dignified and profoundly pensive attitude. I would no doubt have been properly horrified, had it not occurred to me that he and his chaps must be very hungry: that they must have been growing increasingly hungry for at least this month past. They had been engaged for six months (I don't think a single one of them had any clear idea of time, as we at the end of countless ages have. They still belonged to the beginnings of time—had no inherited experience to teach them, as it were), and, of course, as long as there was a piece of paper written over in accordance with some farcical law or other made down the river, it didn't enter anybody's head to trouble how they would live. Certainly they had brought with them some rotten hippo-meat, which couldn't have lasted very long, anyway,

even if the pilgrims hadn't, in the midst of a shocking
hullabaloo, thrown a considerable quantity of it overboard. It looked like a high-handed proceeding; but it
was really a case of legitimate self-defence. You can't
breathe dead hippo waking, sleeping, and eating, and at
the same time keep your precarious grip on existence.
Besides that, they had given them every week three
pieces of brass wire, each about nine inches long; and
the theory was they were to buy their provisions with
that currency in river-side villages. You can see how
that worked. There were either no villages, or the people
were hostile, or the director, who like the rest of us fed
out of tins, with an occasional old he-goat thrown in,
didn't want to stop the steamer for some more or less
recondite reason. So, unless they swallowed the wire
itself, or made loops of it to snare the fishes with, I
don't see what good their extravagant salary could be to
them. I must say it was paid with a regularity worthy
of a large and honourable trading company. For the rest,
the only thing to eat—though it didn't look eatable in
the least—I saw in their possession was a few lumps of
some stuff like half-cooked dough, of a dirty lavender
colour, they kept wrapped in leaves, and now and then
swallowed a piece of, but so small that it seemed done
more for the looks of the thing than for any serious purpose of sustenance. Why in the name of all the gnawing devils of hunger they didn't go for us—they were
thirty to five—and have a good tuck in for once, amazes
me now when I think of it. They were big powerful

men, with not much capacity to weigh the consequences, with courage, with strength, even yet, though
their skins were no longer glossy and their muscles no
longer hard. And I saw that something restraining, one
of those human secrets that baffle probability, had come
into play there. I looked at them with a swift quickening
of interest—not because it occurred to me I might be
eaten by them before very long, though I own to you
that just then I perceived—in a new light, as it were—
how unwholesome the pilgrims looked, and I hoped,
yes, I positively hoped, that my aspect was not so—what
shall I say?—so—unappetizing: a touch of fantastic van-
ity which fitted well with the dream-sensation that per-
vaded all my days at that time. Perhaps I had a little
fever, too. One can't live with one's finger everlastingly
on one's pulse. I had often "a little fever", or a little
touch of other things—the playful paw-strokes of the
wilderness, the preliminary trifling before the more serious onslaught which came in due course. Yes; I looked
at them as you would on any human being, with a
curiosity of their impulses, motives, capacities, weak-
nesses, when brought to the test of an inexorable physical necessity. Restraint! What possible restraint? Was it
superstition, disgust, patience, fear—or some kind of
primitive honour? No fear can stand up to hunger, no
patience can wear it out, disgust simply does not exist
where hunger is; and as to superstition, beliefs, and
what you may call principles, they are less than chaff in
a breeze. Don't you know the devilry of lingering star-

vation, its exasperating torment, its black thoughts, its sombre and brooding ferocity? Well, I do. It takes a man all his inborn strength to fight hunger properly. It's really easier to face bereavement, dishonour, and the perdition of one's soul—than this kind of prolonged hunger. Sad, but true. And these chaps, too, had no earthly reason for any kind of scruple. Restraint! I would just as soon have expected restraint from a hyena prowling amongst the corpses of a battlefield. But there was the fact facing me—the fact dazzling, to be seen, like the foam on the depths of the sea, like a ripple on an unfathomable enigma, a mystery greater—when I thought of it—than the curious, inexplicable note of desperate grief in this savage clamour that had swept by us on the river-bank, behind the blind whiteness of the fog.

'Two pilgrims were quarrelling in hurried whispers as to which bank. "Left." "No, no; how can you? Right, right, of course." "It is very serious," said the manager's voice behind me; "I would be desolated if anything should happen to Mr Kurtz before we came up." I looked at him, and had not the slightest doubt he was sincere. He was just the kind of man who would wish to preserve appearances. That was his restraint. But when he muttered something about going on at once, I did not even take the trouble to answer him. I knew, and he knew, that it was impossible. Were we to let go our hold of the bottom, we would be absolutely in the air—in space. We wouldn't be able to tell where we were going to—whether up or down stream, or across—

till we fetched against one bank or the other—and then we wouldn't know at first which it was. Of course I made no move. I had no mind for a smash-up. You couldn't imagine a more deadly place for a shipwreck. Whether drowned at once or not, we were sure to perish speedily in one way or another. "I authorize you to take all the risks," he said, after a short silence. "I refuse to take any," I said, shortly; which was just the answer he expected, though its tone might have surprised him. "Well, I must defer to your judgement. You are captain," he said, with marked civility. I turned my shoulder to him in sign of my appreciation, and looked into the fog. How long would it last? It was the most hopeless look-out. The approach to this Kurtz grubbing for ivory in the wretched bush was beset by as many dangers as though he had been an enchanted princess sleeping in a fabulous castle. "Will they attack, do you think?" asked the manager, in a confidential tone.

'I did not think they would attack, for several obvious reasons. The thick fog was one. If they left the bank in their canoes they would get lost in it, as we would be if we attempted to move. Still, I had also judged the jungle of both banks quite impenetrable—and yet eyes were in it, eyes that had seen us. The river-side bushes were certainly very thick; but the undergrowth behind was evidently penetrable. However, during the short lift I had seen no canoes anywhere in the reach—certainly not abreast of the steamer. But what made the idea of attack inconceivable to me was the nature of the noise—of the

cries we had heard. They had not the fierce character
boding of immediate hostile intention. Unexpected,
wild, and violent as they had been, they had given me
an irresistible impression of sorrow. The glimpse of the
steamboat had for some reason filled those savages with
unrestrained grief. The danger, if any, I expounded, was
from our proximity to a great human passion let loose.
Even extreme grief may ultimately vent itself in violence—but more generally takes the form of apathy . . .

'You should have seen the pilgrims stare! They had
no heart to grin, or even to revile me: but I believe they
thought me gone mad—with fright, maybe. I delivered
a regular lecture. My dear boys, it was no good bother-
ing. Keep a look-out? Well, you may guess I watched the
fog for the signs of lifting as a cat watches a mouse; but
for anything else our eyes were of no more use to us than
if we had been buried miles deep in a heap of cotton-
wool. It felt like it, too—choking, warm, stifling. Besides,
all I said, though it sounded extravagant, was absolutely
true to fact. What we afterwards alluded to as an attack
was really an attempt at repulse. The action was very far
from being aggressive—it was not even defensive, in the
usual sense: it was undertaken under the stress of desperation, and in its essence was purely protective.

'It developed itself, I should say, two hours after the
fog lifted, and its commencement was at a spot, roughly
speaking, about a mile and a half below Kurtz's station.
We had just floundered and flopped round a bend,
when I saw an islet, a mere grassy hummock of bright

green, in the middle of the stream. It was the only thing of the kind; but as we opened the reach more, I perceived it was the head of a long sandbank, or rather of a chain of shallow patches stretching down the middle of the river. They were discoloured, just awash, and the whole lot was seen just under the water, exactly as a man's backbone is seen running down the middle of his back under the skin. Now, as far as I did see, I could go to the right or to the left of this. I didn't know either channel, of course. The banks looked pretty well alike, the depth appeared the same; but as I had been informed the station was on the west side, I naturally headed for the western passage.

'No sooner had we fairly entered it than I became aware it was much narrower than I had supposed. To the left of us there was the long uninterrupted shoal, and to the right a high, steep bank heavily overgrown with bushes. Above the bush the trees stood in serried ranks. The twigs overhung the current thickly, and from distance to distance a large limb of some tree projected rigidly over the stream. It was then well on in the afternoon, the face of the forest was gloomy, and a broad strip of shadow had already fallen on the water. In this shadow we steamed up—very slowly, as you may imagine. I steered her well inshore—the water being deepest near the bank, as the sounding-pole informed me.

'One of my hungry and forbearing friends was sounding in the bows just below me. This steamboat was exactly like a decked scow. On the deck, there were two little teak-wood houses, with doors and windows. The boiler was in the fore-end, and the machinery right astern. Over the whole there was a light roof, supported on stanchions. The funnel projected through that roof, and in front of the funnel a small cabin built of light planks served for a pilot-house. It contained a couch, two camp-stools, a loaded Martini-Henry leaning in one corner, a tiny table, and the steering-wheel. It had a wide door in front and a broad shutter at each side. All these were always thrown open, of course. I spent my days perched up there on the extreme fore-end of that roof, before the door. At night I slept, or tried to, on the couch. An athletic black belonging to some coast tribe, and educated by my poor predecessor, was the helmsman. He sported a pair of brass earrings, wore a blue cloth wrapper from the waist to the ankles, and thought all the world of himself. He was the most unstable kind of fool I had ever seen. He steered with no end of a swagger while you were by; but if he lost sight of you, he became instantly the prey of an abject funk, and would let that cripple of a steamboat get the upper hand of him in a minute.

'I was looking down at the sounding-pole, and feeling much annoyed to see at each try a little more of it stick out of that river, when I saw my poleman give up the business suddenly, and stretch himself flat on the deck, without even taking the trouble to haul his pole in. He kept hold on it though, and it trailed in the water. At the same time the fireman, whom I could also see below me, sat down abruptly before his furnace and ducked his head. I was amazed. Then I had to look at the river mighty quick, because there was a snag in the fairway. Sticks, little sticks, were flying about—thick: they were whizzing before my nose, dropping below me, striking behind me against my pilot-house. All this time the river, the shore, the woods, were very quiet—perfectly quiet. I could only hear the heavy splashing thump of the stern-wheel and the patter of these things. We cleared the snag clumsily. Arrows, by Jove! We were being shot at! I stepped in quickly to close the shutter on the land-side. That fool-helmsman, his hands on the spokes, was lifting his knees high, stamping his feet, champing his mouth, like a reined-in horse. Confound him! And we were staggering within ten feet of the bank. I had to lean right out to swing the heavy shutter, and I saw a face amongst the leaves on the level with my own, looking at me very fierce and steady and then suddenly, as though a veil had been removed from my eyes, I made out, deep in the tangled gloom, naked breasts, arms, legs, glaring eyes,—the bush was swarming with human limbs in movement, glistening, of bronze colour. The twigs shook, swayed, and rustled, the arrows flew out of them, and then the shutter came to. "Steer her straight," I said to the helmsman. He held his head rigid, face forward; but his eyes rolled, he kept on, lifting and setting down his feet gently, his mouth foamed a little. "Keep quiet!" I said in a fury. I might just as well have ordered a tree not to sway in the wind. I darted out. Below me there

was a great scuffle of feet on the iron deck; confused
exclamations; a voice screamed, "Can you turn back?" I
caught sight of a V-shaped ripple on the water ahead.
What? Another snag! A fusillade burst out under my
feet. The pilgrims had opened with their Winchesters,
and were simply squirting lead into that bush. A deuce
of a lot of smoke came up and drove slowly forward. I
swore at it. Now I couldn't see the ripple or the snag
either. I stood in the doorway, peering, and the arrows
came in swarms. They might have been poisoned, but
they looked as though they wouldn't kill a cat. The bush
began to howl. Our wood-cutters raised a warlike
whoop; the report of a rifle just at my back deafened
me. I glanced over my shoulder, and the pilot-house was
yet full of noise and smoke when I made a dash at the
wheel. The fool-nigger had dropped everything, to
throw the shutter open and let off that Martini-Henry.
He stood before the wide opening, glaring, and I yelled
at him to come back, while I straightened the sudden
twist out of that steamboat. There was no room to turn
even if I had wanted to, the snag was somewhere very
near ahead in that confounded smoke, there was no time
to lose, so I just crowded her into the bank—right into
the bank, where I knew the water was deep.

'We tore slowly along the overhanging bushes in a
whirl of broken twigs and flying leaves. The fusillade
below stopped short, as I had foreseen it would when
the squirts got empty. I threw my head back to a glint-
ing whizz that traversed the pilot-house, in at one shut-

ter-hole and out at the other. Looking past that mad helmsman, who was shaking the empty rifle and yelling at the shore, I saw vague forms of men running bent double, leaping, gliding, indistinct, incomplete, evanescent. Something big appeared in the air before the shutter, the rifle went overboard, and the man stepped back swiftly, looked at me over his shoulder in an extraordinary, profound, familiar manner, and fell upon my feet. The side of his head hit the wheel twice, and the end of what appeared to be a long cane clattered round and knocked over a little camp-stool. It looked as though after wrenching that thing from somebody ashore he had lost his balance in the effort. The thin smoke had blown away, we were clear of the snag, and looking ahead I could see that in another hundred yards or so I would be free to sheer off, away from the bank; but my feet felt so very warm and wet that I had to look down. The man had rolled on his back and stared straight up at me; both his hands clutched that cane. It was the shaft of a spear that, either thrown or lunged through the opening, had caught him in the side just below the ribs; the blade had gone in out of sight, after making a frightful gash; my shoes were full; a pool of blood lay very still, gleaming dark-red under the wheel; his eyes shone with an amazing lustre. The fusillade burst out again. He looked at me anxiously, gripping the spear like something precious, with an air of being afraid I would try to take it away from him. I had to make an effort to free my eyes from his gaze and attend to the

steering. With one hand I felt above my head for the
line of the steam-whistle, and jerked out screech after
screech hurriedly. The tumult of angry and warlike yells
was checked instantly, and then from the depths of the
woods went out such a tremulous and prolonged wail
of mournful fear and utter despair as may be imagined
to follow the flight of the last hope from the earth.
There was a great commotion in the bush; the shower of
arrows stopped, a few dropping shots rang out sharply—
then silence, in which the languid beat of the stern-
wheel came plainly to my ears. I put the helm hard
a-starboard at the moment when the pilgrim in pink
pyjamas, very hot and agitated, appeared in the doorway. "The manager sends me—" he began in an official tone, and stopped short. "Good God!" he said,
glaring at the wounded man.

'We two whites stood over him, and his lustrous and
inquiring glance enveloped us both. I declare it looked
as though he would presently put to us some question
in an understandable language; but he died without
uttering a sound, without moving a limb, without
twitching a muscle. Only in the very last moment, as
though in response to some sign we could not see, to
some whisper we could not hear, he frowned heavily,
and that frown gave to his black death-mask an inconceivably sombre, brooding, and menacing expression.
The lustre of the inquiring glance faded swiftly into
vacant glassiness. "Can you steer?" I asked the agent
eagerly. He looked very dubious; but I made a grab at

his arm, and he understood at once I meant him to steer whether or no. To tell you the truth, I was morbidly anxious to change my shoes and socks. "He is dead," murmured the fellow, immensely impressed. "No doubt about it," said I, tugging like mad at the shoe-laces. "And by the way, I suppose Mr Kurtz is dead as well by this time."

'For the moment that was the dominant thought. There was a sense of extreme disappointment, as though I had found out I had been striving after something altogether without a substance. I couldn't have been more disgusted if I had travelled all this way for the sole purpose of talking with Mr Kurtz. Talking with . . . I flung one shoe overboard, and became aware that that was exactly what I had been looking forward to—a talk with Kurtz. I made the strange discovery that I had never imagined him as doing, you know, but as discoursing. I didn't say to myself, "Now I will never see him," or "Now I will never shake him by the hand," but, "Now I will never hear him." The man presented himself as a voice. Not of course that I did not connect him with some sort of action. Hadn't I been told in all the tones of jealousy and admiration that he had collected, bartered, swindled, or stolen more ivory than all the other agents together? That was not the point. The point was in his being a gifted creature, and that of all his gifts the one that stood out pre-eminently, that carried with it a sense of real presence, was his ability to talk, his words—the gift of expression, the bewildering,

the illuminating, the most exalted and the most con-
temptible, the pulsating stream of light, or the deceitful
flow from the heart of an impenetrable darkness.

'The other shoe went flying unto the devil-god of
that river. I thought, By Jove! it's all over. We are too
late; he has vanished—the gift has vanished, by means
of some spear, arrow, or club. I will never hear that chap
speak after all,—and my sorrow had a startling extrava-
gance of emotion, even such as I had noticed in the
howling sorrow of these savages in the bush. I couldn't
have felt more of lonely desolation somehow, had I been
robbed of a belief or had missed my destiny in life . . .
Why do you sigh in this beastly way, somebody?
Absurd? Well, absurd. Good Lord! mustn't a man
ever—Here, give me some tobacco.' . . .

There was a pause of profound stillness, then a match
flared, and Marlow's lean face appeared, worn, hollow,
with downward folds and dropped eyelids, with an
aspect of concentrated attention; and as he took vigorous
draws at his pipe, it seemed to retreat and advance out
of the night in the regular flicker of the tiny flame. The
match went out.

'Absurd!' he cried. 'This is the worst of trying to tell
. . . Here you all are, each moored with two good
addresses, like a hulk with two anchors, a butcher round
one corner, a policeman round another, excellent
appetites, and temperature normal—you hear—normal
from year's end to year's end. And you say, Absurd!
Absurd be—exploded! Absurd! My dear boys, what can

you expect from a man who out of sheer nervousness had just flung overboard a pair of new shoes! Now I think of it, it is amazing I did not shed tears. I am, upon the whole, proud of my fortitude. I was cut to the quick at the idea of having lost the inestimable privilege of listening to the gifted Kurtz. Of course I was wrong. The privilege was waiting for me. Oh, yes, I heard more than enough. And I was right too. A voice. He was very little more than a voice. And I heard—him—it—this voice—other voices—all of them were so little more than voices—and the memory of that time itself lingers around me, impalpable, like a dying vibration of one immense jabber, silly, atrocious, sordid, savage, or simply mean, without any kind of sense. Voices, voices—even the girl herself—now—'

He was silent for a long time.

'I laid the ghost of his gifts at last with a lie,' he began, suddenly. 'Girl! What? Did I mention a girl? Oh, she is out of it—completely. They—the women I mean—are out of it—should be out of it. We must help them to stay in that beautiful world of their own, lest ours gets worse. Oh, she had to be out of it. You should have heard the disinterred body of Mr Kurtz saying, "My Intended." You would have perceived directly then how completely she was out of it. And the lofty frontal bone of Mr Kurtz! They say the hair goes on growing sometimes, but this—ah—specimen, was impressively bald. The wilderness had patted him on the head, and, behold, it was like a ball—an ivory ball; it had caressed

him, and—lo!—he had withered; it had taken him,
loved him, embraced him, got into his veins, consumed
his flesh, and sealed his soul to its own by the inconceivable ceremonies of some devilish initiation. He was
its spoiled and pampered favourite. Ivory? I should
think so. Heaps of it, stacks of it. The old mud shanty
was bursting with it. You would think there was not a
single tusk left either above or below the ground in the
whole country. "Mostly fossil," the manager had
remarked, disparagingly. It was no more fossil than I
am; but they call it fossil when it is dug up. It appears
these niggers do bury the tusks sometimes—but evidently they couldn't bury this parcel deep enough to
save the gifted Mr Kurtz from his fate. We filled the
steamboat with it, and had to pile a lot on the deck.
Thus he could see and enjoy as long as he could see,
because the appreciation of this favour had remained
with him to the last. You should have heard him say,
"My ivory." Oh yes, I heard him. "My Intended, my
ivory, my station, my river, my—" everything belonged
to him. It made me hold my breath in expectation of
hearing the wilderness burst into a prodigious peal of
laughter that would shake the fixed stars in their places.
Everything belonged to him—but that was a trifle. The
thing was to know what he belonged to, how many
powers of darkness claimed him for their own. That was
the reflection that made you creepy all over. It was
impossible—it was not good for one either—trying to
imagine. He had taken a high seat amongst the devils

of the land—I mean literally. You can't understand. How could you?—with solid pavement under your feet, surrounded by kind neighbours ready to cheer you or to fall on you, stepping delicately between the butcher and the policeman, in the holy terror of scandal and gallows and lunatic asylums—how can you imagine what particular region of the first ages a man's untrammelled feet may take him into by the way of solitude—utter solitude without a policeman—by the way of silence—utter silence, where no warning voice of a kind neighbour can be heard whispering of public opinion? These little things make all the great difference. When they are gone you must fall back upon your own innate strength, upon your own capacity for faithfulness. Of course you may be too much of a fool to go wrong—too dull even to know you are being assaulted by the powers of darkness. I take it, no fool ever made a bargain for his soul with the devil: the fool is too much of a fool, or the devil too much of a devil—I don't know which. Or you may be such a thunderingly exalted creature as to be altogether deaf and blind to anything but heavenly sights and sounds. Then the earth for you is only a standing place—and whether to be like this is your loss or your gain I won't pretend to say. But most of us are neither one nor the other. The earth for us is a place to live in, where we must put up with sights, with sounds, with smells, too, by Jove!—breathe dead hippo, so to speak, and not be contaminated. And there, don't you see? your strength comes in, the faith in your ability for the

digging of unostentatious holes to bury the stuff in—
your power of devotion, not to yourself, but to an
obscure, back-breaking business. And that's difficult
enough. Mind, I am not trying to excuse or even
explain—I am trying to account to myself for—for—Mr
Kurtz—for the shade of Mr Kurtz. This initiated wraith
from the back of Nowhere honoured me with its amazing confidence before it vanished altogether. This was
because it could speak English to me. The original
Kurtz had been educated partly in England, and—as he
was good enough to say himself—his sympathies were
in the right place. His mother was half-English, his
father was half-French. All Europe contributed to the
making of Kurtz; and by-and-by I learned that, most
appropriately, the International Society for the Suppression of Savage Customs had entrusted him with the
making of a report, for its future guidance. And he had
written it, too. I've seen it. I've read it. It was eloquent,
vibrating with eloquence, but too high-strung, I think.
Seventeen pages of close writing he had found time for!
But this must have been before his—let us say—nerves,
went wrong, and caused him to preside at certain midnight dances ending with unspeakable rites, which—as
far as I reluctantly gathered from what I heard at various times—were offered up to him—do you understand?—to Mr Kurtz himself. But it was a beautiful
piece of writing. The opening paragraph, however, in
the light of later information, strikes me now as ominous. He began with the argument that we whites, from

the point of development we had arrived at, "must necessarily appear to them [savages] in the nature of supernatural beings—we approach them with the might as of
a deity," and so on, and so on. "By the simple exercise
of our will we can exert a power for good practically
unbounded," etc., etc. From that point he soared and
took me with him. The peroration was magnificent,
though difficult to remember, you know. It gave me the
notion of an exotic Immensity ruled by an august
Benevolence. It made me tingle with enthusiasm. This
was the unbounded power of eloquence—of words—of
burning noble words. There were no practical hints to
interrupt the magic current of phrases, unless a kind of
note at the foot of the last page, scrawled evidently
much later, in an unsteady hand, may be regarded as the
exposition of a method. It was very simple, and at the
end of that moving appeal to every altruistic sentiment
it blazed at you, luminous and terrifying, like a flash of
lightning in a serene sky: "Exterminate all the brutes!"
The curious part was that he had apparently forgotten
all about that valuable postscriptum, because, later on,
when he in a sense came to himself, he repeatedly
entreated me to take good care of "my pamphlet" (he
called it), as it was sure to have in the future a good
influence upon his career. I had full information about
all these things, and, besides, as it turned out, I was to
have the care of his memory. I've done enough for it to
give me the indisputable right to lay it, if I choose, for
an everlasting rest in the dust-bin of progress, amongst

all the sweepings and, figuratively speaking, all the dead cats of civilization. But then, you see, I can't choose. He won't be forgotten. Whatever he was, he was not common. He had the power to charm or frighten rudimentary souls into an aggravated witch-dance in his honour; he could also fill the small souls of the pilgrims with bitter misgivings: he had one devoted friend at least, and he had conquered one soul in the world that was neither rudimentary nor tainted with self-seeking. No; I can't forget him, though I am not prepared to affirm the fellow was exactly worth the life we lost in getting to him. I missed my late helmsman awfully,—I missed him even while his body was still lying in the pilot-house. Perhaps you will think it passing strange, this regret for a savage who was of no more account than a grain of sand in a black Sahara. Well, don't you see, he had done something, he had steered; for months I had him at my back—a help—an instrument. It was a kind of partnership. He steered for me—I had to look after him, I worried about his deficiencies, and thus a subtle bond had been created, of which I only became aware when it was suddenly broken. And the intimate profundity of that look he gave me when he received his hurt remains to this day in my memory—like a claim of distant kinship affirmed in a supreme moment.

'Poor fool! If he had only left that shutter alone. He had no restraint, no restraint—just like Kurtz—a tree swayed by the wind. As soon as I had put on a dry pair of slippers, I dragged him out, after first jerking the spear out of his side, which operation I confess I performed with my eyes shut tight. His heels leaped together over the little doorstep; his shoulders were pressed to my breast; I hugged him from behind desperately. Oh! he was heavy, heavy; heavier than any man on earth, I should imagine. Then without more ado I tipped him overboard. The current snatched him as though he had been a wisp of grass, and I saw the body roll over twice before I lost sight of it for ever. All the pilgrims and the manager were then congregated on the awning-deck about the pilot-house, chattering at each other like a flock of excited magpies, and there was a scandalized murmur at my heartless promptitude. What they wanted to keep that body hanging about for I can't guess. Embalm it, maybe. But I had also heard another, and a very ominous, murmur on the deck below. My friends the wood-cutters were likewise scandalized, and with a better show of reason—though I admit that the reason itself was quite inadmissible. Oh, quite! I had made up my mind that if my late helmsman was to be eaten, the fishes alone should have him. He had been a very second-rate helmsman while alive, but now he was dead he might have become a first-class temptation, and possibly cause some startling trouble. Besides, I was anxious to take the wheel, the man in pink pyjamas showing himself a hopeless duffer at the business.

'This I did directly the simple funeral was over. We were going half-speed, keeping right in the middle of the stream, and I listened to the talk about me. They

had given up Kurtz, they had given up the station;
Kurtz was dead, and the station had been burnt—and so
on—and so on. The red-haired pilgrim was beside himself with the thought that at least this poor Kurtz had
been properly avenged. "Say! We must have made a
glorious slaughter of them in the bush. Eh? What do
you think? Say?" He positively danced, the bloodthirsty
little gingery beggar. And he had nearly fainted when he
saw the wounded man! I could not help saying, "You
made a glorious lot of smoke, anyhow." I had seen,
from the way the tops of the bushes rustled and flew,
that almost all the shots had gone too high. You can't
hit anything unless you take aim and fire from the
shoulder; but these chaps fired from the hip with their
eyes shut. The retreat, I maintained—and I was right—
was caused by the screeching of the steam-whistle.
Upon this they forgot Kurtz, and began to howl at me
with indignant protests.

'The manager stood by the wheel murmuring confi-
dentially about the necessity of getting well away down
the river before dark at all events, when I saw in the distance a clearing on the river-side and the outlines of
some sort of building. "What's this?" I asked. He
clapped his hands in wonder. "The station!" he cried. I
edged in at once, still going half-speed.

'Through my glasses I saw the slope of a hill inter-
spersed with rare trees and perfectly free from undergrowth. A long decaying building on the summit was
half buried in the high grass; the large holes in the

peaked roof gaped black from afar; the jungle and the
woods made a background. There was no enclosure or
fence of any kind; but there had been one apparently,
for near the house half-a-dozen slim posts remained in a
row, roughly trimmed, and with their upper ends orna-
mented with round carved balls. The rails, or whatever
there had been between, had disappeared. Of course the
forest surrounded all that. The river-bank was clear, and
on the water-side I saw a white man under a hat like a
cartwheel beckoning persistently with his whole arm.
Examining the edge of the forest above and below, I was
almost certain I could see movements—human forms
gliding here and there. I steamed past prudently, then
stopped the engines and let her drift down. The man
on the shore began to shout, urging us to land. "We
have been attacked," screamed the manager. "I know—
I know. It's all right," yelled back the other, as cheerful
as you please. "Come along. It's all right. I am glad."

'His aspect reminded me of something I had seen—
something funny I had seen somewhere. As I manoeu-
vred to get alongside, I was asking myself, "What does
this fellow look like?" Suddenly I got it. He looked like
a harlequin. His clothes had been made of some stuff
that was brown holland probably, but it was covered
with patches all over, with bright patches, blue, red, and
yellow,—patches on the back, patches on the front,
patches on elbows, on knees; coloured binding around
his jacket, scarlet edging at the bottom of his trousers;
and the sunshine made him look extremely gay and

wonderfully neat withal, because you could see how beautifully all this patching had been done. A beardless, boyish face, very fair, no feature to speak of, nose peeling, little blue eyes, smiles and frowns chasing each other over that open countenance like sunshine and shadow on a wind-swept plain. "Look out, captain!" he cried; "there's a snag lodged in here last night." What! Another snag? I confess I swore shamefully. I had nearly holed my cripple, to finish off that charming trip. The harlequin on the bank turned his little pug-nose up to me. "You English?" he asked, all smiles. "Are you?" I shouted from the wheel. The smiles vanished, and he shook his head as if sorry for my disappointment. Then he brightened up. "Never mind!" he cried, encouragingly. "Are we in time?" I asked. "He is up there," he replied, with a toss of the head up the hill, and becoming gloomy all of a sudden. His face was like the autumn sky, overcast one moment and bright the next.

'When the manager, escorted by the pilgrims, all of them armed to the teeth, had gone to the house this chap came on board. "I say, I don't like this. These natives are in the bush," I said. He assured me earnestly it was all right. "They are simple people," he added; "well, I am glad you came. It took me all my time to keep them off." 'But you said it was all right," I cried. "Oh, they meant no harm," he said; and as I stared he corrected himself, "Not exactly." Then vivaciously, "My faith, your pilot-house wants a clean-up!" In the next breath he advised me to keep enough steam on the boiler to blow the whistle in case of any trouble. "One good screech will do more for you than all your rifles. They are simple people," he repeated. He rattled away at such a rate he quite overwhelmed me. He seemed to be trying to make up for lots of silence, and actually hinted, laughing, that such was the case. "Don't you talk with Mr Kurtz?" I said. "You don't talk with that man—you listen to him," he exclaimed with severe exaltation. "But now—" He waved his arm, and in the twinkling of an eye was in the uttermost depths of despondency. In a moment he came up again with a jump, possessed himself of both hands, shook them continuously, while he gabbled: "Brother sailor . . . honour . . . pleasure . . . delight . . . introduce myself . . . Russian . . . son of an arch-priest . . . Government of Tambov . . . What? Tobacco! English tobacco; the excellent English tobacco! Now, that's brotherly. Smoke? Where's a sailor that does not smoke?"

'The pipe soothed him, and gradually I made out he had run away from school, had gone to sea in a Russian ship; ran away again; served some time in English ships; was now reconciled with the arch-priest. He made a point of that. "But when one is young one must see things, gather experience, ideas; enlarge the mind." "Here!" I interrupted. "You can never tell! Here I met Mr Kurtz," he said, youthfully solemn and reproachful. I held my tongue after that. It appears he had persuaded a Dutch trading-house on the coast to fit him out with stores and goods, and had started for the interior with a light heart, and no more idea of what would happen to him than a baby. He had been wandering about that river for nearly two years alone, cut off from everybody and everything. "I am not so young as I look. I am twenty-five," he said. "At first old Van Shuyten would tell me to go to the devil." he narrated with keen enjoyment; "but I stuck to him, and talked and talked, till at last he got afraid I would talk the hind-leg off his favourite dog, so he gave me some cheap things and a few guns, and told me he hoped he would never see my face again. Good old Dutchman. Van Shuyten. I've sent him one small lot of ivory a year ago, so that he can't call me a little thief when I get back. I hope he got it. And for the rest I don't care. I had some wood stacked for you. That was my old house. Did you see?"

'I gave him Towson's book. He made as though he would kiss me, but restrained himself. "The only book I had left, and I thought I had lost it," he said, looking at it ecstatically. "So many accidents happen to a man going about alone, you know. Canoes get upset some-times—and sometimes you've got to clear out so quickly when the people get angry." He thumbed the pages. "You made notes in Russian?" I asked. He nodded. "I thought they were written in cipher," I said. He laughed, then became serious. "I had lots of trouble to keep these people off," he said. "Did they want to kill you?" I asked. "Oh, no!" he cried, and checked himself. "Why did they attack us?" I pursued. He hesitated, then said shamefacedly, "They don't want him to go." "Don't they?" I said, curiously. He nodded a nod full of mystery and wisdom. "I tell you," he cried, "this man has enlarged my mind." He opened his arms wide, staring at me with his little blue eyes that were perfectly round.'

III

'I looked at him, lost in astonishment. There he was before me, in motley, as though he had absconded from a troupe of mimes, enthusiastic, fabulous. His very existence was improbable, inexplicable, and altogether bewildering. He was an insoluble problem. It was inconceivable how he had existed, how he had succeeded in getting so far, how he had managed to remain—why he did not instantly disappear. "I went a little farther," he said, "then still a little farther—till I had gone so far that I don't know how I'll ever get back. Never mind. Plenty time. I can manage. You take Kurtz away quick—quick—I tell you." The glamour of youth enveloped his parti-coloured rags, his destitution, his loneliness, the essential desolation of his futile wanderings. For months—for years—his life hadn't been worth a day's purchase: and there he was gallantly, thoughtlessly alive, to all appearance indestructible solely by the virtue of his few years and of his unreflecting audacity. I was seduced into something like admiration—like envy. Glamour urged him on, glamour kept him unscathed. He surely wanted nothing from the wilderness but space to breathe in and to push on through. His need was to exist, and to move onwards at the greatest possible risk, and with a maximum of privation. If the absolutely pure, uncalculating, unpractical spirit of adventure had ever ruled a human being, it ruled this be-patched youth. I almost envied him the possession of this modest and clear flame. It seemed to have consumed all thought of self so completely, that even while he was talking to you, you forgot that it was he—the man before your eyes—who had gone through these things. I did not envy him his devotion to Kurtz, though. He had not meditated over it. It came to him, and he accepted it with a sort of eager fatalism. I must say that to me it appeared about the most dangerous thing in every way he had come upon so far.

'They had come together unavoidably, like two ships becalmed near each other, and lay rubbing sides at last. I suppose Kurtz wanted an audience, because on a certain occasion, when encamped in the forest, they had talked all night, or more probably Kurtz had talked. "We talked of everything," he said, quite transported at the recollection. "I forgot there was such a thing as sleep. The night did not seem to last an hour. Everything! Everything! . . . Of love, too." "Ah, he talked to you of love?" I said, much amused. "It isn't what you think," he cried, almost passionately. "It was in general. He made me see things—things."

'He threw his arms up. We were on deck at the time, and the headman of my wood-cutters, lounging near by, turned upon him his heavy and glittering eyes. I looked around, and I don't know why, but I assure you that never, never before, did this land, this river, this jungle, the very arch of this blazing sky, appear to me so hopeless and so dark, so impenetrable to human thought, so pitiless to human weakness. "And, ever since, you have been with him, of course?" I said.

'On the contrary. It appears their intercourse had been very much broken by various causes. He had, as he informed me proudly, managed to nurse Kurtz through two illnesses (he alluded to it as you would to some risky feat), but as a rule Kurtz wandered alone, far in the depths of the forest. "Very often coming to this station, I had to wait days and days before he would turn up," he said. "Ah, it was worth waiting for!—sometimes." "What was he doing? exploring or what?" I asked. "Oh, yes, of course"; he had discovered lots of villages, a lake, too—he did not know exactly in what direction; it was dangerous to inquire too much—but mostly his expeditions had been for ivory. "But he had no goods to trade with by that time," I objected. "There's a good lot of cartridges left even yet," he answered, looking away. "To speak plainly, he raided the country," I said. He nodded. "Not alone, surely!" He muttered something about the villages round that lake. "Kurtz got the tribe to follow him, did he?" I suggested. He fidgeted a little. "They adored him," he said. The tone of these words was so extraordinary that I looked at him searchingly. It was curious to see his mingled eagerness and reluctance to speak of Kurtz. The man filled his life, occupied his thoughts, swayed his emotions. "What can you expect?" he burst out; "he came to them with thunder and lightning, you know—and they had never seen anything like it—and very terrible. He could be very terrible. You can't judge Mr Kurtz as you would an ordinary man. No, no, no! Now—just to give you an idea—I don't mind telling you, he wanted to shoot me, too, one day—but I don't judge him." "Shoot you!" I cried. "What for?" "Well, I had a small lot of ivory the chief of that village near my house gave me. You see I used to shoot game for them. Well, he wanted it, and wouldn't hear reason. He declared he would shoot me unless I gave him the ivory and then cleared out of the country, because he could do so, and had a fancy for it, and there was nothing on earth to prevent him killing whom he jolly well pleased. And it was true, too. I gave him the ivory. What did I care! But I didn't clear out. No, no. I couldn't leave him. I had to be careful, of course, till we got friendly again for a time. He had his second illness then. Afterwards I had to keep out of the way; but I didn't mind. He was living for the most part in those villages on the lake. When he came down to the river, sometimes he would take to me, and sometimes it was better for me to be careful. This man suffered too much. He hated all this, and somehow he couldn't get away. When I had a chance I begged him to try and leave while there was time; I offered to go back with him. And he would say yes, and then he would remain; go off on another ivory hunt; disappear for weeks; forget himself amongst these people—forget himself—you know." "Why! he's mad," I said. He protested indignantly. Mr Kurtz couldn't be mad. If I had heard him talk, only two days ago, I wouldn't dare hint at such a thing . . . I had taken up my binoculars while we talked, and was looking at the shore, sweeping the limit of the forest at each side and at the back of the house. The consciousness of there being people in that bush, so silent, so quiet—as silent and quiet as the ruined house on the hill—made me uneasy. There was no sign on the face of nature of this amazing tale that was not so much told as suggested to me in desolate exclamations, completed by shrugs, in interrupted phrases, in hints ending in deep sighs. The woods were unmoved, like a mask—heavy, like the closed door of a prison—they looked with their air of hidden knowledge, of patient expectation, of unapproachable silence. The Russian was explaining to me that it was only lately that Mr Kurtz had come down to the river, bringing along with him all the fighting men of that lake tribe. He had been absent for several months—getting himself adored, I suppose—and had come down unexpectedly, with the intention to all appearance of making a raid either across the river or down stream. Evidently the appetite for more ivory had got the better of the—what shall I say?—less material aspirations. However he had got much worse suddenly. "I heard he was lying helpless, and so I came up—took my chance," said the Russian. "Oh, he is bad, very bad."

I directed my glass to the house. There were no signs of life, but there was the ruined roof, the long mud wall peeping above the grass, with three little square window-holes, no two the same size: all this brought within reach of my hand, as it were. And then I made a brusque movement, and one of the remaining posts of that vanished fence leaped up in the field of my glass. You remember I told you I had been struck at the distance by certain attempts at ornamentation, rather remarkable in the ruinous aspect of the place. Now I had suddenly a nearer view, and its first result was to make me throw my head back as if before a blow. Then I went carefully from post to post with my glass, and I saw my mistake. These round knobs were not ornamental but symbolic; they were expressive and puzzling, striking and disturbing—food for thought and also for the vultures if there had been any looking down from the sky; but at all events for such ants as were industrious enough to ascend the pole. They would have been even more impressive, those heads on the stakes, if their faces had not been turned to the house. Only one, the first I had made out, was facing my way. I was not so shocked as you may think. The start back I had given was really nothing but a movement of surprise. I had expected to see a knob of wood there, you know. I returned deliberately to the first I had seen—and there it was, black, dried, sunken, with closed eyelids—a head that seemed to sleep at the top of that pole, and, with the shrunken dry lips showing a narrow white line of teeth, was smiling, too, smiling continuously at some endless and jocose dream of that eternal slumber.

'I am not disclosing any trade secrets. In fact, the manager said afterwards that Mr Kurtz's methods had ruined the district. I have no opinion on that point, but I want you clearly to understand that there was nothing exactly profitable in these heads being there. They only showed that Mr Kurtz lacked restraint in the gratification of his various lusts, that there was something wanting in him—some small matter which, when the pressing need arose, could not be found under his magnificent eloquence. Whether he knew of this deficiency himself I can't say. I think the knowledge came to him at last—only at the very last. But the wilderness had found him out early, and had taken on him a terrible vengeance for the fantastic invasion. I think it had whispered to him things about himself which he did not know, things of which he had no conception till he took counsel with this great solitude—and the whisper had proved irresistibly fascinating. It echoed loudly within him because he was hollow at the core . . . I put down the glass, and the head that had appeared near enough to be spoken to seemed at once to have leaped away from me into inaccessible distance.

'The admirer of Mr Kurtz was a bit crestfallen. In a hurried, indistinct voice he began to assure me he had not dared to take these—say, symbols—down. He was not afraid of the natives; they would not stir till Mr Kurtz gave the word. His ascendancy was extraordinary.

The camps of these people surrounded the place, and the chiefs came every day to see him. They would crawl . . . "I don't want to know anything of the ceremonies used when approaching Mr Kurtz," I shouted. Curious, this feeling that came over me that such details would be more intolerable than those heads drying on the stakes under Mr Kurtz's windows. After all, that was only a savage sight, while I seemed at one bound to have been transported into some lightless region of subtle horrors, where pure, uncomplicated savagery was a positive relief, being something that had a right to exist—obviously—in the sunshine. The young man looked at me with surprise. I suppose it did not occur to him that Mr Kurtz was no idol of mine. He forgot I hadn't heard any of these splendid monologues on, what was it? on love, justice, conduct of life—or what not. If it had come to crawling before Mr Kurtz, he crawled as much as the veriest savage of them all. I had no idea of the conditions, he said: these heads were the heads of rebels. I shocked him excessively by laughing. Rebels! What would be the next definition I was to hear? There had been enemies, criminals, workers—and these were rebels. Those rebellious heads looked very subdued to me on their sticks. "You don't know how such a life tries a man like Kurtz," cried Kurtz's last disciple. "Well, and you?" I said. "I! I! I am a simple man. I have no great thoughts. I want nothing from anybody. How can you compare me to? . . ." His feelings were too much for speech, and suddenly he broke down. "I don't understand," he groaned. "I've been doing my best to keep him alive, and that's enough. I had no hand in all this. I have no abilities. There hasn't been a drop of medicine or a mouthful of invalid food for months here. He was shamefully abandoned. A man like this, with such ideas. Shamefully! Shamefully! I—I—haven't slept for the last ten nights . . ."

'His voice lost itself in the calm of the evening. The long shadows of the forest had slipped down hill while we talked, had gone far beyond the ruined hovel, beyond the symbolic row of stakes. All this was in the gloom, while we down there were yet in the sunshine, and the stretch of the river abreast of the clearing glittered in a still and dazzling splendour, with a murky and overshadowed bend above and below. Not a living soul was seen on the shore. The bushes did not rustle.

'Suddenly round the corner of the house a group of men appeared, as though they had come up from the ground. They waded waist-deep in the grass, in a compact body, bearing an improvised stretcher in their midst. Instantly, in the emptiness of the landscape, a cry arose whose shrillness pierced the still air like a sharp arrow flying straight to the very heart of the land; and, as if by enchantment, streams of human beings—of naked human beings—with spears in their hands, with bows, with shields, with wild glances and savage movements, were poured into the clearing by the dark-faced and pensive forest. The bushes shook, the grass swayed for a time, and then everything stood still in attentive immobility.

' "Now, if he does not say the right thing to them we are all done for," said the Russian at my elbow. The knot of men with the stretcher had stopped, too, halfway to the steamer, as if petrified. I saw the man on the stretcher sit up, lank and with an uplifted arm, above the shoulders of the bearers. "Let us hope that the man who can talk so well of love in general will find some particular reason to spare us this time," I said. I resented bitterly the absurd danger of our situation, as if to be at the mercy of that atrocious phantom had been a dishonouring necessity. I could not hear a sound, but through my glasses I saw the thin arm extended commandingly, the lower jaw moving, the eyes of that apparition shining darkly far in its bony head that nodded with grotesque jerks. Kurtz—Kurtz—that means short in German—don't it? Well, the name was as true as everything else in his life—and death. He looked at least seven feet long. His covering had fallen off, and his body emerged from it pitiful and appalling as from a winding-sheet. I could see the cage of his ribs all astir, the bones of his arm waving. It was as though an animated image of death carved out of old ivory had been shaking its hand with menaces at a motionless crowd of men made of dark and glittering bronze. I saw him open his mouth wide—it gave him a weirdly voracious aspect, as though he had wanted to swallow all the air, all the earth, all the men before him. A deep voice reached me faintly. He must have been shouting. He fell back suddenly. The stretcher shook as the bearers staggered forward again, and almost at the same time I noticed that the crowd of savages was vanishing without any perceptible movement of retreat, as if the forest that had ejected these beings so suddenly had drawn them in again as the breath is drawn in a long aspiration.

'Some of the pilgrims behind the stretcher carried his arms—two shot-guns, a heavy rifle, and a light revolver-carbine—the thunderbolts of that pitiful Jupiter. The manager bent over him murmuring as he walked beside his head. They laid him down in one of the little cabins—just a room for a bedplace and a camp-stool or two, you know. We had brought his belated correspondence, and a lot of torn envelopes and open letters littered his bed. His hand roamed feebly amongst these papers. I was struck by the fire of his eyes and the composed languor of his expression. It was not so much the exhaustion of disease. He did not seem in pain. This shadow looked satiated and calm, as though for the moment it had had its fill of all the emotions.

'He rustled one of the letters, and looking straight in my face said, "I am glad." Somebody had been writing to him about me. These special recommendations were turning up again. The volume of tone he emitted without effort, almost without the trouble of moving his lips, amazed me. A voice! a voice! It was grave, profound, vibrating, while the man did not seem capable of a whis-

per. However, he had enough strength in him—facti-
tious no doubt—to very nearly make an end of us, as
you shall hear directly.

'The manager appeared silently in the doorway; I
stepped out at once and he drew the curtain after me.
The Russian, eyed curiously by the pilgrims, was staring at the shore. I followed the direction of his glance.

'Dark human shapes could be made out in the distance, flitting indistinctly against the gloomy border of
the forest, and near the river two bronze figures, leaning on tall spears, stood in the sunlight under fantastic
head-dresses of spotted skins, warlike and still in stat-
uesque repose. And from right to left along the lighted
shore moved a wild and gorgeous apparition of a woman.

'She walked with measured steps, draped in striped
and fringed cloths, treading the earth proudly, with a
slight jingle and flash of barbarous ornaments. She carried her head high; her hair was done in the shape of a
helmet; she had brass leggings to the knees, brass wire
gauntlets to the elbow, a crimson spot on her tawny
cheek, innumerable necklaces of glass beads on her neck;
bizarre things, charms, gifts of witch-men, that hung
about her, glittered and trembled at every step. She
must have had the value of several elephant tusks upon
her. She was savage and superb, wild-eyed and magnificent; there was something ominous and stately in her
deliberate progress. And in the hush that had fallen suddenly upon the whole sorrowful land, the immense
wilderness, the colossal body of the fecund and myste-

rious life seemed to look at her, pensive, as though it had been looking at the image of its own tenebrous and passionate soul.

'She came abreast of the steamer, stood still, and faced us. Her long shadow fell to the water's edge. Her face had a tragic and fierce aspect of wild sorrow and of dumb pain mingled with the fear of some struggling, half-shaped resolve. She stood looking at us without a stir, and like the wilderness itself, with an air of brooding over an inscrutable purpose. A whole minute passed, and then she made a step forward. There was a low jingle, a glint of yellow metal, a sway of fringed draperies, and she stopped as if her heart had failed her. The young fellow by my side growled. The pilgrims murmured at my back. She looked at us all as if her life had depended upon the unswerving steadiness of her glance. Suddenly she opened her bared arms and threw them up rigid above her head, as though in an uncontrollable desire to touch the sky, and at the same time the swift shadows darted out on the earth, swept around on the river, gathering the steamer into a shadowy embrace. A formidable silence hung over the scene.

'She turned away slowly, walked on, following the bank, and passed into the bushes to the left. Once only her eyes gleamed back at us in the dusk of the thickets before she disappeared.

' "If she had offered to come aboard I really think I would have tried to shoot her," said the man of patches, nervously. "I had been risking my life every day for the last fortnight to keep her out of the house. She got in one day and kicked up a row about those miserable rags I picked up in the storeroom to mend my clothes with. I wasn't decent. At least it must have been that, for she talked like a fury to Kurtz for an hour, pointing at me now and then. I don't understand the dialect of this tribe. Luckily for me, I fancy Kurtz felt too ill that day to care, or there would have been mischief. I don't understand . . . No—it's too much for me. Ah, well, it's all over now."

'At this moment I heard Kurtz's deep voice behind the curtain: "Save me!—save the ivory, you mean. Don't tell me. Save *me*! Why, I've had to save you. You are interrupting my plans now. Sick! Sick! Not so sick as you would like to believe. Never mind. I'll carry my ideas out yet—I will return. I'll show you what can be done. You with your little peddling notions—you are interfering with me. I will return. I . . ."

'The manager came out. He did me the honour to take me under the arm and lead me aside. "He is very low, very low," he said. He considered it necessary to sigh, but neglected to be consistently sorrowful. "We have done all we could for him—haven't we? But there is no disguising the fact, Mr Kurtz has done more harm than good to the Company. He did not see the time was not ripe for vigorous action. Cautiously, cautiously—that's my principle. We must be cautious yet. The district is closed to us for a time. Deplorable! Upon the whole, the trade will suffer. I don't deny there is a remarkable quantity of ivory—mostly fossil. We must save it, at all events—but look how precarious the position is—and why? Because the method is unsound." "Do you," said I, looking at the shore, "call it 'unsound method'?" "Without doubt," he exclaimed, hotly. "Don't you?" . . .

' "No method at all," I murmured after a while. "Exactly," he exulted. "I anticipated this. Shows a complete want of judgement. It is my duty to point it out in the proper quarter." "Oh," said I, "that fellow—what's his name?—the brickmaker, will make a readable report for you." He appeared confounded for a moment. It seemed to me I had never breathed an atmosphere so vile, and I turned mentally to Kurtz for relief—positively for relief. "Nevertheless I think Mr Kurtz is a remarkable man," I said with emphasis. He started, dropped on me a cold heavy glance, said very quietly "He *was*," and turned his back on me. My hour of favour was over; I found myself lumped along with Kurtz as a partisan of methods for which the time was not ripe: I was unsound! Ah! but it was something to have at least a choice of nightmares.

'I had turned to the wilderness really, not to Mr Kurtz, who, I was ready to admit, was as good as buried. And for a moment it seemed to me as if I also were buried in a vast grave full of unspeakable secrets. I felt an intolerable weight oppressing my breast, the smell of the damp earth, the unseen presence of victorious corruption, the darkness of an impenetrable night . . . The

Russian tapped me on the shoulder. I heard him mumbling and stammering something about "brother seaman—couldn't conceal—knowledge of matters that would affect Mr Kurtz's reputation." I waited. For him evidently Mr Kurtz was not in his grave; I suspect that for him Mr Kurtz was one of the immortals. "Well!" said I at last, "speak out. As it happens, I am Mr Kurtz's friend—in a way."

'He stated with a good deal of formality that had we not been "of the same profession", he would have kept the matter to himself without regard to consequences. "He suspected there was an active ill will towards him on the part of these white men that—" "You are right," I said, remembering a certain conversation I had overheard. "The manager thinks you ought to be hanged." He showed a concern at this intelligence which amused me at first. "I had better get out of the way quietly," he said, earnestly. "I can do no more for Kurtz now, and they would soon find some excuse. What's to stop them? There's a military post three hundred miles from here." "Well, upon my word," said I, "perhaps you had better go if you have any friends amongst the savages near by." "Plenty," he said. "They are simple people— and I want nothing, you know." He stood biting his lip, then: "I don't want any harm to happen to these whites here, but of course I was thinking of Mr Kurtz's reputation—but you are a brother seaman and—" "All right," said I, after a time. "Mr Kurtz's reputation is safe with me." I did not know how truly I spoke.

'He informed me, lowering his voice, that it was Kurtz who had ordered the attack to be made on the steamer. "He hated sometimes the idea of being taken away—and then again . . . But I don't understand these matters. I am a simple man. He thought it would scare you away—that you would give it up, thinking him dead. I could not stop him. Oh, I had an awful time of it this last month." "Very well," I said. "He is all right now." "Ye-e-es," he muttered, not very convinced apparently. "Thanks," said I; "I shall keep my eyes open." "But quiet—eh?" he urged, anxiously. "It would be awful for his reputation if anybody here—" I promised a complete discretion with great gravity. "I have a canoe and three black fellows waiting not very far. I am off. Could you give me a few Martini-Henry cartridges?" I could, and did, with proper secrecy. He helped himself, with a wink at me, to a handful of my tobacco. "Between sailors—you know—good English tobacco." At the door of the pilot-house he turned round— "I say, haven't you a pair of shoes you could spare?" He raised one leg. "Look." The soles were tied with knotted strings sandal-wise under his bare feet. I rooted out an old pair, at which he looked with admiration before tucking it under his left arm. One of his pockets (bright red) was bulging with cartridges, from the other (dark blue) peeped "Towson's Inquiry", etc., etc. He seemed to think himself excellently well equipped for a renewed encounter with the wilderness. "Ah! I'll never, never meet such a man again. You ought to have heard him recite poetry—his own, too, it was, he told me. Poetry!" He rolled his eyes at the recollection of these delights. "Oh, he enlarged my mind!" "Good-bye." said I. He shook hands and vanished in the night. Sometimes I ask myself whether I had ever really seen him—whether it was possible to meet such a phenomenon! . . .

'When I woke up shortly after midnight his warning came to my mind with its hint of danger that seemed, in the starred darkness, real enough to make me get up for the purpose of having a look round. On the hill a big fire burned, illuminating fitfully a crooked corner of the station-house. One of the agents with a picket of a few of our blacks, armed for the purpose, was keeping guard over the ivory; but deep within the forest, red gleams that wavered, that seemed to sink and rise from the ground amongst confused columnar shapes of intense blackness, showed the exact position of the camp where Mr Kurtz's adorers were keeping their uneasy vigil. The monotonous beating of a big drum filled the air with muffled shocks and a lingering vibration. A steady droning sound of many men chanting each to himself some weird incantation came out from the black, flat wall of the woods as the humming of bees comes out of a hive, and had a strange narcotic effect upon my half-awake senses. I believe I dozed off leaning over the rail, till an abrupt burst of yells, an overwhelming outbreak of a pent-up and mysterious frenzy, woke me up in a bewildered wonder. It was cut short all at once, and the

low droning went on with an effect of audible and soothing silence. I glanced casually into the little cabin. A light
was burning within, but Mr Kurtz was not there.

'I think I would have raised an outcry if I had
believed my eyes. But I didn't believe them at first—
the thing seemed so impossible. The fact is I was completely unnerved by a sheer blank fright, pure abstract
terror, unconnected with any distinct shape of physical
danger. What made this emotion so overpowering
was—how shall I define it?—the moral shock I
received, as if something altogether monstrous, intolerable to thought and odious to the soul, had been thrust
upon me unexpectedly. This lasted of course the mer-
est fraction of a second, and then the usual sense of
commonplace, deadly danger, the possibility of a sudden
onslaught and massacre, or something of the kind,
which I saw impending, was positively welcome and
composing. It pacified me, in fact, so much, that I did
not raise an alarm.

'There was an agent buttoned up inside an ulster and
sleeping on a chair on deck within three feet of me. The
yells had not awakened him; he snored very slightly; I
left him to his slumbers and leaped ashore. I did not
betray Mr Kurtz—it was ordered I should never betray
him—it was written I should be loyal to the nightmare
of my choice. I was anxious to deal with this shadow by
myself alone,—and to this day I don't know why I was
so jealous of sharing with anyone the peculiar blackness
of that experience.

'As soon as I got on the bank I saw a trail—a broad trail through the grass. I remember the exultation with which I said to myself, "He can't walk—he is crawling on all-fours—I've got him." The grass was wet with dew. I strode rapidly with clenched fists. I fancy I had some vague notion of falling upon him and giving him a drubbing. I don't know. I had some imbecile thoughts. The knitting old woman with the cat obtruded herself upon my memory as a most improper person to be sitting at the other end of such an affair. I saw a row of pilgrims squirting lead in the air out of Winchesters held to the hip. I thought I would never get back to the steamer, and imagined myself living alone and unarmed in the woods to an advanced age. Such silly things—you know. And I remember I confounded the beat of the drum with the beating of my heart, and was pleased at its calm regularity.

'I kept to the track though—then stopped to listen. The night was very clear; a dark blue space, sparkling with dew and starlight, in which black things stood very still. I thought I could see a kind of motion ahead of me. I was strangely cocksure of everything that night. I actually left the track and ran in a wide semicircle (I verily believe chuckling to myself) so as to get in front of that stir, of that motion I had seen—if indeed I had seen anything. I was circumventing Kurtz as though it had been a boyish game.

'I came upon him, and, if he had not heard me coming, I would have fallen over him, too, but he got up in time. He rose, unsteady, long, pale, indistinct, like a vapour exhaled by the earth, and swayed slightly, misty and silent before me; while at my back the fires loomed between the trees, and the murmur of many voices issued from the forest. I had cut him off cleverly; but when actually confronting him I seemed to come to my senses, I saw the danger in its right proportion. It was by no means over yet. Suppose he began to shout? Though he could hardly stand, there was still plenty of vigour in his voice. "Go away—hide yourself," he said, in that profound tone. It was very awful. I glanced back. We were within thirty yards from the nearest fire. A black figure stood up, strode on long black legs, waving long black arms, across the glow. It had horns—antelope horns, I think—on its head. Some sorcerer, some witch-man, no doubt: it looked fiend-like enough. "Do you know what you are doing?" I whispered. "Perfectly," he answered, raising his voice for that single word: it sounded to me far off and yet loud, like a hail through a speaking-trumpet. If he makes a row we are lost, I thought to myself. This clearly was not a case for fisticuffs, even apart from the very natural aversion I had to beat that Shadow—this wandering and tormented thing. "You will be lost," I said—"utterly lost." One gets sometimes such a flash of inspiration, you know. I did say the right thing, though indeed he could not have been more irretrievably lost than he was at this very moment, when the foundations of our intimacy were being laid—to endure—to endure—even to the end—even beyond.

' "I had immense plans," he muttered irresolutely. "Yes," said I; "but if you try to shout I'll smash your head with—" There was not a stick or a stone near. "I will throttle you for good," I corrected myself. "I was on the threshold of great things," he pleaded, in a voice of longing, with a wistfulness of tone that made my blood run cold. "And now for this stupid scoundrel—" "Your success in Europe is assured in any case," I affirmed, steadily. I did not want to have the throttling of him, you understand—and indeed it would have been very little use for any practical purpose. I tried to break the spell—the heavy, mute spell of the wilderness—that seemed to draw him to its pitiless breast by the awakening of forgotten and brutal instincts, by the memory of gratified and monstrous passions. This alone, I was convinced, had driven him out to the edge of the forest, to the bush, towards the gleam of fires, the throb of drums, the drone of weird incantations; this alone had beguiled his unlawful soul beyond the bounds of permitted aspirations. And, don't you see, the terror of the position was not in being knocked on the head—though I had a very lively sense of that danger, too—but in this, that I had to deal with a being to whom I could not appeal in the name of anything high or low. I had, even like the niggers, to invoke him—himself—his own exalted and incredible degradation. There was nothing either above or below him, and I knew it. He had kicked himself loose of the earth. Confound the man! he had kicked the very earth to pieces. He was alone, and I before him did not know whether I stood on the ground or floated in the air. I've been telling you what we said—repeating the phrases we pronounced—but what's the good? They were common everyday words—the familiar, vague sounds exchanged on every waking day of life. But what of that? They had behind them, to my mind, the terrific suggestiveness of words heard in dreams, of phrases spoken in nightmares. Soul! If anybody had ever struggled with a soul, I am the man. And I wasn't arguing with a lunatic either. Believe me or not, his intelligence was perfectly clear—concentrated, it is true, upon himself with horrible intensity, yet clear; and therein was my only chance—barring, of course, the killing him there and then, which wasn't so good, on account of unavoidable noise. But his soul was mad. Being alone in the wilderness, it had looked within itself, and, by heavens! I tell you, it had gone mad. I had—for my sins, I suppose—to go through the ordeal of looking into it myself. No eloquence could have been so withering to one's belief in mankind as his final burst of sincerity. He struggled with himself, too. I saw it,— I heard it. I saw the inconceivable mystery of a soul that knew no restraint, no faith, and no fear, yet struggling blindly with itself. I kept my head pretty well; but when I had him at last stretched on the couch, I wiped my forehead, while my legs shook under me as though I had carried half a ton on my back down that hill. And yet I had only supported him, his bony arm clasped round my neck—and he was not much heavier than a child.

'When next day we left at noon, the crowd, of whose presence behind the curtain of trees I had been acutely conscious all the time, flowed out of the woods again, filled the clearing, covered the slope with a mass of naked, breathing, quivering, bronze bodies. I steamed up a bit, then swung downstream, and two thousand eyes followed the evolutions of the splashing, thumping, fierce river-demon beating the water with its terrible tail and breathing black smoke into the air. In front of the first rank, along the river, three men, plastered with bright red earth from head to foot, strutted to and fro restlessly. When we came abreast again, they faced the river, stamped their feet, nodded their horned heads, swayed their scarlet bodies; they shook towards the fierce river-demon a bunch of black feathers, a mangy skin with a pendent tail—something that looked like a dried gourd; they shouted periodically together strings of amazing words that resembled no sounds of human language; and the deep murmurs of the crowd, interrupted suddenly, were like the responses of some satanic litany.

'We had carried Kurtz into the pilot-house: there was more air there. Lying on the couch, he stared through the open shutter. There was an eddy in the mass of human bodies, and the woman with helmeted head and tawny cheeks rushed out to the very brink of the stream. She put out her hands, shouted something, and all that wild mob took up the shout in a roaring chorus of articulated, rapid, breathless utterance.

' "Do you understand this?" I asked.

'He kept on looking out past me with fiery, longing eyes, with a mingled expression of wistfulness and hate. He made no answer, but I saw a smile, a smile of indefinable meaning, appear on his colourless lips that a moment after twitched convulsively. "Do I not?" he said slowly, gasping, as if the words had been torn out of him by a supernatural power.

'I pulled the string of the whistle, and I did this because I saw the pilgrims on deck getting out their rifles with an air of anticipating a jolly lark. At the sudden screech there was a movement of abject terror through that wedged mass of bodies. "Don't! don't you frighten them away," cried someone on deck disconsolately. I pulled the string time after time. They broke and ran, they leaped, they crouched, they swerved, they dodged the flying terror of the sound. The three red chaps had fallen flat, face down on the shore, as though they had been shot dead. Only the barbarous and superb woman did not so much as flinch and stretched tragically her bare arms after us over the sombre and glittering river.

'And then that imbecile crowd down on the deck started their little fun, and I could see nothing more for smoke.

'The brown current ran swiftly out of the heart of darkness, bearing us down towards the sea with twice the

speed of our upward progress; and Kurtz's life was running swiftly, too, ebbing, ebbing out of his heart into the
sea of inexorable time. The manager was very placid, he
had no vital anxieties now, he took us both in with a
comprehensive and satisfied glance: the "affair" had
come off as well as could be wished. I saw the time
approaching when I would be left alone of the party of
"unsound method". The pilgrims looked upon me with
disfavour. I was, so to speak, numbered with the dead. It
is strange how I accepted this unforeseen partnership,
this choice of nightmares forced upon me in the tenebrous land invaded by these mean and greedy phantoms.

'Kurtz discoursed. A voice! a voice! It rang deep to
the very last. It survived his strength to hide in the magnificent folds of eloquence the barren darkness of his
heart. Oh, he struggled! he struggled! The wastes of his
weary brain were haunted by shadowy images now—
images of wealth and fame revolving obsequiously
round his unextinguishable gift of noble and lofty
expression. My Intended, my station, my career, my
ideas—these were the subjects for the occasional utterances of elevated sentiments. The shade of the original
Kurtz frequented the bedside of the hollow sham, whose
fate it was to be buried presently in the mould of
primeval earth. But both the diabolic love and the
unearthly hate of the mysteries it had penetrated fought
for the possession of that soul satiated with primitive
emotions, avid of lying fame, of sham distinction, of all
the appearances of success and power.

'Sometimes he was contemptibly childish. He desired to have kings meet him at railway-stations on his return from some ghastly Nowhere, where he intended to accomplish great things. "You show them you have in you something that is really profitable, and then there will be no limits to the recognition of your ability," he would say. "Of course you must take care of the motives—right motives—always." The long reaches that were like one and the same reach, monotonous bends that were exactly alike, slipped past the steamer with their multitude of secular trees looking patiently after this grimy fragment of another world, the forerunner of change, of conquest, of trade, of massacres, of blessings. I looked ahead—piloting. "Close the shutter," said Kurtz suddenly one day; "I can't bear to look at this." I did so. There was a silence. "Oh, but I will wring your heart yet!" he cried at the invisible wilderness.

'We broke down—as I had expected—and had to lie up for repairs at the head of an island. This delay was the first thing that shook Kurtz's confidence. One morning he gave me a packet of papers and a photograph—the lot tied together with a shoe-string. "Keep this for me," he said. "This noxious fool" (meaning the manager) "is capable of prying into my boxes when I am not looking." In the afternoon I saw him. He was lying on his back with closed eyes, and I withdrew quietly, but I heard him mutter, "Live rightly, die, die . . ." I listened. There was nothing more. Was he rehearsing some speech in his sleep, or was it a fragment of a

phrase from some newspaper article? He had been writing for the papers and meant to do so again, "for the
furthering of my ideas. It's a duty."

'His was an impenetrable darkness. I looked at him as
you peer down at a man who is lying at the bottom of
a precipice where the sun never shines. But I had not
much time to give him, because I was helping the
engine-driver to take to pieces the leaky cylinders, to
straighten a bent connecting-rod, and in other such matters. I lived in an infernal mess of rust, filings, nuts,
bolts, spanners, hammers, ratchet-drills—things I
abominate, because I don't get on with them. I tended
the little forge we fortunately had aboard; I toiled
wearily in a wretched scrap-heap—unless I had the
shakes too bad to stand.

'One evening coming in with a candle I was startled
to hear him say a little tremulously, "I am lying here in
the dark waiting for death." The light was within a foot
of his eyes. I forced myself to murmur. "Oh, nonsense!"
and stood over him as if transfixed.

'Anything approaching the change that came over his
features I have never seen before, and hope never to see
again. Oh, I wasn't touched. I was fascinated. It was as
though a veil had been rent. I saw on that ivory face the
expression of sombre pride, of ruthless power, of craven
terror—of an intense and hopeless despair. Did he live
his life again in every detail of desire, temptation, and
surrender during that supreme moment of complete
knowledge? He cried in a whisper at some image, at

some vision—he cried out twice, a cry that was no more than a breath—

' "The horror! The horror!"

'I blew the candle out and left the cabin. The pilgrims were dining in the mess-room, and I took my place opposite the manager, who lifted his eyes to give me a questioning glance, which I successfully ignored. He leaned back, serene, with that peculiar smile of his sealing the unexpressed depths of his meanness. A continuous shower of small flies streamed upon the lamp, upon the cloth, upon our hands and faces. Suddenly the manager's boy put his insolent black head in the doorway, and said in a tone of scathing contempt—

' "Mistah Kurtz—he dead."

'All the pilgrims rushed out to see. I remained, and went on with my dinner. I believe I was considered brutally callous. However, I did not eat much. There was a lamp in there—light, don't you know—and outside it was so beastly, beastly dark. I went no more near the remarkable man who had pronounced a judgement upon the adventures of his soul on this earth. The voice was gone. What else had been there? But I am of course aware that next day the pilgrims buried something in a muddy hole.

'And then they very nearly buried me.

'However, as you see, I did not go to join Kurtz there and then. I did not. I remained to dream the nightmare out to the end, and to show my loyalty to Kurtz once more. Destiny. My Destiny! Droll thing life is—that mysterious arrangement of merciless logic for a futile purpose. The most you can hope from it is some knowledge of yourself—that comes too late—a crop of unextinguishable regrets. I have wrestled with death. It is the most unexciting contest you can imagine. It takes place in an impalpable greyness, with nothing underfoot, with nothing around, without spectators, without clamour, without glory, without the great desire of victory, without the great fear of defeat, in a sickly atmosphere of tepid scepticism, without much belief in your own right, and still less in that of your adversary. If such is the form of ultimate wisdom, then life is a greater riddle than some of us think it to be. I was within a hair's-breadth of the last opportunity for pronouncement, and I found with humiliation that probably I would have nothing to say. This is the reason why I affirm that Kurtz was a remarkable man. He had something to say. He said it. Since I had peeped over the edge myself, I understand better the meaning of his stare, that could not see the flame of the candle, but was wide enough to embrace the whole universe, piercing enough to penetrate all the hearts that beat in the darkness. He had summed up—he had judged. "The horror!" He was a remarkable man. After all, this was the expression of some sort of belief; it had candour, it had conviction, it had a vibrating note of revolt in its whisper, it had the appalling face of a glimpsed truth—the strange commingling of desire and hate. And it is not my own extremity I remember best—a vision of greyness with-

out form filled with physical pain, and a careless contempt for the evanescence of all things—even of this
pain itself. No! It is his extremity that I seem to have
lived through. True, he had made that last stride, he
had stepped over the edge, while I had been permitted
to draw back my hesitating foot. And perhaps in this is
the whole difference; perhaps all the wisdom, and all
truth, and all sincerity, are just compressed into that
inappreciable moment of time in which we step over the
threshold of the invisible. Perhaps! I like to think my
summing-up would not have been a word of careless
contempt. Better his cry—much better. It was an affir-
mation, a moral victory, paid for by innumerable
defeats, by abominable terrors, by abominable satisfac-
tions. But it was a victory! That is why I have remained
loyal to Kurtz to the last, and even beyond, when a long
time after I heard once more, not his own voice, but the
echo of his magnificent eloquence thrown to me from a
soul as translucently pure as a cliff of crystal.

'No, they did not bury me, though there is a period
of time which I remember mistily, with a shuddering
wonder, like a passage through some inconceivable
world that had no hope in it and no desire. I found
myself back in the sepulchral city resenting the sight of
people hurrying through the streets to filch a little
money from each other, to devour their infamous cook-
ery, to gulp their unwholesome beer, to dream their
insignificant and silly dreams. They trespassed upon my
thoughts. They were intruders whose knowledge of life

was to me an irritating pretence, because I felt so sure they could not possibly know the things I knew. Their bearing, which was simply the bearing of commonplace individuals going about their business in the assurance of perfect safety, was offensive to me like the outrageous flauntings of folly in the face of a danger it is unable to comprehend. I had no particular desire to enlighten them, but I had some difficulty in restraining myself from laughing in their faces, so full of stupid importance. I daresay I was not very well at that time. I tottered about the streets—there were various affairs to settle—grinning bitterly at perfectly respectable persons. I admit my behaviour was inexcusable, but then my temperature was seldom normal in these days. My dear aunt's endeavours to "nurse up my strength" seemed altogether beside the mark. It was not my strength that wanted nursing, it was my imagination that wanted soothing. I kept the bundle of papers given me by Kurtz, not knowing exactly what to do with it. His mother had died lately, watched over, as I was told, by his Intended. A clean-shaved man, with an official manner and wearing gold-rimmed spectacles, called on me one day and made inquiries, at first circuitous, afterwards suavely pressing, about what he was pleased to denominate certain "documents". I was not surprised, because I had had two rows with the manager on the subject out there. I had refused to give up the smallest scrap out of that package, and I took the same attitude with the spectacled man. He became darkly menacing at last, and with much heat argued that the Company had the right to every bit of information about its "territories". And said he, "Mr Kurtz's knowledge of unexplored regions must have been necessarily extensive and peculiar—owing to his great abilities and to the deplorable circumstances in which he had been placed: therefore—" I assured him Mr Kurtz's knowledge, however extensive, did not bear upon the problems of commerce or administration. He invoked then the name of science. "It would be an incalculable loss if," etc., etc. I offered him the report on the "Suppression of Savage Customs", with the postscriptum torn off. He took it up eagerly, but ended by sniffing at it with an air of contempt. "This is not what we had a right to expect," he remarked. "Expect nothing else," I said. "There are only private letters." He withdrew upon some threat of legal proceedings, and I saw him no more; but another fellow, calling himself Kurtz's cousin, appeared two days later, and was anxious to hear all the details about his dear relative's last moments. Incidentally he gave me to understand that Kurtz had been essentially a great musician. "There was the making of an immense success," said the man, who was an organist, I believe, with lank grey hair flowing over a greasy coat-collar. I had no reason to doubt his statement; and to this day I am unable to say what was Kurtz's profession, whether he ever had any—which was the greatest of his talents. I had taken him for a painter who wrote for the papers, or else for a journalist who could paint—but even the cousin (who took snuff during the interview) could not tell me what he had been—exactly. He was a universal genius—on that point I agreed with the old chap, who thereupon blew his nose noisily into a large cotton handkerchief and withdrew in senile agitation, bearing off some family letters and memoranda without importance. Ultimately a journalist anxious to know something of the fate of his "dear colleague" turned up. This visitor informed me Kurtz's proper sphere ought to have been politics "on the popular side". He had furry straight eyebrows, bristly hair cropped short, an eye-glass on a broad ribbon, and, becoming expansive, confessed his opinion that Kurtz really couldn't write a bit— "but heavens! how that man could talk. He electrified large meetings. He had faith—don't you see?—he had the faith. He could get himself to believe anything—anything. He would have been a splendid leader of an extreme party." "What party?" I asked. "Any party," answered the other. "He was an—an—extremist." Did I not think so? I assented. Did I know, he asked, with a sudden flash of curiosity, "what it was that had induced him to go out there?" "Yes," said I, and forthwith handed him the famous Report for publication, if he thought fit. He glanced through it hurriedly, mumbling all the time, judged "it would do", and took himself off with this plunder.

'Thus I was left at last with a slim packet of letters and the girl's portrait. She struck me as beautiful—I mean she had a beautiful expression. I know that the sunlight can be made to lie, too, yet one felt that no manipulation of light and pose could have conveyed the delicate shade of truthfulness upon those features. She seemed ready to listen without mental reservation, without suspicion, without a thought for herself. I concluded I would go and give her back her portrait and those letters myself. Curiosity? Yes; and also some other feelings perhaps. All that had been Kurtz's had passed out of my hands: his soul, his body, his station, his plans, his ivory, his career. There remained only his memory and his Intended—and I wanted to give that up, too, to the past, in a way—to surrender personally all that remained of him with me to that oblivion which is the last word of our common fate. I don't defend myself. I had no clear perception of what it was I really wanted. Perhaps it was an impulse of unconscious loyalty, or the fulfilment of one of those ironic necessities that lurk in the facts of human existence. I don't know. I can't tell. But I went.

'I thought his memory was like the other memories of the dead that accumulate in every man's life—a vague impress on the brain of shadows that had fallen on it in their swift and final passage; but before the high and ponderous door, between the tall houses of a street as still and decorous as a well-kept alley in a cemetery, I had a vision of him on the stretcher, opening his mouth voraciously, as if to devour all the earth with all its mankind. He lived then before me; he lived as much as he had ever lived—a shadow insatiable of splendid appearances, of frightful realities; a shadow darker than the shadow of the night, and draped nobly in the folds of a gorgeous eloquence. The vision seemed to enter the house with me—the stretcher, the phantom-bearers, the wild crowd of obedient worshippers, the gloom of the forests, the glitter of the reach between the murky bends, the beat of the drum, regular and muffled like the beating of a heart—the heart of a conquering darkness. It was a moment of triumph for the wilderness, an invading and vengeful rush which, it seemed to me, I would have to keep back alone for the salvation of another soul. And the memory of what I had heard him say afar there, with the horned shapes stirring at my back, in the glow of fires, within the patient woods, those broken phrases came back to me, were heard again in their ominous and terrifying simplicity. I remembered his abject pleading, his abject threats, the colossal scale of his vile desires, the meanness, the torment, the tempestuous anguish of his soul. And later on I seemed to see his collected languid manner, when he said one day, "This lot of ivory now is really mine. The Company did not pay for it. I collected it myself at a very great personal risk. I am afraid they will try to claim it as theirs though. H'm. It is a difficult case. What do you think I ought to do—resist? Eh? I want no more than justice." . . . He wanted no more than justice—no more than justice. I rang the bell before a mahogany door on the first floor, and while I waited he seemed to stare at me out of the glassy panel—stare with that wide and immense stare embrac-

ing, condemning, loathing all the universe. I seemed to
hear the whispered cry, "The horror! The horror!"

'The dusk was falling. I had to wait in a lofty drawing-room with three long windows from floor to ceiling
that were like three luminous and bedraped columns.
The bent gilt legs and backs of the furniture shone in
indistinct curves. The tall marble fireplace had a cold
and monumental whiteness. A grand piano stood mas-
sively in a comer; with dark gleams on the flat surfaces
like a sombre and polished sarcophagus. A high door
opened—closed. I rose.

'She came forward, all in black, with a pale head,
floating towards me in the dusk. She was in mourning.
It was more than a year since his death, more than a
year since the news came; she seemed as though she
would remember and mourn for ever. She took both my
hands in hers and murmured, "I had heard you were
coming." I noticed she was not very young—I mean not
girlish. She had a mature capacity for fidelity, for belief,
for suffering. The room seemed to have grown darker,
as if all the sad light of the cloudy evening had taken
refuge on her forehead. This fair hair, this pale visage,
this pure brow, seemed surrounded by an ashy halo
from which the dark eyes looked out at me. Their glance
was guileless, profound, confident, and trustful. She carried her sorrowful head as though she were proud of
that sorrow, as though she would say, I—I alone know
how to mourn for him as he deserves. But while we were
still shaking hands, such a look of awful desolation came

upon her face that I perceived she was one of those creatures that are not the playthings of Time. For her he had
died only yesterday. And, by Jove! the impression was so
powerful that for me, too, he seemed to have died only
yesterday—nay, this very minute, I saw her and him in
the same instant of time—his death and her sorrow—I
saw her sorrow in the very moment of his death. Do you
understand? I saw them together—I heard them
together. She had said, with a deep catch of the breath,
"I have survived" while my strained ears seemed to hear
distinctly, mingled with her tone of despairing regret, the
summing-up whisper of his eternal condemnation. I
asked myself what I was doing there, with a sensation of
panic in my heart as though I had blundered into a place
of cruel and absurd mysteries not fit for a human being
to behold. She motioned me to a chair. We sat down. I
laid the packet gently on the little table, and she put her
hand over it . . . "You knew him well," she murmured,
after a moment of mourning silence.

‘ "Intimacy grows quickly out there," I said. "I knew
him as well as it is possible for one man to know
another."

‘ "And you admired him," she said. "It was impossible to know him and not to admire him. Was it?"

‘ "He was a remarkable man," I said, unsteadily.
Then before the appealing fixity of her gaze, that
seemed to watch for more words on my lips, I went on.
"It was impossible not to—"

‘ "Love him," she finished eagerly, silencing me into

an appalled dumbness. "How true! how true! But when you think that no one knew him so well as I! I had all his noble confidence. I knew him best."

' "You knew him best," I repeated. And perhaps she did. But with every word spoken the room was growing darker, and only her forehead, smooth and white, remained illumined by the unextinguishable light of belief and love.

' "You were his friend," she went on. "His friend," she repeated, a little louder. "You must have been, if he had given you this, and sent you to me. I feel I can speak to you—and oh! I must speak. I want you—you who have heard his last words—to know I have been worthy of him . . . It is not pride . . . Yes! I am proud to know I understood him better than anyone on earth—he told me so himself. And since his mother died I have had no one no one—to—to—"

'I listened. The darkness deepened. I was not even sure whether he had given me the right bundle. I rather suspect he wanted me to take care of another batch of his papers which, after his death, I saw the manager examining under the lamp. And the girl talked, easing her pain in the certitude of my sympathy; she talked as thirsty men drink. I had heard that her engagement with Kurtz had been disapproved by her people. He wasn't rich enough or something. And indeed I don't know whether he had not been a pauper all his life. He had given me some reason to infer that it was his impatience of comparative poverty that drove him out there.

' ". . . Who was not his friend who had heard him speak once?" she was saying. "He drew men towards him by what was best in them." She looked at me with intensity. "It is the gift of the great," she went on, and the sound of her low voice seemed to have the accompaniment of all the other sounds, full of mystery, desolation, and sorrow, I had ever heard—the ripple of the river, the soughing of the trees swayed by the wind, the murmurs of the crowds, the faint ring of incomprehensible words cried from afar, the whisper of a voice speaking from beyond the threshold of an eternal darkness. "But you have heard him! You know!" she cried.

' "Yes, I know," I said with something like despair in my heart, but bowing my head before the faith that was in her, before that great and saving illusion that shone with an unearthly glow in the darkness, in the triumphant darkness from which I could not have defended her—from which I could not even defend myself.

' "What a loss to me—to us!"—she corrected herself with beautiful generosity; then added in a murmur, "To the world." By the last gleams of twilight I could see the glitter of her eyes, full of tears—of tears that would not fall.

' "I have been very happy—very fortunate—very proud," she went on. "Too fortunate. Too happy for a little while. And now I am unhappy for—for life."

'She stood up; her fair hair seemed to catch all the remaining light in a glimmer of gold. I rose, too.

' "And of all this," she went on, mournfully, "of all

his promise, and of all his greatness, of his generous mind, of his noble heart. nothing remains—nothing but a memory. You and I—"

' "We shall always remember him." I said, hastily.

' "No!" she cried. "It is impossible that all this should be lost—that such a life should be sacrificed to leave nothing—but sorrow. You know what vast plans he had. I knew of them, too—I could not perhaps understand—but others knew of them. Something must remain. His words, at least, have not died."

' "His words will remain," I said.

' "And his example," she whispered to herself. "Men looked up to him—his goodness shone in every act. His example—"

' "True," I said; "his example, too. Yes, his example. I forgot that."

' "But I do not. I cannot—I cannot believe—not yet. I cannot believe that I shall never see him again, that nobody will see him again, never, never, never."

'She put out her arms as if after a retreating figure, stretching them back and with clasped pale hands across the fading and narrow sheen of the window. Never see him! I saw him clearly enough then. I shall see this eloquent phantom as long as I live, and I shall see her, too, a tragic and familiar Shade, resembling in this gesture another one, tragic also, and bedecked with powerless charms, stretching bare brown arms over the glitter of the infernal stream, the stream of darkness. She said suddenly very low, "He died as he lived."

' "His end," said I, with dull anger stirring in me, "was in every way worthy of his life."

' "And I was not with him," she murmured. My anger subsided before a feeling of infinite pity.

' "Everything that could be done—" I mumbled.

' "Ah, but I believed in him more than anyone on earth—more than his own mother, more than—himself. He needed me! Me! I would have treasured every sigh, every word, every sign, every glance."

'I felt like a chill grip on my chest. "Don't," I said, in a muffled voice.

' "Forgive me. I—I—have mourned so long in silence—in silence . . . You were with him—to the last? I think of his loneliness. Nobody near to understand him as I would have understood. Perhaps no one to hear . . ."

' "To the very end," I said, shakily. "I heard his very last words . . ." I stopped in a fright.

' "Repeat them," she murmured in a heart-broken tone. "I want—I want—something—something—to—to live with."

'I was on the point of crying at her, "Don't you hear them?" The dusk was repeating them in a persistent whisper all around us, in a whisper that seemed to swell menacingly like the first whisper of a rising wind. "The horror! The horror!"

' "His last word—to live with," she insisted. "Don't you understand I loved him—I loved him—I loved him!"

'I pulled myself together and spoke slowly.

' "The last word he pronounced was—your name."

'I heard a light sigh and then my heart stood still, stopped dead short by an exulting and terrible cry, by the cry of inconceivable triumph and of unspeakable pain. "I knew it—I was sure!" . . . She knew. She was sure. I heard her weeping; she had hidden her face in her hands. It seemed to me that the house would collapse before I could escape, that the heavens would fall upon my head. But nothing happened. The heavens do not fall for such a trifle. Would they have fallen, I wonder, if I had rendered Kurtz that justice which was his due? Hadn't he said he wanted only justice? But I couldn't. I could not tell her. It would have been too dark—too dark altogether . . .'

Marlow ceased, and sat apart, indistinct and silent, in the pose of a meditating Buddha. Nobody moved for a time. 'We have lost the first of the ebb,' said the Director, suddenly. I raised my head. The offing was barred by a black bank of clouds, and the tranquil waterway leading to the uttermost ends of the earth flowed sombre under an overcast sky—seemed to lead into the heart of an immense darkness.

Typhoon

I

Captain MacWhirr, of the steamer *Nan-Shan*, had a physiognomy that, in the order of material appearances, was the exact counterpart of his mind: it presented no marked characteristics of firmness or stupidity; it had no pronounced characteristics whatever; it was simply ordinary, irresponsive, and unruffled.

The only thing his aspect might have been said to suggest, at times, was bashfulness; because he would sit, in business offices ashore, sunburnt and smiling faintly, with downcast eyes. When he raised them, they were perceived to be direct in their glance and of blue colour. His hair was fair and extremely fine, clasping from temple to temple the bald dome of his skull in a clamp as of fluffy silk. The hair of his face, on the contrary, carroty and flaming, resembled a growth of copper wire clipped short to the line of the lip; while, no matter how close he shaved, fiery metallic gleams passed, when he moved his head, over the surface of his cheeks. He was rather below the medium height, a bit round-shouldered, and so sturdy of limb that his clothes always looked a shade too tight for his arms and legs. As if unable to grasp what is due to the difference of latitudes, he wore a brown bowler hat, a complete suit of a brownish hue, and clumsy black boots. These harbour togs gave to his thick figure an air of stiff and uncouth smartness. A thin silver watch-chain looped his waistcoat, and he never left his ship for the shore without clutching in his powerful, hairy fist an elegant umbrella of the very best quality, but generally unrolled. Young Jukes, the chief mate, attending his commander to the gangway, would sometimes venture to say, with the greatest gentleness, 'Allow me, sir'—and possessing himself of the umbrella deferentially, would elevate the ferrule, shake the folds, twirl a neat furl in a jiffy, and hand it back; going through the performance with a face of such portentous gravity that Mr Solomon Rout, the chief engineer, smoking his morning cigar over the sky-light, would turn away his head in order to hide a smile. 'Oh! aye! The blessed gamp. . . . Thank 'ee, Jukes, thank 'ee,' would mutter Captain MacWhirr, heartily, without looking up.

Having just enough imagination to carry him through each successive day, and no more, he was tranquilly sure of himself; and from the very same cause he was not in the least conceited. It is your imaginative superior who is touchy, overbearing, and difficult to please; but every ship Captain MacWhirr commanded was the floating abode of harmony and peace. It was, in truth, as impossible for him to take a flight of fancy as it would be for a watchmaker to put together a chronometer with nothing except a two-pound hammer and a whip-saw in the way of tools. Yet the uninteresting lives of men so entirely given to the actuality of the bare existence have their mysterious side. It was impossible in Captain MacWhirr's case, for instance, to understand what under heaven could have induced that perfectly satisfactory son of a petty grocer in Belfast to run away to sea. And yet he had done that very thing at the age of fifteen. It was enough, when you thought it over, to give you the idea of an immense, potent, and invisible hand thrust into the ant-heap of the earth, laying hold of shoulders, knocking heads together, and setting the unconscious faces of the multitude towards inconceivable goals and in undreamt-of directions.

His father never really forgave him for this undutiful stupidity. 'We could have got on without him,' he used to say later on, 'but there's the business. And he an only son, too!' His mother wept very much after his disappearance. As it had never occurred to him to leave word behind, he was mourned over for dead till, after eight months, his first letter arrived from Talcahuano. It was short, and contained the statement: 'We had very fine weather on our passage out.' But evidently, in the writer's mind, the only important intelligence was to the effect that his captain had, on the very day of writing, entered him regularly on the ship's articles as Ordinary Seaman. 'Because I can do the work,' he explained. The mother again wept copiously, while the remark, 'Tom's an ass,' expressed the emotions of the father. He was a corpulent man, with a gift for sly chaffing, which to the end of his life he exercised in his intercourse with his son, a little pityingly, as if upon a half-witted person.

MacWhirr's visits to his home were necessarily rare, and in the course of years he despatched other letters to

his parents, informing them of his successive promo-
tions and of his movements upon the vast earth. In these
missives could be found sentences like this: 'The heat
here is very great.' Or: 'On Christmas Day at 4 p.m.
we fell in with some icebergs.' The old people ultimately
became acquainted with a good many names of ships,
and with the names of the skippers who commanded
them—with the names of Scots and English shipowners
—with the names of seas, oceans, straits, promontories—
with outlandish names of lumber-ports, of rice-ports, of
cotton-ports—with the names of islands—with the name
of their son's young woman. She was called Lucy. It did
not suggest itself to him to mention whether he thought
the name pretty. And then they died.

The great day of MacWhirr's marriage came in due
course, following shortly upon the great day when he
got his first command

All these events had taken place many years before
the morning when, in the chart-room of the steamer
Nan-Shan, he stood confronted by the fall of a barometer he had no reason to distrust. The fall—taking into
account the excellence of the instrument, the time of
the year, and the ship's position on the terrestrial
globe—was of a nature ominously prophetic; but the red
face of the man betrayed no sort of inward disturbance.
Omens were as nothing to him, and he was unable to
discover the message of a prophecy till the fulfilment had
brought it home to his very door. 'That's a fall, and no

mistake,' he thought. 'There must be some uncommonly dirty weather knocking about.'

The *Nan-Shan* was on her way from the southward to the treaty port of Fu-chau, with some cargo in her lower holds, and two hundred Chinese coolies returning to their village homes in the province of Fo-kien, after a few years of work in various tropical colonies. The morning was fine, the oily sea heaved without a sparkle, and there was a queer white misty patch in the sky like a halo of the sun. The fore-deck, packed with Chinamen, was full of sombre clothing, yellow faces, and pigtails, sprinkled over with a good many naked shoulders, for there was no wind, and the heat was close. The coolies lounged, talked, smoked, or stared over the rail; some, drawing water over the side, sluiced each other; a few slept on hatches, while several small parties of six sat on their heels surrounding iron trays with plates of rice and tiny teacups; and every single Celestial of them was carrying with him all he had in the world— a wooden chest with a ringing lock and brass on the corners, containing the savings of his labours: some clothes of ceremony, sticks of incense, a little opium maybe, bits of nameless rubbish of conventional value, and a small hoard of silver dollars, toiled for in coal lighters, won in gambling-houses or in petty trading, grubbed out of earth, sweated out in mines, on railway lines, in deadly jungle, under heavy burdens—amassed patiently, guarded with care, cherished fiercely.

A cross swell had set in from the direction of Formosa Channel about ten o'clock, without disturbing these passengers much, because the *Nan-Shan*, with her flat bottom, rolling chocks on bilges, and great breadth of beam, had the reputation of an exceptionally steady ship in a sea-way. Mr Jukes, in moments of expansion on shore, would proclaim loudly that the 'old girl was as good as she was pretty.' It would never have occurred to Captain MacWhirr to express his favourable opinion so loud or in terms so fanciful.

She was a good ship, undoubtedly, and not old either. She had been built in Dumbarton less than three years before, to the order of a firm of merchants in Siam— Messrs Sigg and Son. When she lay afloat, finished in every detail and ready to take up the work of her life, the builders contemplated her with pride.

'Sigg has asked us for a reliable skipper to take her out,' remarked one of the partners; and the other, after reflecting for a while, said: 'I think MacWhirr is ashore just at present.' 'Is he? Then wire him at once. He's the very man,' declared the senior, without a moment's hesitation.

Next morning MacWhirr stood before them unperturbed, having travelled from London by the midnight express after a sudden but undemonstrative parting with his wife. She was the daughter of a superior couple who had seen better days.

'We had better be going together over the ship, Captain,' said the senior partner; and the three men started to view the perfections of the *Nan-Shan* from stem to stern, and from her keelson to the trucks of her two stumpy pole-masts.

Captain MacWhirr had begun by taking off his coat, which he hung on the end of a steam windlass embodying all the latest improvements.

'My uncle wrote of you favourably by yesterday's mail to our good friends—Messrs Sigg, you know—and doubtless they'll continue you out there in command,' said the junior partner. 'You'll be able to boast of being in charge of the handiest boat of her size on the coast of China, Captain,' he added.

'Have you? Thank 'ee,' mumbled vaguely MacWhirr, to whom the view of a distant eventuality could appeal no more than the beauty of a wide landscape to a purblind tourist; and his eyes happening at the moment to be at rest upon the lock of the cabin door, he walked up to it, full of purpose, and began to rattle the handle vigorously, while he observed, in his low, earnest voice, 'You can't trust the workmen nowadays. A brand-new lock, and it won't act at all. Stuck fast. See? See?'

As soon as they found themselves alone in their office across the yard: 'You praised that fellow up to Sigg. What is it you see in him?' asked the nephew, with faint contempt.

'I admit he has nothing of your fancy skipper about him, if that's what you mean,' said the elder man, curtly. 'Is the foreman of the joiners on the *Nan-Shan* outside? . . . Come in, Bates. How is it that you let

Tait's people put us off with a defective lock on the cabin door? The Captain could see directly he set eye on it. Have it replaced at once. The little straws, Bates . . . the little straws. . . .'

The lock was replaced accordingly, and a few days afterwards the *Nan-Shan* steamed out to the East, without MacWhirr having offered any further remark as to her fittings, or having been heard to utter a single word hinting at pride in his ship, gratitude for his appointment, or satisfaction at his prospects.

With a temperament neither loquacious nor taciturn he found very little occasion to talk. There were matters of duty, of course—directions, orders, and so on; but the past being to his mind done with, and the future not there yet, the more general actualities of the day required no comment—because facts can speak for themselves with overwhelming precision.

Old Mr Sigg liked a man of few words, and one that 'you could be sure would not try to improve upon his instructions.' MacWhirr satisfying these requirements, was continued in command of the *Nan-Shan*, and applied himself to the careful navigation of his ship in the China seas. She had come out on a British register, but after some time Messrs Sigg judged it expedient to transfer her to the Siamese flag.

At the news of the contemplated transfer Jukes grew restless, as if under a sense of personal affront. He went about grumbling to himself, and uttering short scornful laughs. 'Fancy having a ridiculous Noah's Ark elephant in the ensign of one's ship,' he said once at the engine-room door. 'Dash me if I can stand it: I'll throw up the billet. Don't it make *you* sick, Mr Rout?' The chief engineer only cleared his throat with the air of a man who knows the value of a good billet.

The first morning the new flag floated over the stern of the *Nan-Shan*, Jukes stood looking at it bitterly from the bridge. He struggled with his feelings for a while, and then remarked, 'Queer flag for a man to sail under, sir.'

'What's the matter with the flag?' inquired Captain MacWhirr. 'Seems all right to me.' And he walked across to the end of the bridge to have a good look.

'Well, it looks queer to me,' burst out Jukes, greatly exasperated, and flung off the bridge.

Captain MacWhirr was amazed at these manners. After a while he stepped quietly into the chart-room, and opened his International Signal Code book at the plate where the flags of all the nations are correctly figured in gaudy rows. He ran his finger over them, and when he came to Siam he contemplated with great attention the red field and the white elephant. Nothing could be more simple; but to make sure, he brought the book out on the bridge for the purpose of comparing the coloured drawing with the real thing at the flagstaff astern. When next Jukes, who was carrying on the duty that day with a sort of suppressed fierceness, happened on the bridge, his commander observed:

'There's nothing amiss with that flag.'

'Isn't there?' mumbled Jukes, falling on his knees before a deck-locker and jerking therefrom viciously a spare lead-line.

'No. I looked up the book. Length twice the breadth and the elephant exactly in the middle. I thought the people ashore would know how to make the local flag. Stands to reason. You were wrong, Jukes. . . .'

'Well, sir,' began Jukes, getting up excitedly, 'all I can say—' He fumbled for the end of the coil of line with trembling hands.

'That's all right.' Captain MacWhirr soothed him, sitting heavily on a little canvas folding-stool he greatly affected. 'All you have to do is to take care they don't hoist the elephant upside-down before they get quite used to it.'

Jukes flung the new lead-line over on the fore-deck with a loud 'Here you are, bosun—don't forget to wet it thoroughly,' and turned with immense resolution towards his commander; but Captain MacWhirr spread his elbows on the bridge-rail comfortably.

'Because it would be, I suppose, understood as a signal of distress,' he went on. 'What do you think? That elephant there, I take it, stands for something in the nature of the Union Jack in the flag. . . .'

'Does it!' yelled Jukes, so that every head on the Nan-Shan's decks looked towards the bridge. Then he sighed, and with sudden resignation: 'It would certainly be a dam' distressful sight,' he said, meekly.

Later in the day, he accosted the chief engineer with a confidential, 'Here, let me tell you the old man's latest.'

Mr Solomon Rout (frequently alluded to as Long Sol, Old Sol, or Father Rout), from finding himself almost invariably the tallest man on board every ship he joined, had acquired the habit of a stooping, leisurely condescension. His hair was scant and sandy, his flat cheeks were pale, his bony wrists and long hands were pale, too, as though he had lived all his life in the shade.

He smiled from on high at Jukes, and went on smoking and glancing about quietly, in the manner of a kind uncle lending an ear to the tale of an excited schoolboy. Then, greatly amused but impassive, he asked:

'And did you throw up the billet?'

'No,' cried Jukes, raising a weary, discouraged voice above the harsh buzz of the *Nan-Shan*'s friction winches. All of them were hard at work, snatching slings of cargo, high up, to the end of long derricks, only, as it seemed, to let them rip down recklessly by the run. The cargo chains groaned in the gins, clinked on coamings, rattled over the side; and the whole ship quivered, with her long grey flanks smoking in wreaths of steam. 'No,' cried Jukes, 'I didn't. What's the good? I might just as well fling my resignation at the bulkhead. I don't believe you can make a man like that understand anything. He simply knocks me over.'

At that moment Captain MacWhirr, back from the shore, crossed the deck, umbrella in hand, escorted by a mournful, self-possessed Chinaman, walking behind in paper-soled silk shoes, and who also carried an umbrella.

The master of the *Nan-Shan*, speaking just audibly and gazing at his boots as his manner was, remarked that it would be necessary to call at Fu-chau this trip, and desired Mr Rout to have steam up to-morrow afternoon at one o'clock sharp. He pushed back his hat to wipe his forehead, observing at the time that he hated going ashore anyhow; while overtopping him Mr Rout, without deigning a word, smoked austerely, nursing his right elbow in the palm of his left hand. Then Jukes was directed in the same subdued voice to keep the forward 'tween-deck clear of cargo. Two hundred coolies were going to be put down there. The Bun Hin Company were sending that lot home. Twenty-five bags of rice would be coming off in a sampan directly, for stores. All seven-years'-men they were, said Captain MacWhirr, with a camphor-wood chest to every man. The carpenter should be set to work nailing three-inch battens along the deck below, fore and aft, to keep these boxes from shifting in a sea-way. Jukes had better look to it at once. 'D'ye hear, Jukes?' This Chinaman here was coming with the ship as far as Fu-chau—a sort of interpreter he would be. Bun Hin's clerk he was, and wanted to have a look at the space. Jukes had better take him forward. 'D'ye hear, Jukes?'

Jukes took care to punctuate these instructions in proper places with the obligatory 'Yes, sir,' ejaculated without enthusiasm. His brusque 'Come along, John; make look see' set the Chinaman in motion at his heels.

'Wanchee look see, all same look see can do,' said Jukes, who having no talent for foreign languages mangled the very pidgin-English cruelly. He pointed at the open hatch. 'Catchee number one piecie place to sleep in. Eh?'

He was gruff, as became his racial superiority, but not unfriendly. The Chinaman, gazing sad and speechless into the darkness of the hatchway, seemed to stand at the head of a yawning grave.

'No catchee rain down there—savee?' pointed out Jukes. 'Suppose all'ee same fine weather, one piecie coolie-man come top-side,' he pursued, warming up imaginatively. 'Make so—Phooooo!' He expanded his chest and blew out his cheeks. 'Savee, John? Breathe—fresh air. Good. Eh? Washee him piecie pants, chow-chow top-side—see, John?'

With his mouth and hands he made exuberant motions of eating rice and washing clothes; and the Chinaman, who concealed his distrust of this pantomime under a collected demeanour tinged by a gentle and refined melancholy, glanced out of his almond eyes from Jukes to the hatch and back again. 'Velly good,' he murmured, in a disconsolate undertone, and hastened smoothly along the decks, dodging obstacles in his course. He disappeared, ducking low under a sling of ten dirty gunny-bags full of some costly merchandise and exhaling a repulsive smell.

Captain MacWhirr meantime had gone on the bridge, and into the chart-room, where a letter, commenced two days before, awaited termination. These long letters began with the words, 'My darling wife,' and the steward, between the scrubbing of the floors and the dusting of chronometer-boxes, snatched at every opportunity to read them. They interested him much more than they possibly could the woman for whose eye they were intended; and this for the reason that they related in minute detail each successive trip of the *Nan-Shan*.

Her master, faithful to facts, which alone his consciousness reflected, would set them down with painstaking care upon many pages. The house in a northern suburb to which these pages were addressed had a bit of garden before the bow-windows, a deep porch of good appearance, coloured glass with imitation lead frame in the front door. He paid five-and-forty pounds a year for it, and did not think the rent too high, because Mrs MacWhirr (a pretentious person with a scraggy neck and a disdainful manner) was admittedly ladylike, and in the neighbourhood considered as 'quite superior.' The only secret of her life was her abject terror of the time when her husband would come home to stay for good. Under the same roof there dwelt also a daughter called Lydia and a son, Tom. These two were but slightly acquainted with their father. Mainly, they knew him as a rare but privileged visitor, who of an evening smoked his pipe in the dining-room and slept in the house. The lanky girl, upon the whole, was rather ashamed of him; the boy was frankly and utterly indifferent in a straightforward, delightful, unaffected way manly boys have.

And Captain MacWhirr wrote home from the coast of China twelve times every year, desiring quaintly to be 'remembered to the children,' and subscribing himself 'your loving husband,' as calmly as if the words so long used by so many men were, apart from their shape, worn-out things, and of a faded meaning.

The China seas north and south are narrow seas. They are seas full of every-day, eloquent facts, such as islands, sand-banks, reefs, swift and changeable currents—tangled facts that nevertheless speak to a seaman in clear and definite language. Their speech appealed to Captain MacWhirr's sense of realities so forcibly that he had given up his state-room below and practically lived all his days on the bridge of his ship, often having his meals sent up, and sleeping at night in the chart-room. And he indited there his home letters. Each of them, without exception, contained the phrase, 'The weather has been very fine this trip,' or some other form of a statement to that effect. And this statement, too, in its wonderful persistence, was of the same perfect accuracy as all the others they contained.

Mr Rout likewise wrote letters; only no one on board knew how chatty he could be, pen in hand, because the chief engineer had enough imagination to keep his desk locked. His wife relished his style greatly. They were a childless couple, and Mrs Rout, a big, high-bosomed, jolly woman of forty, shared with Mr Rout's toothless and venerable mother a little cottage near Teddington. She would run over her correspondence, at breakfast, with lively eyes, and scream out interesting passages in a joyous voice at the deaf old lady, prefacing each extract by the warning shout, 'Solomon says!' She had the trick of firing off Solomon's utterances also upon strangers, astonishing them easily by the unfamiliar text and the unexpectedly jocular vein of these quotations. On the day the new curate called for the first time at the cottage, she found occasion to remark, 'As Solomon says: "the engineers that go down to the sea in ships behold the wonders of sailor nature" '; when a change in the visitor's countenance made her stop and stare.

'Solomon. . . . Oh! . . . Mrs Rout,' stuttered the young man, very red in the face, 'I must say . . . I don't. . . .'

'He's my husband,' she announced in a great shout, throwing herself back in the chair. Perceiving the joke, she laughed immoderately with a handkerchief to her eyes, while he sat wearing a forced smile, and, from his inexperience of jolly women, fully persuaded that she must be deplorably insane. They were excellent friends afterwards; for, absolving her from irreverent intention, he came to think she was a very worthy person indeed; and he learned in time to receive without flinching other scraps of Solomon's wisdom.

'For my part,' Solomon was reported by his wife to have said once, 'give me the dullest ass for a skipper

before a rogue. There is a way to take a fool; but a rogue
is smart and slippery.' This was an airy generalization
drawn from the particular case of Captain MacWhirr's
honesty, which, in itself, had the heavy obviousness of
a lump of clay. On the other hand, Mr Jukes, unable
to generalize, unmarried, and unengaged, was in the
habit of opening his heart after another fashion to an old
chum and former shipmate, actually serving as second
officer on board an Atlantic liner.

First of all he would insist upon the advantages of the
Eastern trade, hinting at its superiority to the Western
ocean service. He extolled the sky, the seas, the ships,
and the easy life of the Far East. The *Nan-Shan*, he
affirmed, was second to none as a sea-boat.

'We have no brass-bound uniforms, but then we are
like brothers here,' he wrote. 'We all mess together and
live like fighting-cocks. . . . All the chaps of the black-
squad are as decent as they make that kind, and old Sol,
the Chief, is a dry stick. We are good friends. As to our
old man, you could not find a quieter skipper. Sometimes you would think he hadn't sense enough to see
anything wrong. And yet it isn't that. Can't be. He has
been in command for a good few years now. He doesn't
do anything actually foolish, and gets his ship along all
right without worrying anybody. I believe he hasn't
brains enough to enjoy kicking up a row. I don't take
advantage of him. I would scorn it. Outside the routine
of duty he doesn't seem to understand more than half of
what you tell him. We get a laugh out of this at times;

but it is dull, too, to be with a man like this—in the long run. Old Sol says he hasn't much conversation. Conversation! O Lord! He never talks. The other day I had been yarning under the bridge with one of the engineers, and he must have heard us. When I came up to take my watch, he steps out of the chart-room and has a good look all round, peeps over at the sidelights, glances at the compass, squints upwards at the stars. That's his regular performance. By-and-by he says: "Was that you talking just now in the port alleyway?" "Yes, sir." " With the third engineer?" "Yes, sir." He walks off to starboard, and sits under the dodger on a little campstool of his, and for half an hour perhaps he makes no sound, except that I heard him sneeze once. Then after a while I hear him getting up over there, and he strolls across to port, where I was. "I can't understand what you can find to talk about," says he. "Two solid hours. I am not blaming you. I see people ashore at it all day long, and then in the evening they sit down and keep at it over the drinks. Must be saying the same things over and over again. I can't understand."

'Did you ever hear anything like that? And he was so patient about it. It made me quite sorry for him. But he is exasperating, too, sometimes. Of course one would not do anything to vex him even if it were worth while. But it isn't. He's so jolly innocent that if you were to put your thumb to your nose and wave your fingers at him he would only wonder gravely to himself what got into you. He told me once quite simply that he found it very difficult to make out what made people always act so queerly. He's too dense to trouble about, and that's the truth.'

Thus wrote Mr Jukes to his chum in the Western ocean trade, out of the fulness of his heart and the liveliness of his fancy.

He had expressed his honest opinion. It was not worth while trying to impress a man of that sort. If the world had been full of such men, life would have probably appeared to Jukes an unentertaining and unprofitable business. He was not alone in his opinion. The sea itself, as if sharing Mr Jukes's good-natured forbearance, had never put itself out to startle the silent man, who seldom looked up, and wandered innocently over the waters with the only visible purpose of getting food, raiment, and house-room for three people ashore. Dirty weather he had known, of course. He had been made wet, uncomfortable, tired in the usual way, felt at the time and presently forgotten. So that upon the whole he had been justified in reporting fine weather at home. But he had never been given a glimpse of immeasurable strength and of immoderate wrath, the wrath that passes exhausted but never appeased—the wrath and fury of the passionate sea. He knew it existed, as we know that crime and abominations exist; he had heard of it as a peaceable citizen in a town hears of battles, famines, and floods, and yet knows nothing of what these things mean—though, indeed, he may have been mixed up in a street row, have gone without his dinner once, or been soaked to the skin in a shower. Captain MacWhirr had sailed over the surface of the oceans as some men go skimming over the years of existence to sink gently into a placid grave, ignorant of life to the last, without ever having been made to see all it may contain of perfidy, of violence, and of terror. There are on sea and land such men thus fortunate—or thus disdained by destiny or by the sea.

II

Observing the steady fall of the barometer, Captain MacWhirr thought, 'There's some dirty weather knocking about.' This is precisely what he thought. He had had an experience of moderately dirty weather—the term dirty as applied to the weather implying only moderate discomfort to the seaman. Had he been informed by an indisputable authority that the end of the world was to be finally accomplished by a catastrophic disturbance of the atmosphere, he would have assimilated the information under the simple idea of dirty weather, and no other, because he had no experience of cataclysms, and belief does not necessarily imply comprehension. The wisdom of his country had pronounced by means of an Act of Parliament that before he could be considered as fit to take charge of a ship he should be able to answer certain simple questions on the subject of circular storms such as hurricanes, cyclones, typhoons; and apparently he had answered them, since he was now in command of the *Nan-Shan* in the China seas during the season of typhoons. But if he had answered he remembered nothing of it. He was, however, conscious of being made uncomfortable by the clammy heat. He came out on the bridge, and found no relief to this oppression. The air seemed thick. He gasped like a fish, and began to believe himself greatly out of sorts.

The *Nan-Shan* was ploughing a vanishing furrow upon the circle of the sea that had the surface and the shimmer of an undulating piece of grey silk. The sun, pale and without rays, poured down leaden heat in a strangely indecisive light, and the Chinamen were lying prostrate about the decks. Their bloodless, pinched, yellow faces were like the faces of bilious invalids. Captain MacWhirr noticed two of them especially, stretched out on their backs below the bridge. As soon as they had closed their eyes they seemed dead. Three others, however, were quarrelling barbarously away forward; and one big fellow, half naked, with herculean shoulders, was hanging limply over a winch; another, sitting on the deck, his knees up and his head drooping sideways in a girlish attitude, was plaiting his pigtail with infinite languor depicted in his whole person and in the very movement of his fingers. The smoke struggled with difficulty out of the funnel, and instead of streaming away spread itself out like an infernal sort of cloud, smelling of sulphur and raining soot all over the decks.

'What the devil are you doing there, Mr Jukes?' asked Captain MacWhirr.

This unusual form of address, though mumbled rather than spoken, caused the body of Mr Jukes to start as though it had been probed under the fifth rib. He had had a low bench brought on the bridge, and sitting on it, with a length of rope curled about his feet and a piece of canvas stretched over his knees, was pushing a sail-needle vigorously. He looked up, and his surprise gave to his eyes an expression of innocence and candour.

'I am only roping some of that new set of bags we made last trip for whipping up coals,' he remonstrated, gently. 'We shall want them for the next coaling, sir.'

'What became of the others ?'

'Why, worn out, of course, sir.'

Captain MacWhirr, after glaring down irresolutely at his chief mate, disclosed the gloomy and cynical conviction that more than half of them had been lost overboard, 'if only the truth was known,' and retired to the other end of the bridge. Jukes, exasperated by this unprovoked attack, broke the needle at the second stitch, and dropping his work got up and cursed the heat in a violent undertone.

The propeller thumped, the three Chinamen forward had given up squabbling very suddenly, and the one who had been plaiting his tail clasped his legs and stared dejectedly over his knees. The lurid sunshine cast faint and sickly shadows. The swell ran higher and swifter every moment, and the ship lurched heavily in the smooth, deep hollows of the sea.

'I wonder where that beastly swell comes from,' said Jukes aloud, recovering himself after a stagger.

'North-east,' grunted the literal MacWhirr, from his side of the bridge. 'There's some dirty weather knocking about. Go and look at the glass.'

When Jukes came out of the chart-room, the cast of his countenance had changed to thoughtfulness and concern. He caught hold of the bridge-rail and stared ahead.

The temperature in the engine-room had gone up to a hundred and seventeen degrees. Irritated voices were ascending through the skylight and through the fiddle of the stokehold in a harsh and resonant uproar, mingled with angry clangs and scrapes of metal, as if men with limbs of iron and throats of bronze had been quarrelling down there. The second engineer was falling foul of the stokers for letting the steam go down. He was a man with arms like a blacksmith, and generally feared; but that afternoon the stokers were answering him back recklessly, and slammed the furnace doors with the fury of despair. Then the noise ceased suddenly, and the second engineer appeared, emerging out of the stokehold streaked with grime and soaking wet like a chimney-sweep coming out of a well. As soon as his head was clear of the fiddle he began to scold Jukes for not trimming properly the stokehold ventilators; and in answer Jukes made with his hands deprecatory soothing signs meaning: No wind—can't be helped—you can see for yourself. But the other wouldn't hear reason. His teeth flashed angrily in his dirty face. He didn't mind, he said, the trouble of punching their blanked heads down there, blank his soul, but did the condemned sailors think you could keep steam up in the God-forsaken boilers simply by knocking the blanked stokers about? No, by George! You had to get some draught, too—may he be everlastingly blanked for a swab-headed deck-hand if you didn't! And the chief, too, rampaging before the steam-gauge and carrying on like a lunatic up and down the engine-room ever since noon. What did Jukes think he was stuck up there for, if he couldn't get one of his decayed, good-for-nothing deck-cripples to turn the ventilators to the wind?

The relations of the 'engine-room' and the 'deck' of the *Nan-Shan* were, as is known, of a brotherly nature; therefore Jukes leaned over and begged the other in a restrained tone not to make a disgusting ass of himself; the skipper was on the other side of the bridge. But the second declared mutinously that he didn't care a rap who was on the other side of the bridge, and Jukes, passing in a flash from lofty disapproval into a state of exaltation, invited him in unflattering terms to come up and twist the beastly things to please himself, and catch such wind as a donkey of his sort could find. The second rushed up to the fray. He flung himself at the port ventilator as though he meant to tear it out bodily and toss it overboard. All he did was to move the cowl round a few inches, with an enormous expenditure of force, and seemed spent in the effort. He leaned against the back of the wheel-house, and Jukes walked up to him.

'Oh, Heavens!' ejaculated the engineer in a feeble voice. He lifted his eyes to the sky, and then let his glassy stare descend to meet the horizon that, tilting up to an angle of forty degrees, seemed to hang on a slant for a while and settled down slowly. 'Heavens! Phew! What's up, anyhow?'

Jukes, straddling his long legs like a pair of compasses, put on an air of superiority. 'We're going to catch it this time,' he said. 'The barometer is tumbling down like anything, Harry. And you trying to kick up that silly row. . . .'

The word 'barometer' seemed to revive the second engineer's mad animosity. Collecting afresh all his energies, he directed Jukes in a low and brutal tone to shove the unmentionable instrument down his gory throat. Who cared for his crimson barometer? It was the steam—the steam—that was going down; and what between the firemen going faint and the chief going silly, it was worse than a dog's life for him; he didn't care a tinker's curse how soon the whole show was blown out of the water. He seemed on the point of having a cry, but after regaining his breath he muttered darkly, 'I'll faint them,' and dashed off. He stopped upon the fiddle long enough to shake his fist at the unnatural daylight, and dropped into the dark hole with a whoop.

When Jukes turned, his eyes fell upon the rounded back and the big red ears of Captain MacWhirr, who had come across. He did not look at his chief officer, but said at once, 'That's a very violent man, that second engineer.'

'Jolly good second, anyhow,' grunted Jukes. 'They can't keep up steam,' he added, rapidly, and made a grab at the rail against the coming lurch.

Captain MacWhirr, unprepared, took a run and brought himself up with a jerk by an awning stanchion.

'A profane man,' he said, obstinately. 'If this goes on, I'll have to get rid of him the first chance.'

'It's the heat,' said Jukes. 'The weather's awful. It would make a saint swear. Even up here I feel exactly as if I had my head tied up in a woollen blanket.'

Captain MacWhirr looked up. 'D'ye mean to say, Mr Jukes, you ever had your head tied up in a blanket? What was that for?'

'It's a manner of speaking, sir,' said Jukes, stolidly.

'Some of you fellows do go on! What's that about saints swearing? I wish you wouldn't talk so wild. What sort of saint would that be that would swear? No more saint than yourself, I expect. And what's a blanket got to do with it—or the weather either. . . . The heat does not make me swear—does it? It's filthy bad temper. That's what it is. And what's the good of your talking like this?'

Thus Captain MacWhirr expostulated against the use of images in speech, and at the end electrified Jukes by a contemptuous snort, followed by words of passion and resentment: 'Damme! I'll fire him out of the ship if he don't look out.'

And Jukes, incorrigible, thought: 'Goodness me! Somebody's put a new inside to my old man. Here's temper, if you like. Of course it's the weather; what else? It would make an angel quarrelsome—let alone a saint.'

All the Chinamen on deck appeared at their last gasp.

At its setting the sun had a diminished diameter and an expiring brown, rayless glow, as if millions of centuries elapsing since the morning had brought it near its end. A dense bank of cloud became visible to the northward; it had a sinister dark olive tint, and lay low and motionless upon the sea, resembling a solid obstacle in the path of the ship. She went floundering towards it like an exhausted creature driven to its death. The coppery twilight retired slowly, and the darkness brought out overhead a swarm of unsteady, big stars, that, as if blown upon, flickered exceedingly and seemed to hang very near the earth. At eight o'clock Jukes went into the chart-room to write up the ship's log.

He copied neatly out of the rough-book the number of miles, the course of the ship, and in the column for 'wind' scrawled the word 'calm' from top to bottom of the eight hours since noon. He was exasperated by the continuous, monotonous rolling of the ship. The heavy inkstand would slide away in a manner that suggested perverse intelligence in dodging the pen. Having written in the large space under the head of 'Remarks' 'Heat very oppressive,' he stuck the end of the pen-holder in his teeth, pipe fashion, and mopped his face carefully.

'Ship rolling heavily in a high cross swell,' he began

again, and commented to himself, 'Heavily is no word for it.' Then he wrote: 'Sunset threatening, with a low bank of clouds to N. and E. Sky clear overhead.'

Sprawling over the table with arrested pen, he glanced out of the door, and in that frame of his vision he saw all the stars flying upwards between the teak-wood jambs on a black sky. The whole lot took flight together and disappeared, leaving only a blackness flecked with white flashes, for the sea was as black as the sky and speckled with foam afar. The stars that had flown to the roll came back on the return swing of the ship, rushing downwards in their glittering multitude, not of fiery points, but enlarged to tiny discs brilliant with a clear wet sheen.

Jukes watched the flying big stars for a moment, and then wrote: '8 p.m. Swell increasing. Ship labouring and taking water on her decks. Battened down the coolies for the night. Barometer still falling.' He paused, and thought to himself, 'Perhaps nothing whatever'll come of it.' And then he closed resolutely his entries: 'Every appearance of a typhoon coming on.'

On going out he had to stand aside, and Captain MacWhirr strode over the doorstep without saying a word or making a sign.

'Shut the door, Mr Jukes, will you?' he cried from within.

Jukes turned back to do so, muttering ironically: 'Afraid to catch cold, I suppose.' It was his watch below, but he yearned for communion with his kind;

and he remarked cheerily to the second mate: 'Doesn't look so bad, after all—does it ?'

The second mate was marching to and fro on the bridge, tripping down with small steps one moment, and the next climbing with difficulty the shifting slope of the deck. At the sound of Jukes's voice he stood still, facing forward, but made no reply.

'Hallo! That's a heavy one,' said Jukes, swaying to meet the long roll till his lowered head touched the planks. This time the second mate made in his throat a noise of an unfriendly nature.

He was an oldish, shabby little fellow, with bad teeth and no hair on his face. He had been shipped in a hurry in Shanghai, that trip when the second officer brought from home had delayed the ship three hours in port by contriving (in some manner Captain MacWhirr could never understand) to fall overboard into an empty coal-lighter lying alongside, and had to be sent ashore to the hospital with concussion of the brain and a broken limb or two.

Jukes was not discouraged by the unsympathetic sound. 'The Chinamen must be having a lovely time of it down there,' he said. 'It's lucky for them the old girl has the easiest roll of any ship I've ever been in. There now! This one wasn't so bad.'

'You wait,' snarled the second mate.

With his sharp nose, red at the tip, and his thin pinched lips he always looked as though he were raging inwardly; and he was concise in his speech to the point of rudeness. All his time off duty he spent in his cabin with the door shut, keeping so still in there that he was supposed to fall asleep as soon as he had disappeared; but the man who came in to wake him for his watch on deck would invariably find him with his eyes wide open, flat on his back in the bunk, and glaring irritably from a soiled pillow. He never wrote any letters, did not seem to hope for news from anywhere; and though he had been heard once to mention West Hartlepool, it was with extreme bitterness, and only in connection with the extortionate charges of a boarding-house. He was one of those men who are picked up at need in the ports of the world. They are competent enough, appear hopelessly hard up, show no evidence of any sort of vice, and carry about them all the signs of manifest failure. They come aboard on an emergency, care for no ship afloat, live in their own atmosphere of casual connection amongst their shipmates who know nothing of them, and make up their minds to leave at inconvenient times. They clear out with no words of leave-taking in some God-forsaken port other men would fear to be stranded in, and go ashore in company of a shabby sea-chest, corded like a treasure-box, and with an air of shaking the ship's dust off their feet.

'You wait,' he repeated, balanced in great swings with his back to Jukes, motionless and implacable.

'Do you mean to say we are going to catch it hot?' asked Jukes with boyish interest.

'Say? . . . I say nothing. You don't catch me,'

snapped the little second mate, with a mixture of pride, scorn, and cunning, as if Jukes's question had been a trap cleverly detected. 'Oh, no! None of you here shall make a fool of me if I know it,' he mumbled to himself.

Jukes reflected rapidly that this second mate was a mean little beast, and in his heart he wished poor Jack Allen had never smashed himself up in the coal-lighter. The far-off blackness ahead of the ship was like another night seen through the starry night of the earth—the starless night of the immensities beyond the created universe, revealed in its appalling stillness through a low fissure in the glittering sphere of which the earth is the kernel.

'Whatever there might be about,' said Jukes, 'we are steaming straight into it.'

'*You've* said it,' caught up the second mate, always with his back to Jukes. 'You've said it, mind—not I.'

'Oh, go to Jericho!' said Jukes, frankly; and the other emitted a triumphant little chuckle.

'You've said it,' he repeated.

'And what of that?'

'I've known some real good men get into trouble with their skippers for saying a dam' sight less,' answered the second mate feverishly. 'Oh, no! You don't catch me.'

'You seem deucedly anxious not to give yourself away,' said Jukes, completely soured by such absurdity. 'I wouldn't be afraid to say what I think.'

'Aye, to me. That's no great trick. I am nobody, and well I know it.'

The ship, after a pause of comparative steadiness
started upon a series of rolls, one worse than the other,
and for a time Jukes, preserving his equilibrium, was too
busy to open his mouth. As soon as the violent swinging had quieted down somewhat, he said: 'This is a bit
too much of a good thing. Whether anything is coming
or not I think she ought to be put head on to that swell.
The old man is just gone in to lie down. Hang me if I
don't speak to him.'

But when he opened the door of the chart-room he
saw his captain reading a book. Captain MacWhirr was
not lying down: he was standing up with one hand
grasping the edge of the bookshelf and the other holding
open before his face a thick volume. The lamp wriggled
in the gimbals, the loosened books toppled from side to
side on the shelf, the long barometer swung in jerky circles, the table altered its slant every moment. In the
midst of all this stir and movement Captain MacWhirr,
holding on, showed his eyes above the upper edge, and
asked, 'What's the matter?'

'Swell getting worse, sir.'

'Noticed that in here,' muttered Captain MacWhirr.
'Anything wrong?'

Jukes, inwardly disconcerted by the seriousness of the
eyes looking at him over the top of the book, produced
an embarrassed grin.

'Rolling like old boots,' he said, sheepishly.

'Aye! Very heavy—very heavy. What do you want?'

At this Jukes lost his footing and began to flounder.

'I was thinking of our passengers,' he said, in the manner of a man clutching at a straw.

'Passengers ?' wondered the Captain, gravely. 'What passengers ?'

'Why, the Chinamen, sir,' explained Jukes, very sick of this conversation.

'The Chinamen! Why don't you speak plainly? Couldn't tell what you meant. Never heard a lot of coolies spoken of as passengers before. Passengers, indeed! What's come to you?'

Captain MacWhirr, closing the book on his forefinger, lowered his arm and looked completely mystified. 'Why are you thinking of the Chinamen, Mr Jukes ?' he inquired.

Jukes took a plunge, like a man driven to it. 'She's rolling her decks full of water, sir. Thought you might put her head on perhaps—for a while. Till this goes down a bit—very soon, I dare say. Head to the eastward. I never knew a ship roll like this.'

He held on in the doorway, and Captain MacWhirr, feeling his grip on the shelf inadequate, made up his mind to let go in a hurry, and fell heavily on the couch.

'Head to the eastward ?' he said, struggling to sit up. 'That's more than four points off her course.'

'Yes, sir. Fifty degrees. . . . Would just bring her head far enough round to meet this. . . .'

Captain MacWhirr was now sitting up. He had not dropped the book, and he had not lost his place.

'To the eastward ?' he repeated, with dawning astonishment. 'To the . . . Where do you think we are bound to? You want me to haul a full-powered steamship four points off her course to make the Chinamen comfortable! Now, I've heard more than enough of mad things done in the world—but this. . . . If I didn't know you, Jukes, I would think you were in liquor. Steer four points off. . . . And what afterwards? Steer four points over the other way, I suppose, to make the course good. What put it into your head that I would start to tack a steamer as if she were a sailing-ship?'

'Jolly good thing she isn't,' threw in Jukes, with bitter readiness. 'She would have rolled every blessed stick out of her this afternoon.'

'Aye! And you just would have had to stand and see them go,' said Captain MacWhirr, showing a certain animation. 'It's a dead calm, isn't it?'

'It is, sir. But there's something out of the common coming, for sure.'

'Maybe. I suppose you have a notion I should be getting out of the way of that dirt,' said Captain MacWhirr, speaking with the utmost simplicity of manner and tone, and fixing the oilcloth on the floor with a heavy stare. Thus he noticed neither Jukes's discomfiture nor the mixture of vexation and astonished respect on his face.

'Now, here's this book,' he continued with deliberation, slapping his thigh with the closed volume. 'I've been reading the chapter on the storms there.'

This was true. He had been reading the chapter on the storms. When he had entered the chart-room, it was with no intention of taking the book down. Some influence in the air—the same influence, probably, that caused the steward to bring without orders the Captain's sea-boots and oilskin coat up to the chart-room—had as it were guided his hand to the shelf; and without taking the time to sit down he had waded with a conscious effort into the terminology of the subject. He lost himself amongst advancing semi-circles, left- and right-hand quadrants, the curves of the tracks, the probable bearing of the centre, the shifts of wind and the readings of barometer. He tried to bring all these things into a definite relation to himself, and ended by becoming contemptuously angry with such a lot of words and with so much advice, all head-work and supposition, without a glimmer of certitude.

'It's the damnedest thing, Jukes,' he said. 'If a fellow was to believe all that's in there, he would be running most of his time all over the sea trying to get behind the weather.'

Again he slapped his leg with the book; and Jukes opened his mouth, but said nothing.

'Running to get behind the weather! Do you understand that, Mr Jukes? It's the maddest thing!' ejaculated Captain MacWhirr, with pauses, gazing at the floor profoundly. 'You would think an old woman had been writing this. It passes me. If that thing means anything useful, then it means that I should at once alter the course away, away to the devil somewhere, and come booming down on Fu-chau from the northward at the tail of this dirty weather that's supposed to be knocking about in our way. From the north! Do you understand, Mr Jukes? Three hundred extra miles to the distance, and a pretty coal bill to show. I couldn't bring myself to do that if every word in there was gospel truth, Mr Jukes. Don't you expect me. . . .'

And Jukes, silent, marvelled at this display of feeling and loquacity.

'But the truth is that you don't know if the fellow is right, anyhow. How can you tell what a gale is made of till you get it? He isn't aboard here, is he? Very well. Here he says that the centre of them things bears eight points off the wind; but we haven't got any wind, for all the barometer falling. Where's his centre now?'

'We will get the wind presently,' mumbled Jukes.

'Let it come, then,' said Captain MacWhirr, with dignified indignation. 'It's only to let you see, Mr Jukes, that you don't find everything in books. All these rules for dodging breezes and circumventing the winds of heaven, Mr Jukes, seem to me the maddest thing, when you come to look at it sensibly.'

He raised his eyes, saw Jukes gazing at him dubiously, and tried to illustrate his meaning.

'About as queer as your extraordinary notion of dodging the ship head to sea, for I don't know how long, to make the Chinamen comfortable; whereas all we've got to do is to take them to Fu-chau, being timed to get there before noon on Friday. If the weather delays me—very well. There's your log-book to talk straight about the weather. But suppose I went swinging off my course and came in two days late, and they asked me: "Where have you been all that time, Captain?" What could I say to that? "Went around to dodge the bad weather," I would say. "It must've been dam' bad," they would say. "Don't know," I would have to say; "I've dodged clear of it." See that, Jukes? I have been thinking it all out this afternoon.'

He looked up again in his unseeing, unimaginative way. No one had ever heard him say so much at one time. Jukes, with his arms open in the doorway, was like a man invited to behold a miracle. Unbounded wonder was the intellectual meaning of his eye, while incredulity was seated in his whole countenance.

'A gale is a gale, Mr Jukes,' resumed the Captain, 'and a full-powered steamship has got to face it. There's just so much dirty weather knocking about the world, and the proper thing is to go through it with none of what old Captain Wilson of the *Melita* calls "storm strategy." The other day ashore I heard him hold forth about it to a lot of shipmasters who came in and sat at a table next to mine. It seemed to me the greatest nonsense. He was telling them how he out-manoeuvred, I think he said, a terrific gale, so that it never came nearer than fifty miles to him. A neat piece of head-work he called it. How he knew there was a terrific gale fifty miles off beats me altogether. It was like listening to a crazy man. I would have thought Captain Wilson was old enough to know better.'

Captain MacWhirr ceased for a moment, then said, 'It's your watch below, Mr Jukes?'

Jukes came to himself with a start. 'Yes, sir.'

'Leave orders to call me at the slightest change,' said the Captain. He reached up to put the book away, and tucked his legs upon the couch. 'Shut the door so that it don't fly open, will you? I can't stand a door banging. They've put a lot of rubbishy locks into this ship, I must say.'

Captain MacWhirr closed his eyes.

He did so to rest himself. He was tired, and he experienced that state of mental vacuity which comes at the end of an exhaustive discussion that has liberated some belief matured in the course of meditative years. He had indeed been making his confession of faith, had he only known it; and its effect was to make Jukes, on the other side of the door, stand scratching his head for a good while.

Captain MacWhirr opened his eyes.

He thought he must have been asleep. What was that loud noise? Wind? Why had he not been called? The lamp wriggled in its gimbals, the barometer swung in circles, the table altered its slant every moment; a pair of limp sea-boots with collapsed tops went sliding past the couch. He put out his hand instantly, and captured one.

Jukes's face appeared in a crack of the door: only his face, very red, with staring eyes. The flame of the lamp leaped, a piece of paper flew up, a rush of air enveloped Captain MacWhirr. Beginning to draw on the boot, he directed an expectant gaze at Jukes's swollen, excited features.

'Came on like this,' shouted Jukes, 'five minutes ago . . . all of a sudden.'

The head disappeared with a bang, and a heavy splash and patter of drops swept past the closed door as if a pailful of melted lead had been flung against the house. A whistling could be heard now upon the deep vibrating noise outside. The stuffy chart-room seemed as full of draughts as a shed. Captain MacWhirr collared the other sea-boot on its violent passage along the floor. He was not flustered, but he could not find at once the opening for inserting his foot. The shoes he had flung off were scurrying from end to end of the cabin, gambolling playfully over each other like puppies. As soon as he stood up he kicked at them viciously, but without effect.

He threw himself into the attitude of a lunging fencer, to reach after his oilskin coat; and afterwards he staggered all over the confined space while he jerked himself into it. Very grave, straddling his legs far apart, and stretching his neck, he started to tie deliberately the strings of his sou'-wester under his chin, with thick fingers that trembled slightly. He went through all the movements of a woman putting on her bonnet before a glass, with a strained, listening attention, as though he had expected every moment to hear the shout of his name in the confused clamour that had suddenly beset his ship. Its increase filled his ears while he was getting

ready to go out and confront whatever it might mean.
It was tumultuous and very loud—made up of the rush
of the wind, the crashes of the sea, with that prolonged
deep vibration of the air, like the roll of an immense and
remote drum beating the charge of the gale.

He stood for a moment in the light of the lamp, thick,
clumsy, shapeless in his panoply of combat, vigilant and
red-faced.

'There's a lot of weight in this,' he muttered.

As soon as he attempted to open the door the wind
caught it. Clinging to the handle, he was dragged out
over the doorstep, and at once found himself engaged
with the wind in a sort of personal scuffle whose object
was the shutting of that door. At the last moment a
tongue of air scurried in and licked out the flame of the
lamp.

Ahead of the ship he perceived a great darkness lying
upon a multitude of white flashes; on the starboard
beam a few amazing stars drooped, dim and fitful, above
an immense waste of broken seas, as if seen through a
mad drift of smoke.

On the bridge a knot of men, indistinct and toiling,
were making great efforts in the light of the wheel-house
windows that shone mistily on their heads and backs.
Suddenly darkness closed upon one pane, then on
another. The voices of the lost group reached him after
the manner of men's voices in a gale, in shreds and fragments of forlorn shouting snatched past the ear. All at

once Jukes appeared at his side, yelling, with his head down.

'Watch—put in—wheelhouse shutters glass—afraid—blow in.'

Jukes heard his commander upbraiding.

'This—come—anything—warning—call me.'

He tried to explain, with the uproar pressing on his lips.

'Light air—remained—bridge—sudden—northeast—could turn—thought—you—sure—hear.'

They had gained the shelter of the weather-cloth, and could converse with raised voices, as people quarrel.

'I got the hands along to cover up all the ventilators. Good job I had remained on deck. I didn't think you would be asleep, and so . . . What did you say, sir? What?'

'Nothing,' cried Captain MacWhirr. 'I said—all right.'

'By all the powers! We've got it this time,' observed Jukes in a howl.

'You haven't altered her course?' inquired Captain MacWhirr, straining his voice.

'No, sir. Certainly not. Wind came out right ahead. And here comes the head sea.'

A plunge of the ship ended in a shock as if she had landed her forefoot upon something solid. After a moment of stillness a lofty flight of sprays drove hard with the wind upon their faces.

'Keep her at it as long as we can,' shouted Captain MacWhirr.

Before Jukes had squeezed the salt water out of his eyes all the stars had disappeared.

III

Jukes was as ready a man as any half-dozen young mates that may be caught by casting a net upon the waters; and though he had been somewhat taken aback by the startling viciousness of the first squall, he had pulled himself together on the instant, had called out the hands and had rushed them along to secure such openings about the deck as had not been already battened down earlier in the evening. Shouting in his fresh, stentorian voice, 'Jump, boys, and bear a hand!' he led in the work, telling himself the while that he had 'just expected this.'

But at the same time he was growing aware that this was rather more than he had expected. From the first stir of the air felt on his cheek the gale seemed to take upon itself the accumulated impetus of an avalanche. Heavy sprays enveloped the *Nan-Shan* from stem to stern, and instantly in the midst of her regular rolling she began to jerk and plunge as though she had gone mad with fright.

Jukes thought, 'This is no joke.' While he was exchanging explanatory yells with his captain, a sudden

lowering of the darkness came upon the night, falling
before their vision like something palpable. It was as if
the masked lights of the world had been turned down.
Jukes was uncritically glad to have his captain at hand.
It relieved him as though that man had, by simply coming on deck, taken most of the gale's weight upon his
shoulders. Such is the prestige, the privilege, and the
burden of command.

Captain MacWhirr could expect no relief of that sort
from any one on earth. Such is the loneliness of command. He was trying to see, with that watchful manner
of a seaman who stares into the wind's eye as if into the
eye of an adversary, to penetrate the hidden intention
and guess the aim and force of the thrust. The strong
wind swept at him out of a vast obscurity; he felt under
his feet the uneasiness of his ship, and he could not even
discern the shadow of her shape. He wished it were not
so; and very still he waited, feeling stricken by a blind
man's helplessness.

To be silent was natural to him, dark or shine. Jukes,
at his elbow, made himself heard yelling cheerily in the
gusts, 'We must have got the worst of it at once, sir.'
A faint burst of lightning quivered all round, as if
flashed into a cavern—into a black and secret chamber
of the sea, with a floor of foaming crests.

It unveiled for a sinister, fluttering moment a ragged
mass of clouds hanging low, the lurch of the long outlines of the ship, the black figures of men caught on the

bridge, heads forward, as if petrified in the act of butting. The darkness palpitated down upon all this, and then the real thing came at last.

It was something formidable and swift, like the sudden smashing of a vial of wrath. It seemed to explode all round the ship with an overpowering concussion and a rush of great waters, as if an immense dam had been blown up to windward. In an instant the men lost touch of each other. This is the disintegrating power of a great wind: it isolates one from one's kind. An earthquake, a landslip, an avalanche, overtake a man incidentally, as it were—without passion. A furious gale attacks him like a personal enemy, tries to grasp his limbs, fastens upon his mind, seeks to rout his very spirit out of him.

Jukes was driven away from his commander. He fancied himself whirled a great distance through the air. Everything disappeared—even, for a moment, his power of thinking; but his hand had found one of the rail-stanchions. His distress was by no means alleviated by an inclination to disbelieve the reality of this experience. Though young, he had seen some bad weather, and had never doubted his ability to imagine the worst; but this was so much beyond his powers of fancy that it appeared incompatible with the existence of any ship whatever. He would have been incredulous about himself in the same way, perhaps, had he not been so harassed by the necessity of exerting a wrestling effort against a force trying to tear him away from his hold. Moreover, the conviction of not being utterly destroyed returned to him through the sensations of being half-drowned, bestially shaken, and partly choked.

It seemed to him he remained there precariously alone with the stanchion for a long, long time. The rain poured on him, flowed, drove in sheets. He breathed in gasps; and sometimes the water he swallowed was fresh and sometimes it was salt. For the most part he kept his eyes shut tight, as if suspecting his sight might be destroyed in the immense flurry of the elements. When he ventured to blink hastily, he derived some moral support from the green gleam of the starboard light shining feebly upon the flight of rain and sprays. He was actually looking at it when its ray fell upon the uprearing sea which put it out. He saw the head of the wave topple over, adding the might of its crash to the tremendous uproar raging around him, and almost at the same instant the stanchion was wrenched away from his embracing arms. After a crushing thump on his back he found himself suddenly afloat and borne upwards. His first irresistible notion was that the whole China Sea had climbed on the bridge. Then, more sanely, he concluded himself gone overboard. All the time he was being tossed, flung, and rolled in great volumes of water, he kept on repeating mentally, with the utmost precipitation, the words: 'My God! My God! My God! My God!'

All at once, in a revolt of misery and despair, he formed the crazy resolution to get out of that. And he began to thresh about with his arms and legs. But as soon as he commenced his wretched struggles he dis-

covered that he had become somehow mixed up with a
face, an oilskin coat, somebody's boots. He clawed fero-
ciously all these things in turn, lost them, found them
again, lost them once more, and finally was himself
caught in the firm clasp of a pair of stout arms. He
returned the embrace closely round a thick solid body.
He had found his captain.

They tumbled over and over, tightening their hug.
Suddenly the water let them down with a brutal bang;
and, stranded against the side of the wheelhouse, out of
breath and bruised, they were left to stagger up in the
wind and hold on where they could.

Jukes came out of it rather horrified, as though he
had escaped some unparalleled outrage directed at his
feelings. It weakened his faith in himself. He started
shouting aimlessly to the man he could feel near him in
that fiendish blackness, 'Is it you, sir? Is it you, sir?' till
his temples seemed ready to burst. And he heard in
answer a voice, as if crying far away, as if screaming to
him fretfully from a very great distance, the one word
'Yes!' Other seas swept again over the bridge. He
received them defencelessly right over his bare head,
with both his hands engaged in holding.

The motion of the ship was extravagant. Her lurches
had an appalling helplessness: she pitched as if taking a
header into a void, and seemed to find a wall to hit
every time. When she rolled she fell on her side headlong, and she would be righted back by such a demol-
ishing blow that Jukes felt her reeling as a clubbed man

reels before he collapses. The gale howled and scuffled about gigantically in the darkness, as though the entire world were one black gully. At certain moments the air streamed against the ship as if sucked through a tunnel with a concentrated solid force of impact that seemed to lift her clean out of the water and keep her up for an instant with only a quiver running through her from end to end. And then she would begin her tumbling again as if dropped back into a boiling cauldron. Jukes tried hard to compose his mind and judge things coolly.

The sea, flattened down in the heavier gusts, would uprise and overwhelm both ends of the *Nan-Shan* in snowy rushes of foam, expanding wide, beyond both rails, into the night. And on this dazzling sheet, spread under the blackness of the clouds and emitting a bluish glow, Captain MacWhirr could catch a desolate glimpse of a few tiny specks black as ebony, the tops of the hatches, the battened companions, the heads of the covered winches, the foot of a mast. This was all he could see of his ship. Her middle structure, covered by the bridge which bore him, his mate, the closed wheelhouse where a man was steering shut up with the fear of being swept overboard together with the whole thing in one great crash—her middle structure was like a half-tide rock awash upon a coast. It was like an outlying rock with the water boiling up, streaming over, pouring off, beating round—like a rock in the surf to which shipwrecked people cling before they let go—only it rose, it sank, it rolled continuously, without respite and rest, like a rock that should have miraculously struck adrift from a coast and gone wallowing upon the sea.

The *Nan-Shan* was being looted by the storm with a senseless, destructive fury: trysails torn out of the extra gaskets, double-lashed awnings blown away, bridge swept clean, weather-cloths burst, rails twisted, light-screens smashed—and two of the boats had gone already. They had gone unheard and unseen, melting, as it were, in the shock and smother of the wave. It was only later, when upon the white flash of another high sea hurling itself amidships, Jukes had a vision of two pairs of davits leaping black and empty out of the solid black-ness, with one overhauled fall flying and an iron-bound block capering in the air, that he became aware of what had happened within about three yards of his back.

He poked his head forward, groping for the ear of his commander. His lips touched it—big, fleshy, very wet. He cried in an agitated tone, 'Our boats are going now, sir.'

And again he heard that voice, forced and ringing feebly, but with a penetrating effect of quietness in the enormous discord of noises, as if sent out from some remote spot of peace beyond the black wastes of the gale; again he heard a man's voice—the frail and indomitable sound that can be made to carry an infin-ity of thought, resolution and purpose, that shall be pro-nouncing confident words on the last day, when heavens fall, and justice is done—again he heard it, and it was crying to him, as if from very, very far—'All right.'

He thought he had not managed to make himself understood. 'Our boats—I say boats—the boats, sir! Two gone!'

The same voice, within a foot of him and yet so remote, yelled sensibly, 'Can't be helped.'

Captain MacWhirr had never turned his face, but Jukes caught some more words on the wind.

'What can—expect—when hammering through—such——Bound to leave—something behind—stands to reason.'

Watchfully Jukes listened for more. No more came. This was all Captain MacWhirr had to say; and Jukes could picture to himself rather than see the broad squat back before him. An impenetrable obscurity pressed down upon the ghostly glimmers of the sea. A dull conviction seized upon Jukes that there was nothing to be done.

If the steering-gear did not give way, if the immense volumes of water did not burst the deck in or smash one of the hatches, if the engines did not give up, if way could be kept on the ship against this terrific wind, and she did not bury herself in one of these awful seas, of whose white crests alone, topping high above her bows, he could now and then get a sickening glimpse—then there was a chance of her coming out of it. Something within him seemed to turn over, bringing uppermost the feeling that the *Nan-Shan* was lost.

'She's done for,' he said to himself, with a surprising mental agitation, as though he had discovered an unexpected meaning in this thought. One of these things was bound to happen. Nothing could be prevented now, and nothing could be remedied. The men on board did not count, and the ship could not last. This weather was too impossible.

Jukes felt an arm thrown heavily over his shoulders; and to this overture he responded with great intelligence by catching hold of his captain round the waist.

They stood clasped thus in the blind night, bracing each other against the wind, cheek to cheek and lip to ear, in the manner of two hulks lashed stem to stern together.

And Jukes heard the voice of his commander hardly any louder than before, but nearer, as though, starting to march athwart the prodigious rush of the hurricane, it had approached him, bearing that strange effect of quietness like the serene glow of a halo.

'D'ye know where the hands got to?' it asked, vigorous and evanescent at the same time, overcoming the strength of the wind, and swept away from Jukes instantly.

Jukes didn't know. They were all on the bridge when the real force of the hurricane struck the ship. He had no idea where they had crawled to. Under the circumstances they were nowhere, for all the use that could be made of them. Somehow the Captain's wish to know distressed Jukes.

'Want the hands, sir?' he cried, apprehensively.

'Ought to know,' asserted Captain MacWhirr. 'Hold hard.'

They held hard. An outburst of unchained fury, a vicious rush of the wind absolutely steadied the ship; she rocked only, quick and light like a child's cradle, for a terrific moment of suspense, while the whole atmosphere, as it seemed, streamed furiously past her, roaring away from the tenebrous earth.

It suffocated them, and with eyes shut they tightened their grasp. What from the magnitude of the shock might have been a column of water running upright in the dark, butted against the ship, broke short, and fell on her bridge, crushingly, from on high, with a dead burying weight.

A flying fragment of that collapse, a mere splash, enveloped them in one swirl from their feet over their heads, filling violently their ears, mouths and nostrils with salt water. It knocked out their legs, wrenched in haste at their arms, seethed away swiftly under their chins; and opening their eyes, they saw the piled-up masses of foam dashing to and fro amongst what looked like the fragments of a ship. She had given way as if driven straight in. Their panting hearts yielded, too, before the tremendous blow; and all at once she sprang up again to her desperate plunging, as if trying to scramble out from under the ruins.

The seas in the dark seemed to rush from all sides to keep her back where she might perish. There was hate

in the way she was handled, and a ferocity in the blows
that fell. She was like a living creature thrown to the
rage of a mob: hustled terribly, struck at, borne up,
flung down, leaped upon. Captain MacWhirr and Jukes
kept hold of each other, deafened by the noise, gagged
by the wind; and the great physical tumult beating
about their bodies, brought, like an unbridled display
of passion, a profound trouble to their souls. One of
those wild and appalling shrieks that are heard at times
passing mysteriously overhead in the steady roar of a
hurricane, swooped, as if borne on wings, upon the ship,
and Jukes tried to outscream it.

'Will she live through this?'

The cry was wrenched out of his breast. It was as
unintentional as the birth of a thought in the head, and
he heard nothing of it himself. It all became extinct at
once—thought, intention, effort—and of his cry the
inaudible vibration added to the tempest waves of the
air.

He expected nothing from it. Nothing at all. For
indeed what answer could be made? But after a while he
heard with amazement the frail and resisting voice in his
ear, the dwarf sound, unconquered in the giant tumult.

'She may!'

It was a dull yell, more difficult to seize than a whisper. And presently the voice returned again, half sub-
merged in the vast crashes, like a ship battling against
the waves of an ocean.

'Let's hope so!' it cried—small, lonely and unmoved,

a stranger to the visions of hope or fear; and it flickered into disconnected words: 'Ship. . . . This. . . . Never—Anyhow . . . for the best.' Jukes gave it up.

Then, as if it had come suddenly upon the one thing fit to withstand the power of a storm, it seemed to gain force and firmness for the last broken shouts:

'Keep on hammering . . . builders . . . good men. . . . And chance it . . . engines. . . . Rout . . . good man.'

Captain MacWhirr removed his arm from Jukes's shoulders, and thereby ceased to exist for his mate, so dark it was; Jukes, after a tense stiffening of every muscle, would let himself go limp all over. The gnawing of profound discomfort existed side by side with an incredible disposition to somnolence, as though he had been buffeted and worried into drowsiness. The wind would get hold of his head and try to shake it off his shoulders; his clothes, full of water, were as heavy as lead, cold and dripping like an armour of melting ice: he shivered—it lasted a long time; and with his hands closed hard on his hold, he was letting himself sink slowly into the depths of bodily misery. His mind became concentrated upon himself in an aimless, idle way, and when something pushed lightly at the back of his knees he nearly, as the saying is, jumped out of his skin.

In the start forward he bumped the back of Captain MacWhirr, who didn't move; and then a hand gripped his thigh. A lull had come, a menacing lull of the wind, the holding of a stormy breath—and he felt himself pawed all over. It was the boatswain. Jukes recognized these hands, so thick and enormous that they seemed to belong to some new species of man.

The boatswain had arrived on the bridge, crawling on all fours against the wind, and had found the chief mate's legs with the top of his head. Immediately he crouched and began to explore Jukes's person upwards with prudent, apologetic touches, as became an inferior.

He was an ill-favoured, undersized, gruff sailor of fifty, coarsely hairy, short-legged, long-armed, resembling an elderly ape. His strength was immense; and in his great lumpy paws, bulging like brown boxing-gloves on the end of furry forearms, the heaviest objects were handled like playthings. Apart from the grizzled pelt on his chest, the menacing demeanour and the hoarse voice, he had none of the classical attributes of his rating. His good nature almost amounted to imbecility: the men did what they liked with him, and he had not an ounce of initiative in his character, which was easy-going and talkative. For these reasons Jukes disliked him; but Captain MacWhirr, to Jukes's scornful disgust, seemed to regard him as a first-rate petty officer.

He pulled himself up by Jukes's coat, taking that liberty with the greatest moderation, and only so far as it was forced upon him by the hurricane.

'What is it, bosun, what is it?' yelled Jukes, impatiently. What could that fraud of a bosun want on the bridge? The typhoon had got on Jukes's nerves. The husky bellowings of the other, though unintelligible, seemed to suggest a state of lively satisfaction. There could be no mistake. The old fool was pleased with something.

The boatswain's other hand had found some other body, for in a changed tone he began to inquire: 'Is it you, sir? Is it you, sir?' The wind strangled his howls.

'Yes!' cried Captain MacWhirr.

IV

All that the boatswain, out of a superabundance of yells, could make clear to Captain MacWhirr was the bizarre intelligence that 'All them Chinamen in the fore 'tween deck have fetched away, sir.'

Jukes to leeward could hear these two shouting within six inches of his face, as you may hear on a still night half a mile away two men conversing across a field. He heard Captain MacWhirr's exasperated 'What? What?' and the strained pitch of the other's hoarseness. 'In a lump . . . seen them myself. . . . Awful sight, sir . . . thought . . . tell you.'

Jukes remained indifferent, as if rendered irresponsible by the force of the hurricane, which made the very thought of action utterly vain. Besides, being very young, he had found the occupation of keeping his heart completely steeled against the worst so engrossing that he had come to feel an overpowering dislike towards any other form of activity whatever. He was not scared; he knew this because, firmly believing he would never see another sunrise, he remained calm in that belief.

These are the moments of do-nothing heroics to which even good men surrender at times. Many officers of ships can no doubt recall a case in their experience when just such a trance of confounded stoicism would come all at once over a whole ship's company. Jukes, however, had no wide experience of men or storms. He conceived himself to be calm—inexorably calm; but as a matter of fact he was daunted; not abjectly, but only so far as a decent man may, without becoming loathsome to himself.

It was rather like a forced-on numbness of spirit. The long, long stress of a gale does it; the suspense of the interminably culminating catastrophe; and there is a bodily fatigue in the mere holding on to existence within the excessive tumult; a searching and insidious fatigue that penetrates deep into a man's breast to cast down and sadden his heart, which is incorrigible, and of all the gifts of the earth—even before life itself—aspires to peace.

Jukes was benumbed much more than he supposed. He held on—very wet, very cold, stiff in every limb; and in a momentary hallucination of swift visions (it is said that a drowning man thus reviews all his life) he beheld all sorts of memories altogether unconnected with his present situation. He remembered his father, for instance: a worthy business man, who at an unfortunate crisis in his affairs went quietly to bed and died forthwith in a state of resignation. Jukes did not recall these circumstances, of course, but remaining otherwise unconcerned he seemed to see distinctly the poor man's face; a certain game of nap played when quite a boy in Table Bay on board a ship, since lost with all hands; the thick eyebrows of his first skipper; and without any emotion, as he might years ago have walked listlessly into her room and found her sitting there with a book, he remembered his mother—dead, too, now—the resolute woman, left badly off, who had been very firm in his bringing up.

It could not have lasted more than a second, perhaps not so much. A heavy arm had fallen about his shoulders; Captain MacWhirr's voice was speaking his name into his ear.

'Jukes! Jukes!'

He detected the tone of deep concern. The wind had thrown its weight on the ship, trying to pin her down amongst the seas. They made a clean breach over her, as over a deep-swimming log; and the gathered weight of crashes menaced monstrously from afar. The breakers flung out of the night with a ghostly light on their crests—the light of sea-foam that in a ferocious, boiling-up pale flash showed upon the slender body of the ship the toppling rush, the downfall, and the seething mad scurry of each wave. Never for a moment could she shake herself clear of the water; Jukes, rigid, perceived in her motion the ominous sign of haphazard floundering. She was no longer struggling intelligently. It was the beginning of the end; and the note of busy concern in Captain MacWhirr's voice sickened him like an exhibition of blind and pernicious folly.

The spell of the storm had fallen upon Jukes. He was penetrated by it, absorbed by it; he was rooted in it with a rigour of dumb attention. Captain MacWhirr persisted in his cries, but the wind got between them like a solid wedge. He hung round Jukes's neck as heavy as a millstone, and suddenly the sides of their heads knocked together.

'Jukes! Mr. Jukes, I say!'

He had to answer that voice that would not be silenced. He answered in the customary manner: '. . . Yes, sir.'

And directly, his heart, corrupted by the storm that breeds a craving for peace, rebelled against the tyranny of training and command.

Captain MacWhirr had his mate's head fixed firm in the crook of his elbow, and pressed it to his yelling lips mysteriously. Sometimes Jukes would break in, admonishing hastily: 'Look out, sir!' or Captain MacWhirr would bawl an earnest exhortation to 'Hold hard, there!' and the whole black universe seemed to reel together with the ship. They paused. She floated yet. And Captain MacWhirr would resume his shouts. '. . . . Says . . . whole lot . . . fetched away. . . . Ought to see . . . what's the matter.'

Directly the full force of the hurricane had struck the ship, every part of her deck became untenable; and the sailors, dazed and dismayed, took shelter in the port alleyway under the bridge. It had a door aft, which they shut; it was very black, cold, and dismal. At each heavy

fling of the ship they would groan all together in the
dark, and tons of water could be heard scuttling about
as if trying to get at them from above. The boatswain
had been keeping up a gruff talk, but a more unreason-
able lot of men, he said afterwards, he had never been
with. They were snug enough there, out of harm's way,
and not wanted to do anything, either; and yet they did
nothing but grumble and complain peevishly like so
many sick kids. Finally, one of them said that if there
had been at least some light to see each other's noses by,
it wouldn't be so bad. It was making him crazy, he
declared, to lie there in the dark waiting for the blamed
hooker to sink.

'Why don't you step outside, then, and be done with
it at once?' the boatswain turned on him.

This called up a shout of execration. The boatswain
found himself overwhelmed with reproaches of all sorts.
They seemed to take it ill that a lamp was not instantly
created for them out of nothing. They would whine
after a light to get drowned by—anyhow! And though
the unreason of their revilings was patent—since no one
could hope to reach the lamp-room, which was forward—he became greatly distressed. He did not think it
was decent of them to be nagging at him like this. He
told them so, and was met by general contumely. He
sought refuge, therefore, in an embittered silence. At the
same time their grumbling and sighing and muttering
worried him greatly, but by-and-by it occurred to him
that there were six globe lamps hung in the 'tween-deck,

and that there could be no harm in depriving the coolies of one of them.

The *Nan-Shan* had an athwartship coal-bunker, which, being at times used as cargo space, communicated. by an iron door with the fore 'tween-deck. It was empty then, and its manhole was the foremost one in the alleyway. The boatswain could get in, therefore, without coming out on deck at all; but to his great surprise he found he could induce no one to help him in taking off the manhole cover. He groped for it all the same, but one of the crew lying in his way refused to budge.

'Why, I only want to get you that blamed light you are crying for,' he expostulated, almost pitifully.

Somebody told him to go and put his head in a bag. He regretted he could not recognize the voice, and that it was too dark to see, otherwise, as he said, he would have put a head on *that* son of a sea-cook, anyway, sink or swim. Nevertheless, he had made up his mind to show them he could get a light, if he were to die for it.

Through the violence of the ship's rolling, every movement was dangerous. To be lying down seemed labour enough. He nearly broke his neck dropping into the bunker. He fell on his back, and was sent shooting helplessly from side to side in the dangerous company of a heavy iron bar—a coal-trimmer's slice probably— left down there by somebody. This thing made him as nervous as though it had been a wild beast. He could not see it, the inside of the bunker coated with coal-dust being perfectly and impenetrably black; but he

heard it sliding and clattering, and striking here and
there, always in the neighbourhood of his head. It
seemed to make an extraordinary noise, too—to give
heavy thumps as though it had been as big as a bridge
girder. This was remarkable enough for him to notice
while he was flung from port to starboard and back
again, and clawing desperately the smooth sides of the
bunker in the endeavour to stop himself. The door into
the 'tween-deck not fitting quite true, he saw a thread
of dim light at the bottom.

Being a sailor, and a still active man, he did not want
much of a chance to regain his feet; and as luck would
have it, in scrambling up he put his hand on the iron
slice, picking it up as he rose. Otherwise he would have
been afraid of the thing breaking his legs, or at least
knocking him down again. At first he stood still. He felt
unsafe in this darkness that seemed to make the ship's
motion unfamiliar, unforeseen, and difficult to counter-
act. He felt so much shaken for a moment that he dared
not move for fear of 'taking charge again.' He had no
mind to get battered to pieces in that bunker.

He had struck his head twice; he was dazed a little.
He seemed to hear yet so plainly the clatter and bangs of
the iron slice flying about his ears that he tightened his
grip to prove to himself he had it there safely in his
hand. He was vaguely amazed at the plainness with
which down there he could hear the gale raging. Its
howls and shrieks seemed to take on, in the emptiness of
the bunker, something of the human character, of

human rage and pain—being not vast but infinitely poignant. And there were, with every roll, thumps, too—profound, ponderous thumps, as if a bulk object of five-ton weight or so had got play in the hold. But there was no such thing in the cargo. Something on deck? Impossible. Or alongside? Couldn't be.

He thought all this quickly, clearly, competently, like a seaman, and in the end remained puzzled. This noise, though, came deadened from outside, together with the washing and pouring of water on deck above his head. Was it the wind? Must be. It made down there a row like the shouting of a big lot of crazed men. And he discovered in himself a desire for a light, too—if only to get drowned by—and a nervous anxiety to get out of that bunker as quickly as possible.

He pulled back the bolt: the heavy iron plate turned on its hinges; and it was as though he had opened the door to the sounds of the tempest. A gust of hoarse yelling met him: the air was still; and the rushing of water overhead was covered by a tumult of strangled, throaty shrieks that produced an effect of desperate confusion. He straddled his legs the whole width of the doorway and stretched his neck. And at first he perceived only what he had come to seek: six small yellow flames swinging violently on the great body of the dusk.

It was stayed like the gallery of a mine, with a row of stanchions in the middle, and cross beams overhead, penetrating into the gloom ahead—indefinitely. And to port there loomed, like the caving in of one of the sides, a bulky mass with a slanting outline. The whole place, with the shadows and the shapes, moved all the time. The boatswain glared: the ship lurched to starboard, and a great howl came from that mass that had the slant of fallen earth.

Pieces of wood whizzed past. Planks, he thought, inexpressibly startled, and flinging back his head. At his feet a man went sliding over, open-eyed, on his back, straining with uplifted arms for nothing: and another came bounding like a detached stone with his head between his legs and his hands clenched. His pigtail whipped in the air; he made a grab at the boatswain's legs, and from his opened hand a bright white disc rolled against the boatswain's foot. He recognized a silver dollar, and yelled at it with astonishment. With a precipitated sound of trampling and shuffling of bare feet, and with guttural cries, the mound of writhing bodies piled up to port detached itself from the ship's side and, sliding, inert and struggling, shifted to starboard, with a dull, brutal thump. The cries ceased. The boatswain heard a long moan through the roar and whistling of the wind; he saw an inextricable confusion of heads and shoulders, naked soles kicking upwards, fists raised, tumbling backs, legs, pigtails, faces.

'Good Lord!' he cried, horrified, and banged-to the iron door upon this vision.

This was what he had come on the bridge to tell. He could not keep it to himself; and on board ship there is only one man to whom it is worth while to unburden yourself. On his passage back the hands in the alleyway swore at him for a fool. Why didn't he bring that lamp? What the devil did the coolies matter to anybody? And when he came out, the extremity of the ship made what went on inside of her appear of little moment.

At first he thought he had left the alleyway in the very moment of her sinking. The bridge ladders had been washed away, but an enormous sea filling the after-deck floated him up. After that he had to lie on his stomach for some time, holding to a ring-bolt, getting his breath now and then, and swallowing salt water. He struggled farther on his hands and knees, too frightened and distracted to turn back. In this way he reached the after part of the wheelhouse. In that comparatively shel-tered spot he found the second mate. The boatswain was pleasantly surprised—his impression being that everybody on deck must have been washed away a long time ago. He asked eagerly where the captain was.

The second mate was lying low, like a malignant lit-tle animal under a hedge.

'Captain? Gone overboard, after getting us into this mess.' The mate, too, for all he knew or cared. Another fool. Didn't matter. Everybody was going by-and-by.

The boatswain crawled out again into the strength of the wind; not because he much expected to find any-body, he said, but just to get away from 'that man.' He crawled out as outcasts go to face an inclement world. Hence his great joy at finding Jukes and the Captain. But what was going on in the 'tween-deck was to him a minor matter by that time. Besides, it was difficult to make yourself heard. But he managed to convey the idea that the Chinamen had broken adrift together with their boxes, and that he had come up on purpose to report this. As to the hands, they were all right. Then, appeased, he subsided on the deck in a sitting posture, hugging with his arms and legs the stand of the engine-room telegraph—an iron casting as thick as a post. When that went, why, he expected he would go, too. He gave no more thought to the coolies.

Captain MacWhirr had made Jukes understand that he wanted him to go down below—to see.

'What am I to do then, sir?' And the trembling of his whole wet body caused Jukes's voice to sound like bleating.

'See first . . . Bosun . . . says . . . adrift.'

'That bosun is a confounded fool,' howled Jukes, shakily.

The absurdity of the demand made upon him revolted Jukes. He was as unwilling to go as if the moment he had left the deck the ship were sure to sink.

'I must know . . . can't leave. . . .'

'They'll settle, sir.'

'Fight . . . bosun says they fight. . . . Why? Can't have . . . fighting . . . board ship. . . . Much rather keep you here . . . case. . . . I should . . . washed overboard myself. . . . Stop it . . . some way. You see and tell me . . . through engine-room tube. Don't want you . . .

come up here . . . too often. Dangerous . . . moving about . . . deck.'

Jukes, held with his head in chancery, had to listen to what seemed horrible suggestions.

'Don't want . . . you get lost . . . so long . . . ship isn't. . . . Rout. . . . Good man . . . Ship . . . may . . . through this . . . all right yet.'

All at once Jukes understood he would have to go.

'Do you think she may?' he screamed.

But the wind devoured the reply, out of which Jukes heard only the one word, pronounced with great energy '. . . . Always. . . .'

Captain MacWhirr released Jukes, and bending over the boatswain, yelled 'Get back with the mate.' Jukes only knew that the arm was gone off his shoulders. He was dismissed with his orders—to do what? He was exasperated into letting go his hold carelessly, and on the instant was blown away. It seemed to him that nothing could stop him from being blown right over the stern. He flung himself down hastily, and the boatswain, who was following, fell on him.

'Don't you get up yet, sir,' cried the boatswain. 'No hurry!'

A sea swept over. Jukes understood the boatswain to splutter that the bridge ladders were gone. 'I'll lower you down, sir, by your hands,' he screamed. He shouted also something about the smoke-stack being as likely to go overboard as not. Jukes thought it very possible, and imagined the fires were out, the ship helpless. . . . The boatswain by his side kept on yelling. 'What? What is it?' Jukes cried distressfully; and the other repeated, 'What would my old woman say if she saw me now?'

In the alleyway, where a lot of water had got in and splashed in the dark, the men were still as death, till Jukes stumbled against one of them and cursed him savagely for being in the way. Two or three voices then asked, eager and weak, 'Any chance for us, sir?'

'What's the matter with you fools?' he said, brutally. He felt as though he could throw himself down amongst them and never move any more. But they seemed cheered; and in the midst of obsequious warnings, 'Look out! Mind that manhole lid, sir,' they lowered him into the bunker. The boatswain tumbled down after him, and as soon as he had picked himself up he remarked, 'She would say, "Serve you right, you old fool, for going to sea." '

The boatswain had some means, and made a point of alluding to them frequently. His wife—a fat woman—and two grown-up daughters kept a greengrocer's shop in the East-end of London.

In the dark, Jukes, unsteady on his legs, listened to a faint thunderous patter. A deadened screaming went on steadily at his elbow, as it were; and from above the louder tumult of the storm descended upon these near sounds. His head swam. To him, too, in that bunker, the motion of the ship seemed novel and menacing, sapping his resolution as though he had never been afloat before.

He had half a mind to scramble out again; but the

remembrance of Captain MacWhirr's voice made this impossible. His orders were to go and see. What was the good of it? he wanted to know. Enraged, he told himself he would see—of course. But the boatswain, staggering clumsily, warned him to be careful how he opened that door; there was a blamed fight going on. And Jukes, as if in great bodily pain, desired irritably to know what the devil they were fighting for.

'Dollars! Dollars, sir. All their rotten chests got burst open. Blamed money skipping all over the place, and they are tumbling after it head over heels—tearing and biting like anything. A regular little hell in there.'

Jukes convulsively opened the door. The short boatswain peered under his arm.

One of the lamps had gone out, broken perhaps. Rancorous, guttural cries burst out loudly on their ears, and a strange panting sound, the working of all these straining breasts. A hard blow hit the side of the ship: water fell above with a stunning shock, and in the forefront of the gloom, where the air was reddish and thick, Jukes saw a head bang the deck violently, two thick calves waving on high, muscular arms twined round a naked body, a yellow-face, open-mouthed and with a set wild stare, look up and slide away. An empty chest clattered turning over; a man fell head first with a jump, as if lifted by a kick; and farther off, indistinct, others streamed like a mass of rolling stones down a bank, thumping the deck with their feet and flourishing their arms wildly. The hatchway ladder was loaded with coolies swarming on it like bees on a branch. They hung on the steps in a crawling, stirring cluster, beating madly with their fists the underside of the battened hatch, and the headlong rush of the water above was heard in the intervals of their yelling. The ship heeled over more, and they began to drop off: first one, then two, then all the rest went away together, falling straight off with a great cry.

Jukes was confounded. The boatswain, with gruff anxiety, begged him, 'Don't you go in there, sir.'

The whole place seemed to twist upon itself, jumping incessantly the while; and when the ship rose to a sea Jukes fancied that all these men would be shot upon him in a body. He backed out, swung the door to, and with trembling hands pushed at the bolt. . . .

As soon as his mate had gone, Captain MacWhirr, left alone on the bridge, sidled and staggered as far as the wheelhouse. Its door being hinged forward, he had to fight the gale for admittance, and when at last he managed to enter, it was with an instantaneous clatter and a bang, as though he had been fired through the wood. He stood within, holding on to the handle.

The steering-gear leaked steam, and in the confined space the glass of the binnacle made a shiny oval of light in a thin white fog. The wind howled, hummed, whistled, with sudden booming gusts that rattled the doors and shutters in the vicious patter of sprays. Two coils of lead-line and a small canvas bag hung on a long lanyard, swung wide off, and came back clinging to the bulkheads. The gratings underfoot were nearly afloat; with every sweeping blow of a sea, water squirted violently through the cracks all round the door, and the man at the helm had flung down his cap, his coat, and stood propped against the gear-casing in a striped cotton shirt open on his breast. The little brass wheel in his hands had the appearance of a bright and fragile toy. The cords of his neck stood hard and lean, a dark patch lay in the hollow of his throat, and his face was still and sunken as in death.

Captain MacWhirr wiped his eyes. The sea that had nearly taken him overboard had, to his great annoyance, washed his sou'-wester hat off his bald head. The fluffy, fair hair, soaked and darkened, resembled a mean skein of cotton threads festooned round his bare skull. His face, glistening with sea-water, had been made crimson with the wind, with the sting of sprays. He looked as though he had come off sweating from before a furnace.

'You here?' he muttered, heavily.

The second mate had found his way into the wheel-house some time before. He had fixed himself in a corner with his knees up, a fist pressed against each temple; and this attitude suggested rage, sorrow, resignation, surrender, with a sort of concentrated unforgiveness. He said mournfully and defiantly, 'Well, it's my watch below now: ain't it?'

The steam gear clattered, stopped, clattered again; and the helmsman's eyeballs seemed to project out of a hungry face as if the compass-card behind the binnacle glass had been meat. God knows how long he had been left there to steer, as if forgotten by all his shipmates. The bells had not been struck; there had been no reliefs; the ship's routine had gone down wind; but he was trying to keep her head north-north-east. The rudder might have been gone for all he knew, the fires out, the engines broken down, the ship ready to roll over like a corpse. He was anxious not to get muddled and lose control of her head, because the compass-card swung far both ways, wriggling on the pivot, and sometimes seemed to whirl right round. He suffered from mental stress. He was horribly afraid, also, of the wheelhouse going. Mountains of water kept on tumbling against it. When the ship took one of her desperate dives the corners of his lips twitched.

Captain MacWhirr looked up at the wheelhouse clock. Screwed to the bulk-head, it had a white face on which the black hands appeared to stand quite still. It was half-past one in the morning.

'Another day,' he muttered to himself.

The second mate heard him, and lifting his head as one grieving amongst ruins, 'You won't see it break,' he exclaimed. His wrists and his knees could be seen to shake violently. 'No, by God! You won't. . . .'

He took his face again between his fists.

The body of the helmsman had moved slightly, but his head didn't budge on his neck,—like a stone head fixed to look one way from a column. During a roll that all but took his booted legs from under him, and in the very stagger to save himself, Captain MacWhirr said austerely, 'Don't you pay any attention to what that man says.' And then with an indefinable change of tone, very grave, he added, 'He isn't on duty.'

The sailor said nothing.

The hurricane boomed, shaking the little place, which seemed air-tight; and the light of the binnacle flickered all the time.

'You haven't been relieved,' Captain MacWhirr went on, looking down. 'I want you to stick to the helm, though, as long as you can. You've got the hang of her. Another man coming here might make a mess of it. Wouldn't do. No child's play. And the hands are probably busy with a job down below. . . . Think you can?'

The steering-gear leaped into an abrupt short clatter, stopped smouldering like an ember; and the still man, with a motionless gaze, burst out, as if all the passion in him had gone into his lips 'By Heavens, sir! I can steer for ever if nobody talks to me.'

'Oh! aye! All right. . . .' The Captain lifted his eyes for the first time to the man, '. . . Hackett.'

And he seemed to dismiss this matter from his mind. He stooped to the engine-room speaking-tube, blew in, and bent his head. Mr Rout below answered, and at once Captain MacWhirr put his lips to the mouthpiece.

With the uproar of the gale around him he applied alternately his lips and his ear, and the engineer's voice mounted to him, harsh and as if out of the heat of an engagement. One of the stokers was disabled, the others had given in, the second engineer and the donkey-man were firing-up. The third engineer was standing by the steam-valve. The engines were being tended by hand. How was it above?

'Bad enough. It mostly rests with you,' said Captain MacWhirr. Was the mate down there yet? No? Well, he would be presently. Would Mr Rout let him talk through the speaking-tube?—through the deck speaking-tube, because he—the Captain—was going out on the bridge directly. There was some trouble among the Chinamen. They were fighting, it seemed. Couldn't allow fighting anyhow. . . .

Mr Rout had gone away, and Captain MacWhirr could feel against his ear the pulsation of the engines, like the beat of the ship's heart. Mr Rout's voice down there shouted something distantly. The ship pitched headlong, the pulsation leaped with a hissing tumult, and stopped dead. Captain MacWhirr's face was impassive, and his eyes were fixed aimlessly on the crouching shape of the second mate. Again Mr Rout's voice cried out in the depths, and the pulsating beats recommenced, with slow strokes—growing swifter.

Mr Rout had returned to the tube. 'It don't matter much what they do,' he said, hastily; and then, with irritation, 'She takes these dives as if she never meant to come up again.'

'Awful sea,' said the Captain's voice from above.

'Don't let me drive her under,' barked Solomon Rout up the pipe.

'Dark and rain. Can't see what's coming,' uttered the voice. 'Must—keep—her—moving—enough to steer—and chance it,' it went on to state distinctly.

'I am doing as much as I dare.'

'We are—getting—smashed up—a good deal up here,' proceeded the voice mildly. 'Doing—fairly well—though. Of course, if the wheelhouse should go . . . .'

Mr Rout, bending an attentive ear, muttered peevishly something under his breath.

But the deliberate voice up there became animated to ask: 'Jukes turned up yet?' Then, after a short wait, 'I wish he would bear a hand. I want him to be done and come up here in case of anything. To look after the ship. I am all alone. The second mate's lost. . . .'

'What?' shouted Mr Rout into the engine-room, taking his head away. Then up the tube he cried, 'Gone overboard?' and clapped his ear to.

'Lost his nerve,' the voice from above continued in a matter-of-fact tone. 'Damned awkward circumstance.'

Mr Rout, listening with bowed neck, opened his eyes wide at this. However, he heard something like the sounds of a scuffle and broken exclamations coming down to him. He strained his hearing; and all the time Beale, the third engineer, with his arms uplifted, held between the palms of his hands the rim of a little black wheel projecting at the side of a big copper pipe. He seemed to be poising it above his head, as though it were a correct attitude in some sort of game

To steady himself, he pressed his shoulder against the

white bulkhead, one knee bent, and a sweat-rag tucked in his belt hanging on his hip. His smooth cheek was begrimed and flushed, and the coal dust on his eyelids, like the black pencilling of a make-up, enhanced the liquid brilliance of the whites, giving to his youthful face something of a feminine, exotic and fascinating aspect. When the ship pitched he would with hasty movements of his hands screw hard at the little wheel.

'Gone crazy,' began the Captain's voice suddenly in the tube. 'Rushed at me. . . . Just now. Had to knock him down. . . . This minute. You heard, Mr Rout?'

'The devil!' muttered Mr Rout. 'Look out, Beale!'

His shout rang out like the blast of a warning trumpet, between the iron walls of the engine-room. Painted white, they rose high into the dusk of the skylight, sloping like a roof; and the whole lofty space resembled the interior of a monument, divided by floors of iron grating, with lights flickering at different levels, and a mass of gloom lingering in the middle, within the columnar stir of machinery under the motionless swelling of the cylinders. A loud and wild resonance, made up of all the noises of the hurricane, dwelt in the still warmth of the air. There was in it the smell of hot metal, of oil, and a slight mist of steam. The blows of the sea seemed to traverse it in an unringing, stunning shock, from side to side.

Gleams, like pale long flames, trembled upon the polish of metal; from the flooring below, the enormous crank-heads emerged in their turns with a flash of brass and steel—going over; while the connecting-rods, big-jointed, like skeleton limbs, seemed to thrust them down and pull them up again with an irresistible precision. And deep in the half-light other rods dodged deliberately to and fro, crossheads nodded, discs of metal rubbed smoothly against each other, slow and gentle, in a commingling of shadows and gleams.

Sometimes all those powerful and unerring movements would slow down simultaneously, as if they had been the functions of a living organism, stricken suddenly by the blight of languor; and Mr Rout's eyes would blaze darker in his long sallow face. He was fighting this fight in a pair of carpet slippers. A short shiny jacket barely covered his loins, and his white wrists protruded far out of the tight sleeves, as though the emergency had added to his stature, had lengthened his limbs, augmented his pallor, hollowed his eyes.

He moved, climbing high up, disappearing low down, with a restless, purposeful industry, and when he stood still, holding the guard-rail in front of the starting-gear, he would keep glancing to the right at the steam-gauge, at the water-gauge, fixed upon the white wall in the light of a swaying lamp. The mouths of two speaking-tubes gaped stupidly at his elbow, and the dial of the engine-room telegraph resembled a clock of large diameter, bearing on its face curt words instead of figures. The grouped letters stood out heavily black, around the pivot-head of the indicator, emphatically symbolic of loud exclamations: AHEAD, ASTERN, SLOW, HALF, STAND

BY; and the fat black hand pointed downwards to the word FULL, which, thus singled out, captured the eye as a sharp cry secures attention.

The wood-encased bulk of the low-pressure cylinder, frowning portly from above, emitted a faint wheeze at every thrust, and except for that low hiss the engines worked their steel limbs headlong or slow with a silent, determined smoothness. And all this, the white walls, the moving steel, the floor plates under Solomon Rout's feet, the floors of iron grating above his head, the dusk and the gleams, uprose and sank continuously, with one accord, upon the harsh wash of the waves against the ship's side. The whole loftiness of the place, booming hollow to the great voice of the wind, swayed at the top like a tree, would go over bodily, as if borne down this way and that by the tremendous blasts.

'You've got to hurry up,' shouted Mr Rout, as soon as he saw Jukes appear in the stokehold doorway.

Jukes's glance was wandering and tipsy; his red face was puffy, as though he had overslept himself. He had had an arduous road, and had travelled over it with immense vivacity, the agitation of his mind corresponding to the exertions of his body. He had rushed up out of the bunker, stumbling in the dark alleyway amongst a lot of bewildered men who, trod upon, asked 'What's up, sir?' in awed mutters all round him;—down the stokehold ladder, missing many iron rungs in his hurry, down into a place deep as a well, black as Tophet, tipping over back and forth like a see-saw. The water in the bilges thundered at each roll, and lumps of coal skipped to and fro, from end to end, rattling like an avalanche of pebbles on a slope of iron.

Somebody in there moaned with pain, and somebody else could be seen crouching over what seemed the prone body of a dead man; a lusty voice blasphemed; and the glow under each fire-door was like a pool of flaming blood radiating quietly in a velvety blackness.

A gust of wind struck upon the nape of Jukes's neck and next moment he felt it streaming about his wet ankles. The stokehold ventilators hummed: in front of the six fire-doors two wild figures, stripped to the waist, staggered and stooped, wrestling with two shovels.

'Hallo! Plenty of draught now,' yelled the second engineer at once, as though he had been all the time looking out for Jukes. The donkeyman, a dapper little chap with a dazzling fair skin and a tiny, gingery moustache, worked in a sort of mute transport. They were keeping a full head of steam, and a profound rumbling, as of an empty furniture van trotting over a bridge, made a sustained bass to all the other noises of the place.

'Blowing off all the time,' went on yelling the second. With a sound as of a hundred scoured saucepans, the orifice of a ventilator spat upon his shoulder a sudden gush of salt water, and he volleyed a stream of curses upon all things on earth including his own soul, ripping and raving, and all the time attending to his business. With a sharp clash of metal the ardent pale glare of the fire opened upon his bullet head, showing

his spluttering lips, his insolent face, and with another
clang closed like the white-hot wink of an iron eye.

'Where's the blooming ship? Can you tell me? blast
my eyes! Under water—or what? It's coming down here
in tons. Are the condemned cowls gone to Hades? Hey?
Don't you know anything—you jolly sailor-man you . . . ?'

Jukes, after a bewildered moment, had been helped
by a roll to dart through; and as soon as his eyes took
in the comparative vastness, peace and brilliance of the
engine-room, the ship, setting her stern heavily in the
water, sent him charging head down upon Mr Rout.

The chief's arm, long like a tentacle, and straighten-
ing as if worked by a spring, went out to meet him, and
deflected his rush into a spin towards the speaking-
tubes. At the same time Mr Rout repeated earnestly:

'You've got to hurry up, whatever it is.'

Jukes yelled 'Are you there, sir?' and listened. Nothing. Suddenly the roar of the wind fell straight into his
ear, but presently a small voice shoved aside the shouting hurricane quietly.

'You, Jukes?—Well?'

Jukes was ready to talk: it was only time that seemed
to be wanting. It was easy enough to account for everything. He could perfectly imagine the coolies battened
down in the reeking -deck, lying sick and scared
between the rows of chests. Then one of these chests—
or perhaps several at once—breaking loose in a roll,
knocking out others, sides splitting, lids flying open, and
all these clumsy Chinamen rising up in a body to save

their property. Afterwards every fling of the ship would hurl that tramping, yelling mob here and there, from side to side, in a whirl of smashed wood, torn clothing, rolling dollars. A struggle once started, they would be unable to stop themselves. Nothing could stop them now except main force. It was a disaster. He had seen it, and that was all he could say. Some of them must be dead, he believed. The rest would go on fighting . . . .

He sent up his words, tripping over each other, crowding the narrow tube. They mounted as if into a silence of an enlightened comprehension dwelling alone up there with a storm. And Jukes wanted to be dismissed from the face of that odious trouble intruding on the great need of the ship.

V

He waited. Before his eyes the engines turned with slow labour, that in the moment of going off into a mad fling would stop dead at Mr Rout's shout, 'Look out, Beale!' They paused in an intelligent immobility, stilled in midstroke, a heavy crank arrested on the cant, as if conscious of danger and the passage of time. Then, with a 'Now, then!' from the chief, and the sound of a breath expelled through clenched teeth, they would accomplish the interrupted revolution and begin another.

There was the prudent sagacity of wisdom and the deliberation of enormous strength in their movements. This was their work—this patient coaxing of a dis-

tracted ship over the fury of the waves and into the very
eye of the wind. At times Mr Rout's chin would sink on
his breast, and he watched them with knitted eyebrows
as if lost in thought.

The voice that kept the hurricane out of Jukes's ear
began: 'Take the hands with you . . . ,' and left off
unexpectedly.

'What could I do with them, sir?'

A harsh, abrupt, imperious clang exploded suddenly.
The three pairs of eyes flew up to the telegraph dial to
see the hand jump from FULL to STOP, as if snatched by
a devil. And then these three men in the engine-room
had the intimate sensation of a check upon the ship, of
a strange shrinking, as if she had gathered herself for a
desperate leap.

'Stop her!' bellowed Mr Rout.

Nobody—not even Captain MacWhirr, who alone on
deck had caught sight of a white line of foam coming
on at such a height that he couldn't believe his eyes—
nobody was to know the steepness of that sea and the
awful depth of the hollow the hurricane had scooped out
behind the running wall of water.

It raced to meet the ship, and, with a pause, as of
girding the loins, the *Nan-Shan* lifted her bows and
leaped. The flames in all the lamps sank, darkening the
engine-room. One went out. With a tearing crash and
a swirling, raving tumult, tons of water fell upon the
deck, as though the ship had darted under the foot of a
cataract.

Down there they looked at each other, stunned.

'Swept from end to end, by God!' bawled Jukes.

She dipped into the hollow straight down, as if going over the edge of the world. The engine-room toppled forward menacingly, like the inside of a tower nodding in an earthquake. An awful racket, of iron things falling, came from the stokehold. She hung on this appalling slant long enough for Beale to drop on his hands and knees and begin to crawl as if he meant to fly on all fours out of the engine-room, and for Mr Rout to turn his head slowly, rigid, cavernous, with the lower jaw dropping. Jukes had shut his eyes, and his face in a moment became hopelessly blank and gentle, like the face of a blind man.

At last she rose slowly, staggering, as if she had to lift a mountain with her bows.

Mr Rout shut his mouth; Jukes blinked; and little Beale stood up hastily.

'Another one like this, and that's the last of her,' cried the chief.

He and Jukes looked at each other, and the same thought came into their heads. The Captain! Everything must have been swept away. Steering-gear gone—ship like a log. All over directly.

'Rush!' ejaculated Mr Rout thickly, glaring with enlarged, doubtful eyes at Jukes, who answered him by an irresolute glance.

The clang of the telegraph gong soothed them

instantly. The black hand dropped in a flash from STOP to FULL.

'Now then, Beale!' cried Mr Rout.

The steam hissed low. The piston-rods slid in and out. Jukes put his ear to the tube. The voice was ready for him. It said: 'Pick up all the money. Bear a hand now. I'll want you up here.' And that was all.

'Sir?' called up Jukes. There was no answer.

He staggered away like a defeated man from the field of battle. He had got, in some way or other, a cut above his left eyebrow—a cut to the bone. He was not aware of it in the least: quantities of the China Sea, large enough to break his neck for him, had gone over his head, had cleaned, washed, and salted that wound. It did not bleed, but only gaped red; and this gash over the eye, his dishevelled hair, the disorder of his clothes, gave him the aspect of a man worsted in a fight with fists.

'Got to pick up the dollars.' He appealed to Mr Rout, smiling pitifully at random.

'What's that?' asked Mr Rout, wildly. 'Pick up . . . ? I don't care. . . .' Then, quivering in every muscle, but with an exaggeration of paternal tone, 'Go away now, for God's sake. You deck people'll drive me silly. There's that second mate been going for the old man. Don't you know? You fellows are going wrong for want of something to do. . . .'

At these words Jukes discovered in himself the begin-

nings of anger. Want of something to do—indeed. . . .
Full of hot scorn against the chief, he turned to go the
way he had come. In the stokehold the plump donkey-
man toiled with his shovel mutely, as if his tongue had
been cut out; but the second was carrying on like a
noisy, undaunted maniac, who had preserved his skill
in the art of stoking under a marine boiler.

'Hallo, you wandering officer! Hey! Can't you get
some of your slush-slingers to wind up a few of them
ashes? I am getting choked with them there. Curse it!
Hallo! Hey! Remember the articles: *Sailors and firemen
to assist each other*. Hey! D'ye hear?'

Jukes was climbing out frantically, and the other, lifting up his face after him, howled, 'Can't you speak?
What are you poking about here for? What's your
game, anyhow?'

A frenzy possessed Jukes. By the time he was back
amongst the men in the darkness of the alleyway, he felt
ready to wring all their necks at the slightest sign of
hanging back. The very thought of it exasperated him.
He couldn't hang back. They shouldn't.

The impetuosity with which he came amongst them
carried them along. They had already been excited and
startled at all his comings and goings—by the fierceness
and rapidity of his movements; and more felt than seen
in his rushes, he appeared formidable—busied with
matters of life and death that brooked no delay. At the
first word, he heard them drop into the bunker one after
another, obediently, with heavy thumps.

They were not clear as to what would have to be done. 'What is it? What is it?' they were asking each other. The boatswain tried to explain; the sounds of a great scuffle surprised them: and the mighty shocks, reverberating awfully in the black bunker, kept them in mind of their danger. When the boatswain threw open the door it seemed that an eddy of the hurricane, stealing through the iron sides of the ship, had set all these bodies whirling like dust: there came to them a confused uproar, a tempestuous tumult, a fierce mutter, gusts of screams dying away, and the tramping of feet mingling with the blows of the sea.

For a moment they glared amazed, blocking the doorway. Jukes pushed through them brutally. He said nothing, and simply darted in. Another lot of coolies on the ladder, struggling suicidally to break through the battened hatch to a swamped deck, fell off as before, and he disappeared under them like a man overtaken by a landslide.

The boatswain yelled excitedly: 'Come along. Get the mate out. He'll be trampled to death. Come on.'

They charged in, stamping on breasts, on fingers, on faces, catching their feet in heaps of clothing, kicking broken wood; but before they could get hold of him Jukes emerged waist deep in a multitude of clawing hands. In the instant he had been lost to view, all the buttons of his jacket had gone, its back had got split up to the collar, his waistcoat had been torn open. The central struggling mass of Chinamen went over to the roll, dark, indistinct, helpless, with a wild gleam of many eyes in the dim light of the lamps.

'Leave me alone—damn you. I am all right,' screeched Jukes. 'Drive them forward. Watch your chance when she pitches. Forward with 'em. Drive them against the bulkhead. Jam 'em up.'

The rush of the sailors into the seething 'tween-deck was like a splash of cold water into a boiling cauldron. The commotion sank for a moment.

The bulk of Chinamen were locked in such a compact scrimmage that, linking their arms and aided by an appalling dive of the ship, the seamen sent it forward in one great shove, like a solid block. Behind their backs small clusters and loose bodies tumbled from side to side.

The boatswain performed prodigious feats of strength. With his long arms open, and each great paw clutching at a stanchion, he stopped the rush of seven entwined Chinamen rolling like a boulder. His joints cracked; he said, 'Ha!' and they flew apart. But the carpenter showed the greater intelligence. Without saying a word to anybody he went back into the alleyway, to fetch several coils of cargo gear he had seen there—chain and rope. With these life-lines were rigged.

There was really no resistance. The struggle, however it began, had turned into a scramble of blind panic. If the coolies had started up after their scattered dollars they were by that time fighting only for their footing. They took each other by the throat merely to save themselves from being hurled about. Whoever got a hold anywhere would kick at the others who caught at his legs and hung on, till a roll sent them flying together across the deck.

The coming of the white devils was a terror. Had they come to kill? The individuals torn out of the ruck became very limp in the seamen's hands: some, dragged aside by the heels, were passive, like dead bodies, with open, fixed eyes. Here and there a coolie would fall on his knees as if begging for mercy; several, whom the excess of fear made unruly, were hit with hard fists between the eyes, and cowered; while those who were hurt submitted to rough handling, blinking rapidly without a plaint. Faces streamed with blood; there were raw places on the shaven heads, scratches, bruises, torn wounds, gashes. The broken porcelain out of the chests was mostly responsible for the latter. Here and there a Chinaman, wild-eyed, with his tail unplaited, nursed a bleeding sole.

They had been ranged closely, after having been shaken into submission, cuffed a little to allay excitement, addressed in gruff words of encouragement that sounded like promises of evil. They sat on the deck in ghastly, drooping rows, and at the end the carpenter, with two hands to help him, moved busily from place to place, setting taut and hitching the life-lines. The boatswain, with one leg and one arm embracing a stanchion, struggled with a lamp pressed to his breast, trying to get a light and growling all the time like an industrious gorilla. The figures of seamen stooped repeatedly, with the movements of gleaners, and everything was being flung into the bunker: clothing, smashed wood, broken china, and the dollars, too, gathered up in men's jackets. Now and then a sailor would stagger towards the doorway with his arms full of rubbish; and dolorous, slanting eyes followed his movements.

With every roll of the ship the long rows of sitting Celestials would sway forward brokenly, and her headlong dives knocked together the line of shaven polls from end to end. When the wash of water rolling on the deck died away for a moment, it seemed to Jukes, yet quivering from his exertions, that in his mad struggle down there he had overcome the wind somehow: that a silence had fallen upon the ship, a silence in which the sea struck thunderously at her sides.

Everything had been cleared out of the 'tween-deck—all the wreckage, as the men said. They stood erect and tottering above the level of heads and drooping shoulders. Here and there a coolie sobbed for his breath. Where the high light fell, Jukes could see the salient ribs of one, the yellow, wistful face of another; bowed necks; or would meet a dull stare directed at his face. He was amazed that there had been no corpses; but the lot of them seemed at their last gasp, and they appeared to him more pitiful than if they had been all dead.

Suddenly one of the coolies began to speak. The light came and went on his lean, straining face; he threw his head up like a baying hound. From the bunker came the sounds of knocking and the tinkle of some dollars rolling loose; he stretched out his arm, his mouth yawned black, and the incomprehensible guttural hooting sounds, that did not seem to belong to a human language, penetrated Jukes with a strange emotion as if a brute had tried to be eloquent.

Two more started mouthing what seemed to Jukes fierce denunciations; the others stirred with grunts and growls. Jukes ordered the hands out of the 'tween-decks hurriedly. He left last himself, backing through the door, while the grunts rose to a loud murmur and hands were extended after him as after a malefactor. The boatswain shot the bolt, and remarked uneasily, 'Seems as if the wind had dropped, sir.'

The seamen were glad to get back into the alleyway. Secretly each of them thought that at the last moment he could rush out on deck—and that was a comfort. There is something horribly repugnant in the idea of being drowned under a deck. Now they had done with the Chinamen, they again became conscious of the ship's position.

Jukes on coming out of the alleyway found himself up to the neck in the noisy water. He gained the bridge, and discovered he could detect obscure shapes as if his sight had become preternaturally acute. He saw faint outlines. They recalled not the familiar aspect of the *Nan-Shan*, but something remembered—an old dismantled steamer he had seen years ago rotting on a mudbank. She recalled that wreck.

There was no wind, not a breath, except the faint currents created by the lurches of the ship. The smoke tossed out of the funnel was settling down upon her deck. He breathed it as he passed forward. He felt the deliberate throb of the engines, and heard small sounds that seemed to have survived the great uproar: the knocking of broken fittings, the rapid tumbling of some piece of wreckage on the bridge. He perceived dimly the squat shape of his captain holding on to a twisted bridge-rail, motionless and swaying as if rooted to the planks. The unexpected stillness of the air oppressed Jukes.

'We have done it, sir,' he gasped.

'Thought you would,' said Captain MacWhirr.

'Did you?' murmured Jukes to himself.

'Wind fell all at once,' went on the Captain.

Jukes burst out: 'If you think it was an easy job——'

But his captain, clinging to the rail, paid no attention. 'According to the books the worst is not over yet.'

'If most of them hadn't been half dead with sea-sickness and fright, not one of us would have come out of that 'tween-deck alive,' said Jukes.

'Had to do what's fair by them,' mumbled MacWhirr, stolidly. 'You don't find everything in books.'

'Why, I believe they would have risen on us if I hadn't ordered the hands out of that pretty quick,' continued Jukes with warmth.

After the whisper of their shouts, their ordinary tones, so distinct, rang out very loud to their ears in the amazing stillness of the air. It seemed to them they were talking in a dark and echoing vault.

Through a jagged aperture in the dome of clouds the light of a few stars fell upon the black sea, rising and falling confusedly. Sometimes the head of a watery cone would topple on board and mingle with the rolling flurry of foam on the swamped deck, and the *Nan-Shan* wallowed heavily at the bottom of a circular cistern of clouds. This ring of dense vapours, gyrating madly round the calm of the centre, encompassed the ship like a motionless and unbroken wall of an aspect inconceivably sinister. Within, the sea, as if agitated by an internal commotion, leaped in peaked mounds that jostled each other, slapping heavily against her sides; and a low moaning sound, the infinite plaint of the storm's fury, came from beyond the limits of the menacing calm. Captain MacWhirr remained silent, and Jukes's ready ear caught suddenly the faint, long-drawn roar of some immense wave rushing unseen under that thick blackness, which made the appalling boundary of his vision.

'Of course,' he started resentfully, 'they thought we had caught at the chance to plunder them. Of course! You said—pick up the money. Easier said than done. They couldn't tell what was in our heads. We came in, smash—right into the middle of them. Had to do it by a rush.'

'As long as it's done . . . ,' mumbled the Captain, without attempting to look at Jukes. 'Had to do what's fair.'

'We shall find yet there's the devil to pay when this is over,' said Jukes, feeling very sore. 'Let them only recover a bit, and you'll see. They will fly at our throats, sir. Don't forget, sir, she isn't a British ship now. These brutes know it well, too. The damned Siamese flag.'

'We are on board, all the same,' remarked Captain MacWhirr.

'The trouble's not over yet,' insisted Jukes, prophetically, reeling and catching on. 'She's a wreck,' he added, faintly.

'The trouble's not over yet,' assented Captain MacWhirr, half aloud. . . . 'Look out for her a minute.'

'Are you going off the deck, sir?' asked Jukes, hurriedly, as if the storm were sure to pounce upon him as soon as he had been left alone with the ship.

He watched her, battered and solitary, labouring heavily in a wild scene of mountainous black waters lit by the gleams of distant worlds. She moved slowly, breathing into the still core of the hurricane the excess of her strength in a white cloud of steam—and the deep-toned vibration of the escape was like the defiant trumpeting of a living creature of the sea impatient for the renewal of the contest. It ceased suddenly. The still air moaned. Above Jukes's head a few stars shone into a pit of black vapours. The inky edge of the cloud-disc frowned upon the ship under the patch of glittering sky. The stars, too, seemed to look at her intently, as if for the last time, and the cluster of their splendour sat like a diadem on a lowering brow.

Captain MacWhirr had gone into the chart-room. There was no light there; but he could feel the disorder of that place where he used to live tidily. His armchair was upset. The books had tumbled out on the floor: he scrunched a piece of glass under his boot. He groped for the matches, and found a box on a shelf with a deep ledge. He struck one, and puckering the corners of his eyes, held out the little flame towards the barometer whose glittering top of glass and metals nodded at him continuously.

It stood very low—incredibly low, so low that Captain MacWhirr grunted. The match went out, and hurriedly he extracted another, with thick, stiff fingers.

Again a little flame flared up before the nodding glass and metal of the top. His eyes looked at it narrowed with attention, as if expecting an imperceptible sign. With his grave face he resembled a booted and misshapen pagan burning incense before the oracle of a Joss. There was no mistake. It was the lowest reading he had ever seen in his life.

Captain MacWhirr emitted a low whistle. He forgot himself till the flame diminished to a blue spark, burnt his fingers and vanished. Perhaps something had gone wrong with the thing!

There was an aneroid glass screwed above the couch. He turned that way, struck another match, and discovered the white face of the other instrument looking at him from the bulkhead, meaningly, not to be gainsaid, as though the wisdom of men were made unerring by the indifference of matter. There was no room for doubt now. Captain MacWhirr pshawed at it, and threw the match down.

The worst was to come, then—and if the books were right this worst would be very bad. The experience of the last six hours had enlarged his conception of what heavy weather could be like. 'It'll be terrific,' he pronounced, mentally. He had not consciously looked at anything by the light of the matches except at the barometer; and yet somehow he had seen that his water-bottle and the two tumblers had been flung out of their stand. It seemed to give him a more intimate knowledge of the tossing the ship had gone through. 'I wouldn't have believed it,' he thought. And his table had been cleared, too; his rulers, his pencils, the inkstand—all the things that had their safe appointed places—they were gone, as if a mischievous hand had plucked them out one by one and flung them on the wet floor. The hurricane had broken in upon the orderly arrangements of his privacy. This had never happened before, and the feeling of dismay reached the very seat of his composure. And the worst was to come yet! He was glad the trouble in the 'tween-deck had been discovered in time. If the ship had to go after all, then, at least, she wouldn't be going to the bottom with a lot of people in her fighting teeth and claw. That would have been odious. And in that feeling there was a humane intention and a vague sense of the fitness of things.

These instantaneous thoughts were yet in their

essence heavy and slow, partaking of the nature of the
man. He extended his hand to put back the matchbox
in its corner of the shelf. There were always matches
there—by his order. The steward had his instructions
impressed upon him long before. 'A box . . . just there,
see? Not so very full . . . where I can put my hand on
it, steward. Might want a light in a hurry. Can't tell on
board ship *what* you might want in a hurry. Mind, now.'

And of course on his side he would be careful to put
it back in its place scrupulously. He did so now, but
before he removed his hand it occurred to him that perhaps he would never have occasion to use that box any
more. The vividness of the thought checked him and for
an infinitesimal fraction of a second his fingers closed
again on the small object as though it had been the
symbol of all these little habits that chain us to the
weary round of life. He released it at last, and letting
himself fall on the settee, listened for the first sounds
of returning wind.

Not yet. He heard only the wash of water, the heavy
splashes, the dull shocks of the confused seas boarding
his ship from all sides. She would never have a chance to
clear her decks.

But the quietude of the air was startlingly tense and
unsafe, like a slender hair holding a sword suspended
over his head. By this awful pause the storm penetrated
the defences of the man and unsealed his lips. He spoke
out in the solitude and the pitch darkness of the cabin, as
if addressing another being awakened within his breast.

'I shouldn't like to lose her,' he said half aloud.

He sat unseen, apart from the sea, from his ship, isolated, as if withdrawn from the very current of his own existence, where such freaks as talking to himself surely had no place. His palms reposed on his knees, he bowed his short neck and puffed heavily, surrendering to a strange sensation of weariness he was not enlightened enough to recognize for the fatigue of mental stress.

From where he sat he could reach the door of a washstand locker. There should have been a towel there. There was. Good. . . . He took it out, wiped his face, and afterwards went on rubbing his wet head. He towelled himself with energy in the dark, and then remained motionless with the towel on his knees. A moment passed, of a stillness so profound that no one could have guessed there was a man sitting in that cabin. Then a murmur arose.

'She may come out of it yet.'

When Captain MacWhirr came out on deck, which he did brusquely, as though he had suddenly become conscious of having stayed away too long, the calm had lasted already more than fifteen minutes—long enough to make itself intolerable even to his imagination. Jukes, motionless on the forepart of the bridge, began to speak at once. His voice, blank and forced as though he were talking through hard-set teeth, seemed to flow away on all sides into the darkness, deepening again upon the sea.

'I had the wheel relieved. Hackett began to sing out

that he was done. He's lying in there alongside the steer-ing-gear with a face like death. At first I couldn't get anybody to crawl out and relieve the poor devil. That bosun's worse than no good, I always said. Thought I would have had to go myself and haul out one of them by the neck.'

'Ah, well,' muttered the Captain. He stood watchful by Jukes's side.

'The second mate's in there, too, holding his head. Is he hurt, sir?'

'No—crazy,' said Captain MacWhirr, curtly.

'Looks as if he had a tumble, though.'

'I had to give him a push,' explained the Captain

Jukes gave an impatient sigh.

'It will come very sudden,' said Captain MacWhirr, 'and from over there, I fancy. God only knows though. These books are only good to muddle your head and make you jumpy It will be bad, and there's an end. If we only can steam her round in time to meet it. . . .'

A minute passed. Some of the stars winked rapidly and vanished.

'You left them pretty safe?' began the Captain abruptly, as though the silence were unbearable.

'Are you thinking of the coolies, sir? I rigged life-lines all ways across that 'tween-deck.'

'Did you? Good idea, Mr Jukes.'

'I didn't . . . think you cared to . . . know,' said Jukes—the lurching of the ship cut his speech as though somebody had been jerking him around while he talked—'how I got on with . . . that infernal job. We did it. And it may not matter in the end.'

'Had to do what's fair, for all—they are only China-men. Give them the same chance with ourselves—hang it all. She isn't lost yet. Bad enough to be shut up below in a gale——'

'That's what I thought when you gave me the job, sir, interjected Jukes, moodily.

'—without being battered to pieces,' pursued Captain MacWhirr with rising vehemence. 'Couldn't let that go on in my ship, if I knew she hadn't five minutes to live. Couldn't bear it, Mr Jukes.'

A hollow echoing noise, like that of a shout rolling in a rocky chasm, approached the ship and went away again. The last star, blurred, enlarged, as if returning to the fiery mist of its beginning, struggled with the colos-sal depth of blackness hanging over the ship—and went out.

'Now for it!' muttered Captain MacWhirr. 'Mr Jukes.'

'Here, sir.'

The two men were growing indistinct to each other.

'We must trust her to go through it and come out on the other side. That's plain and straight. There's no room for Captain Wilson's storm-strategy here.'

'No, sir.'

'She will be smothered and swept again for hours,' mumbled the Captain. 'There's not much left by this time above deck for the sea to take away—unless you or me.'

'Both, sir,' whispered Jukes, breathlessly.

'You are always meeting trouble half way, Jukes,' Captain MacWhirr remonstrated quaintly. 'Though it's a fact that the second mate is no good. D'ye hear, Mr Jukes? You would be left alone if . . .'

Captain MacWhirr interrupted himself, and Jukes, glancing on all sides, remained silent.

'Don't you be put out by anything,' the Captain continued, mumbling rather fast. 'Keep her facing it. They may say what they like, but the heaviest seas run with the wind. Facing it—always facing it—that's the way to get through. You are a young sailor. Face it. That's enough for any man. Keep a cool head.'

'Yes, sir,' said Jukes, with a flutter of the heart.

In the next few seconds the Captain spoke to the engine-room and got an answer.

For some reason Jukes experienced an access of confidence, a sensation that came from outside like a warm breath, and made him feel equal to every demand. The distant muttering of the darkness stole into his ears. He noted it unmoved, out of that sudden belief in himself, as a man safe in a shirt of mail would watch a point.

The ship laboured without intermission amongst the black hills of water, paying with this hard tumbling the price of her life. She rumbled in her depths, shaking a white plummet of steam into the night, and Jukes's thought skimmed like a bird through the engine-room, where Mr Rout—good man—was ready. When the rumbling ceased it seemed to him that there was a pause of every sound, a dead pause in which Captain MacWhirr's voice rang out startlingly.

'What's that? A puff of wind?'—it spoke much louder than Jukes had ever heard it before—'On the bow. That's right. She may come out of it yet.'

The mutter of the winds drew near apace. In the forefront could be distinguished a drowsy waking plaint passing on, and far off the growth of a multiple clamour, marching and expanding. There was the throb as of many drums in it, a vicious rushing note, and like the chant of a tramping multitude.

Jukes could no longer see his captain distinctly. The darkness was absolutely piling itself upon the ship. At most he made out movements, a hint of elbows spread out, of a head thrown up.

Captain MacWhirr was trying to do up the top button of his oilskin coat with unwonted haste. The hurricane, with its power to madden the seas, to sink ships, to uproot trees, to overturn strong walls and dash the very birds of the air to the ground, had found this taciturn man in its path, and, doing its utmost, had managed to wring out a few words. Before the renewed wrath of winds swooped on his ship, Captain MacWhirr was moved to declare, in a tone of vexation, as it were: 'I wouldn't like to lose her.'

He was spared that annoyance.

VI

On a bright sunshiny day, with the breeze chasing her smoke far ahead, the *Nan-Shan* came into Fu-chau. Her arrival was at once noticed on shore, and the seamen in harbour said: 'Look! Look at that steamer. What's that? Siamese—isn't she? Just look at her!'

She seemed, indeed, to have been used as a running target for the secondary batteries of a cruiser. A hail of minor shells could not have given her upper works a more broken, torn, and devastated aspect: and she had about her the worn, weary air of ships coming from the far ends of the world—and indeed with truth, for in her short passage she had been very far; sighting, verily, even the coast of the Great Beyond, whence no ship ever returns to give up her crew to the dust of the earth. She was incrusted and grey with salt to the trucks of her masts and to the top of her funnel; as though (as some facetious seaman said) 'the crowd on board had fished her out somewhere from the bottom of the sea and brought her in here for salvage.' And further, excited by the felicity of his own wit, he offered to give five pounds for her—'as she stands.'

Before she had been quite an hour at rest, a meagre little man, with a red-tipped nose and a face cast in an angry mould, landed from a sampan on the quay of the Foreign Concession, and incontinently turned to shake his fist at her.

A tall individual, with legs much too thin for a rotund stomach, and with watery eyes, strolled up and remarked, 'Just left her—eh? Quick work.'

He wore a soiled suit of blue flannel with a pair of dirty cricketing shoes; a dingy grey moustache drooped from his lip, and daylight could be seen in two places between the rim and the crown of his hat

'Hallo! what are you doing here?' asked the ex-second-mate of the *Nan-Shan*, shaking hands hurriedly.

'Standing by for a job—chance worth taking—got a quiet hint,' explained the man with the broken hat, in jerky, apathetic wheezes.

The second shook his fist again at the *Nan-Shan*. 'There's a fellow there that ain't fit to have the command of a scow,' he declared, quivering with passion, while the other looked about listlessly.

'Is there?'

But he caught sight on the quay of a heavy seaman's chest, painted brown under a fringed sailcloth cover, and lashed with new manila line. He eyed it with awakened interest.

'I would talk and raise trouble if it wasn't for that damned Siamese flag. Nobody to go to—or I would make it hot for him. The fraud! Told his chief engineer—that's another fraud for you—I had lost my nerve. The greatest lot of ignorant fools that ever sailed the seas. No! You can't think . . .'

'Got your money all right?' inquired his seedy acquaintance suddenly.

'Yes. Paid me off on board,' raged the second mate. ' "Get your breakfast on shore," says he.'

'Mean skunk!' commented the tall man, vaguely, and passed his tongue on his lips. 'What about having a drink of some sort?'

'He struck me,' hissed the second mate.

'No! Struck! You don't say?' The man in blue began to bustle about sympathetically. 'Can't possibly talk here. I want to know all about it. Struck—eh? Let's get a fellow to carry your chest. I know a quiet place where they have some bottled beer. . . .'

Mr Jukes, who had been scanning the shore through a pair of glasses, informed the chief engineer afterwards that 'our late second mate hasn't been long in finding a friend. A chap looking uncommonly like a bummer. I saw them walk away together from the quay.'

The hammering and banging of the needful repairs did not disturb Captain MacWhirr. The steward found in the letter he wrote, in a tidy chart-room, passages of such absorbing interest that twice he was nearly caught in the act. But Mrs MacWhirr, in the drawing-room of the forty-pound house, stifled a yawn—perhaps out of self-respect—for she was alone.

She reclined in a plush-bottomed and gilt hammock-chair near a tiled fireplace, with Japanese fans on the mantel and a glow of coals in the grate. Lifting her hands, she glanced wearily here and there into the many pages. It was not her fault they were so prosy, so completely uninteresting—from 'My darling wife' at the

beginning, to 'Your loving husband' at the end. She
couldn't be really expected to understand all these ship
affairs. She was glad, of course, to hear from him, but
she had never asked herself why, precisely.

'. . . They are called typhoons . . . The mate did not
seem to like it . . . Not in books . . . Couldn't think of
letting it go on. . . .'

The paper rustled sharply. '. . . A calm that lasted
more than twenty minutes,' she read perfunctorily; and
the next words her thoughtless eyes caught, on the top of
another page, were: 'see you and the children again. . . .'
She had a movement of impatience. He was always
thinking of coming home. He had never had such a
good salary before. What was the matter now?

It did not occur to her to turn back overleaf to look.
She would have found it recorded there that between 4
and 6 a.m. on December 25th, Captain MacWhirr did
actually think that his ship could not possibly live
another hour in such a sea, and that he would never see
his wife and children again. Nobody was to know this
(his letters got mislaid so quickly)—nobody whatever
but the steward, who had been greatly impressed by that
disclosure. So much so, that he tried to give the cook
some idea of the 'narrow squeak we all had' by saying
solemnly, 'The old man himself had a darn' poor opinion of our chance.'

'How do you know?' asked, contemptuously, the
cook, an old soldier. 'He hasn't told you, maybe?'

'Well, he did give me a hint to that effect,' the steward brazened it out.

'Get along with you! He will be coming to tell *me* next,' jeered the old cook, over his shoulder.

Mrs MacWhirr glanced farther, on the alert. '. . . Do what's fair. . . . Miserable objects. . . Only three with a broken leg each, and one . . . Thought had better keep the matter quiet . . . hope to have done the fair thing. . . .'

She let fall her hands. No: there was nothing more about coming home. Must have been merely expressing a pious wish. Mrs MacWhirr's mind was set at ease, and a black marble clock, priced by the local jeweller at £3 18s. 6d., had a discreet stealthy tick.

The door flew open, and a girl in the long-legged, short-frocked period of existence, flung into the room. A lot of colourless, rather lanky hair was scattered over her shoulders. Seeing her mother, she stood still, and directed her pale prying eyes upon the letter.

'From father,' murmured Mrs MacWhirr. 'What have you done with your ribbon?'

The girl put her hands up to her head and pouted.

'He's well,' continued Mrs MacWhirr, languidly. 'At least I think so. He never says.' She had a little laugh. The girl's face expressed a wandering indifference, and Mrs MacWhirr surveyed her with fond pride.

'Go and get your hat,' she said after a while. 'I am

going out to do some shopping. There is a sale at Linom's.'

'Oh, how jolly!' uttered the child, impressively, in unexpectedly grave vibrating tones, and bounded out of the room.

It was a fine afternoon, with a grey sky and dry sidewalks. Outside the draper's Mrs MacWhirr smiled upon a woman in a black mantle of generous proportions armoured in jet and crowned with flowers blooming falsely above a bilious matronly countenance. They broke into a swift little babble of greetings and exclamations both together, very hurried, as if the street were ready to yawn open and swallow all that pleasure before it could be expressed.

Behind them the high glass doors were kept on the swing. People couldn't pass, men stood aside waiting patiently, and Lydia was absorbed in poking the end of her parasol between the stone flags. Mrs MacWhirr talked rapidly.

'Thank you very much. He's not coming home yet. Of course it's very sad to have him away, but it's such a comfort to know he keeps so well.' Mrs MacWhirr drew breath. 'The climate there agrees with him,' she added, beamingly, as if poor MacWhirr had been away touring in China for the sake of his health.

Neither was the chief engineer coming home yet. Mr Rout knew too well the value of a good billet.

'Solomon says wonders will never cease,' cried Mrs Rout joyously at the old lady in her armchair by the fire.

Mr Rout's mother moved slightly, her withered hands lying in black half-mittens on her lap.

The eyes of the engineer's wife fairly danced on the paper. 'That captain of the ship he is in—a rather simple man, you remember, mother?—has done something rather clever, Solomon says.'

'Yes, my dear,' said the old woman meekly, sitting with bowed silvery head, and that air of inward stillness characteristic of very old people who seem lost in watching the last flickers of life. 'I think I remember.'

Solomon Rout, Old Sol, Father Sol, the Chief, 'Rout, good man'—Mr Rout, the condescending and paternal friend of youth, had been the baby of her many children—all dead by this time. And she remembered him best as a boy of ten— long before he went away to serve his apprenticeship in some great engineering works in the North. She had seen so little of him since, she had gone through so many years, that she had now to retrace her steps very far back to recognize him plainly in the mist of time. Sometimes it seemed that her daughter-in-law was talking of some strange man.

Mrs Rout junior was disappointed. 'H'm. H'm.' She turned the page. 'How provoking! He doesn't say what it is. Says I couldn't understand how much there was in it. Fancy! What could it be so very clever? What a wretched man not to tell us!'

She read on without further remark soberly, and at last sat looking into the fire. The chief wrote just a word or two of the typhoon; but something had moved him to express an increased longing for the companionship of the jolly woman. 'If it hadn't been that mother must be looked after, I would send you your passage-money to-day. You could set up a small house out here. I would have a chance to see you sometimes then. We are not growing younger. . . .'

'He's well, mother,' sighed Mrs Rout, rousing herself.

'He always was a strong healthy boy,' said the old woman, placidly.

But Mr Jukes's account was really animated and very full. His friend in the Western Ocean trade imparted it freely to the other officers of his liner. 'A chap I know writes to me about an extraordinary affair that happened on board his ship in that typhoon—you know—that we read of in the papers two months ago. It's the funniest thing! Just see for yourself what he says. I'll show you his letter.'

There were phrases in it calculated to give the impression of light-hearted, indomitable resolution. Jukes had written them in good faith, for he felt thus when he wrote. He described with lurid effect the scenes in the 'tween-deck. '. . . It struck me in a flash that those confounded Chinamen couldn't tell we weren't a desperate kind of robbers. 'Tisn't good to part the Chinaman from his money if he is the stronger party. We need have been desperate indeed to go thieving in such weather, but what could these beggars know of us? So, without thinking of it twice, I got the hands away in a jiffy. Our work was done —that the old man had set his heart on. We cleared out without staying to inquire how they felt. I am convinced that if they had not been so unmercifully shaken, and afraid—each individual one of them—to stand up, we would have been torn to pieces. Oh! It was pretty complete, I can tell you; and you may run to and fro across the Pond to the end of time before you find yourself with such a job on your hands.'

After this he alluded professionally to the damage done to the ship, and went on thus:

'It was when the weather quieted down that the situation became confoundedly delicate. It wasn't made any better by us having been lately transferred to the Siamese flag; though the skipper can't see that it makes any difference—'as long as *we* are on board'—he says. There are feelings that this man simply hasn't got—and there's an end of it. You might just as well try to make a bedpost understand. But apart from this it is an infernally lonely state for a ship to be going about the China seas with no proper consuls, not even a gunboat of her own anywhere, nor a body to go to in case of some trouble.

'My notion was to keep these Johnnies under hatches for another fifteen hours or so; as we weren't much farther than that from Fu-chau. We would find there, most likely, some sort of a man-of-war, and once under her guns we were safe enough; for surely any skipper of a man-of-war—English, French or Dutch—would see white men through as far as row on board goes. We could get rid of them and their money afterwards by

delivering them to their Mandarin or Taotai, or whatever they call these chaps in goggles you see being carried about in sedan-chairs through their stinking streets.

'The old man wouldn't see it somehow. He wanted to
keep the matter quiet. He got that notion into his head,
and a steam windlass couldn't drag it out of him. He
wanted as little fuss made as possible, for the sake of the
ship's name and for the sake of the owners—"for the
sake of all concerned," says he, looking at me very hard.
It made me angry hot. Of course you couldn't keep a
thing like that quiet; but the chests had been secured in
the usual manner and were safe enough for any earthly
gale, while this had been an altogether fiendish business
I couldn't give you even an idea of.

'Meantime, I could hardly keep on my feet. None of
us had a spell of any sort for nearly thirty hours, and
there the old man sat rubbing his chin, rubbing the top
of his head, and so bothered he didn't even think of
pulling his long boots off.

' "I hope, sir," says I, "you won't be letting them out
on deck before we make ready for them in some shape
or other." Not, mind you, that I felt very sanguine
about controlling these beggars if they meant to take
charge. A trouble with a cargo of Chinamen is no child's
play. I was dam' tired, too. "I wish," said I, "you would
let us throw the whole lot of these dollars down to them
and leave them to fight it out amongst themselves, while
we get a rest."

' "Now you talk wild, Jukes," says he, looking up in

his slow way that makes you ache all over, somehow. "We must plan out something that would be fair to all parties."

'I had no end of work on hand, as you may imagine, so I set the hands going, and then I thought I would turn in a bit. I hadn't been asleep in my bunk ten minutes when in rushes the steward and begins to pull at my leg.

' "For God's sake, Mr Jukes, come out! Come on deck quick, sir. Oh, do come out!"

'The fellow scared all the sense out of me. I didn't know what had happened: another hurricane—or what. Could hear no wind.

' "The Captain's letting them out. Oh, he is letting them out! Jump on deck, sir, and save us. The chief engineer has just run below for his revolver."

'That's what I understood the fool to say. However, Father Rout swears he went in there only to get a clean pocket-handkerchief. Anyhow, I made one jump into my trousers and flew on deck aft. There was certainly a good deal of noise going on forward of the bridge. Four of the hands with the bosun were at work abaft. I passed up to them some of the rifles all the ships on the China coast carry in the cabin and led them on the bridge. On the way I ran against Old Sol, looking startled and sucking at an unlighted cigar.

' "Come along," I shouted to him.

'We charged, the seven of us, up to the chart-room. All was over. There stood the old man with his sea-boots still drawn up to the hips and in shirt-sleeves—got warm thinking it out, I suppose. Bun-hin's dandy clerk at his elbow as dirty as a sweep, was still green in the face. I could see directly I was in for something.

' "What the devil are these monkey tricks, Mr Jukes?" asks the old man, as angry as ever he could be. I tell you frankly it made me lose my tongue. "For God's sake, Mr Jukes," says he, "do take away these rifles from the men. Somebody's sure to get hurt before long if you don't. Damme, if this ship isn't worse than Bedlam! Look sharp now. I want you up here to help me and Bun-hin's Chinaman to count that money. You wouldn't mind lending a hand, too, Mr Rout, now you're here. The more of us the better."

'He had settled it all in his mind while I was having a snooze. Had we been an English ship, or only going to land our cargo of coolies in an English port, like Hong-Kong, for instance, there would have been no end of inquiries and bother, claims for damages and so on. But these Chinamen know their officials better than we do.

'The hatches had been taken off already, and they were all on deck after a night and a day down below. It made you feel queer to see so many gaunt, wild faces together. The beggars stared about at the sky, at the sea, at the ship, as though they had expected the whole thing to have been blown to pieces. And no wonder! They had had a doing that would have shaken the soul out of a white man. But then they say a Chinaman has no soul. He has, though, something about him that is deuced

tough. There was a fellow (amongst others of the badly
hurt) who had had his eye all but knocked out. It stood
out of his head the size of half a hen's egg. This would
have laid out a white man on his back for a month: and
yet there was that chap elbowing here and there in the
crowd and talking to the others as if nothing had been
the matter. They made a great hubbub amongst themselves, and whenever the old man showed his bald head
on the foreside of the bridge, they would all leave off
jawing and look at him from below.

'It seems that after he had done his thinking he made
that Bun-hin's fellow go down and explain to them the
only way they could get their money back. He told me
afterwards that, all the coolies having worked in the
same place and for the same length of time, he reckoned
he would be doing the fair thing by them as near as possible if he shared all the cash we had picked up equally
among the lot. You couldn't tell one man's dollars from
another's, he said, and if you asked each man how much
money he brought on board he was afraid they would
lie, and he would find himself a long way short. I think
he was right there. As to giving up the money to any
Chinese official he could scare up in Fu-chau, he said he
might just as well put the lot in his own pocket at once
for all the good it would be to them. I suppose they
thought so, too.

'We finished the distribution before dark. It was
rather a sight: the sea running high, the ship a wreck to
look at, these Chinamen staggering up on the bridge one

by one for their share, and the old man still booted, and in his shirt-sleeves, busy paying out at the chart-room door, perspiring like anything, and now and then coming down sharp on myself or Father Rout about one thing or another not quite to his mind. He took the share of those who were disabled himself to them on the No. 2 hatch. There were three dollars left over, and these went to the three most damaged coolies, one to each. We turned-to afterwards, and shovelled out on deck heaps of wet rags, all sorts of fragments of things without shape, and that you couldn't give a name to, and let them settle the ownership themselves.

'This certainly is coming as near as can be to keeping the thing quiet for the benefit of all concerned. What's your opinion, you pampered mail-boat swell? The old chief says that this was plainly the only thing that could be done. The skipper remarked to me the other day, "There are things you find nothing about in books." I think that he got out of it very well for such a stupid man.'